LOST WOMEN

By the same author

Marina Bay Sins
Rich Kill, Poor Kill
Bloody Foreigners

LOST WOMEN

An Inspector Low Novel

Neil Humphreys

MUSWELL
PRESS

First published by Muswell Press in 2023
Copyright © Neil Humphreys 2023

Neil Humphreys has asserted his right to be
identified as the author of this work in accordance
with the Copyright, Designs and Patents Act, 1988

*This book is a work of fiction and, except in the case
of historical fact, any resemblance to actual persons,
living or dead, is purely coincidental*

A CIP catalogue record for this book
is available from the British Library

Typeset in Bembo by M Rules
Printed and bound by
CPI Group (UK) Ltd, Croydon CR0 4YY

ISBN: 978-1-73912-380-2
eISBN: 978-1-73912-381-9

Muswell Press
London N6 5HQ
www.muswell-press.co.uk

For a glossary of popular Singapore terms and Singlish phrases, see p.339

LOST WOMEN

PROLOGUE

Alan Edwards had expected to see more blood. His initial reaction had surprised him. He'd never seen a murder victim before, let alone one with its throat sliced open. And yet, Edwards remained unexpectedly calm.

Instead, he was struck by the colour. The blood looked black.

He shone his torch through the windscreen. The flies were already hovering outside the lorry. The maggots would soon follow.

Being an ornithology hobbyist of sorts, Edwards was no stranger to nature's brutality. The wildlife of Rainham Marshes feasted on death. The Thames Estuary kept the swampy grassland attractive for Edwards' beloved wildfowl and waders.

And the peregrine falcons killed them.

The lorry wasn't a total shock either. Industrial parks and haulage firms filled the riverbanks recently abandoned by Ford. Gentrification was making its way through East London, but it hadn't yet reached this part of the River Thames.

Drug dealers and traffickers plugged the gaps in the meantime. Rainham Marshes offered solitude for Edwards' migratory species and privacy for anyone keen on a coke deal. The seasonal birds were temporary. The drug dealers were not. On his pre-dawn treks through the scrub, Edwards had pretended not to see them for years.

But he couldn't miss a dead Chinese lorry driver.

That was the other thing. Lorry drivers were not Chinese, not around here. They were usually white and nearly always British, especially in recent years, but never Chinese.

And they were never dead.

The long grass danced around the lorry as the cold air filled Edwards' lungs. For the first time, he realised that he was terrified. He had already called the police, talking gibberish, listing one large, white lorry in a ditch and one dead Chinese driver in the cab like he was ordering a take-away. And he had followed the firm instructions to wait on the scene; alone, deep inside the Rainham Marshes, with nothing but a torch, a pair of binoculars, a thermos flask and a cheese and pickle sandwich for protection.

Edwards stepped away from the lorry, already making swift, instinctive calculations of his own. The driver hadn't committed suicide, not like that. He had willingly driven to an isolated spot. The lorry was parked in a ditch, its tyre marks obvious in the boggy terrain. The lorry came in. No other vehicle went out.

Edwards wasn't alone.

The old man moved quickly. He knew the area well, even in the dark. The familiar woodland was easy to navigate. His bicycle wasn't far away, just behind the lorry. Soon, he'd be home with his wife, sipping sugary tea and eating custard creams, his hands still shaking as he held the mug and attempted to make light of the slumped driver, the torn flesh and the flies, those damn flies.

2

And eventually, he'd return, for his lapwings and little egrets, and he'd forget the man's open eyes, frozen at the time of death, capturing that moment of realisation.

But Edwards wouldn't forget. He wouldn't forget anything, not after she emerged through the long grass and hurried towards him. She was unsteady on her feet, stumbling through the marsh in high heels. Her clothes were all wrong, for the environment and the weather. The hot pants and crop top belonged in a nightclub, not in an Essex swamp before dawn.

The only thing that made sense was the knife. She waved the blade in front of Edwards' face. Instinctively, the retiree raised his hands.

"Help."

She was barely speaking.

"Help."

She was already crying.

Her Chinese face and her foreign accent didn't belong here ether.

"Help. Please."

Edwards was already following her back to the lorry. They were running, his terror dissipating, his confusion giving way to something unexpected. Empathy.

"*Lai lai.* Come."

"Yes, OK." Edwards held out his torch to light the way.

She grabbed his elbow, not to intimidate, but for support. She was shaking, tripping through the scrub. Edwards patted her hand.

"It'll be OK."

He had no idea what he was saying. But he knew the police were on their way. Fate would take care of the rest.

Edwards heard the banging before they reached the back of the lorry. There was screaming, high-pitched and desperate, coming from inside. She was already grabbing the bottom of the roller shutters.

"Open." She wasn't strong enough.

"Open." She was louder now, barking at Edwards.

"Maybe we should wait for the police."

Edwards thought about his wife, his favourite armchair, the sugary tea and the custard creams. He heard the screaming and hesitated.

"The police will be here any second."

"Please."

Later, her mascara-streaked face would stay with Edwards longer than the wide-eyed dead driver. He already knew that the child-like wailing inside that lorry would never leave him.

He grabbed the cold metal with both hands.

Together, they pushed the shutters above their heads.

Edwards struggled to comprehend the chaos that followed. But he remembered a dozen Asian women running towards him.

They all had knives.

Chapter 1

P olice Constable Jamie Henderson was already bored. Illegals in lorries were dull. He saw them all the time, snaking their way through the Thames Estuary, mostly alive, occasionally dead, but always a lot of paperwork.

At least the latest lot were pretty.

"I'd give her one." He nudged his colleague in the ribs.

"Shut up, Jamie," PC Stuart Walker said, blowing his fingers. His hands were already frozen. He was struggling with his notes and the dithering old man.

"So you were bird-watching, Mr Edwards," Walker said, leaning into his own car.

He had offered the pensioner a back seat and some warmth. Neither had stopped the shaking.

"So am I," PC Henderson quipped.

He leered at the girls, still sheltering in the back of the lorry. Until social services arrived, there was nowhere else for a dozen women to wait in the Rainham Marshes. They had dropped their knives. They were in the care of two uniformed officers now. They were safe.

"Especially that one." Henderson pointed at the woman with the longest legs and the hardest face. She was wearing hot pants and stilettos, the perfect combo.

"I've always had a thing for high heels." Henderson's torch found the woman's eyes. "I like 'em tall."

"For god's sake, Jamie, give it a rest."

The sun was slowly rising above the boggy swampland, but the air was still chilly. Walker loathed the cold and early morning calls. His mate wasn't helping.

"Now, Mr Edwards, you called us after you found the driver, but before you found the girls in the back. Is that right?"

"*We* found the girls in the back."

Walker was losing patience. "Who's 'we', Mr Edwards? You said you were alone?"

"I was alone. I've been coming here alone for years. My wife thinks I'm a sad old git, getting up at 4 o'clock in the morning to look for 'poxy birds', as she calls 'em, but I like it. Keeps me fit. It's better than fishing, especially in this weather."

Edwards went to sip his tea from his thermos flask, but both men noticed his shaking hands. Edwards changed his mind. "It's daft, really."

"What is?"

"To reach sixty-eight years old and never see a dead body—not a murdered one anyway—I suppose you see them all the time."

"One is too many, sir."

"Yeah, I reckon you're right, mate. That's why I can't stop bloody shaking. She didn't shake though, her with the knife. That's why I thought it was her. She came at me with a knife, running like a bloody maniac through the bushes."

"Who did?"

"Her over there, the one sitting on the back of the lorry."

Henderson looked disgusted. "Ah, not her with the high heels?"

"Just tell me what happened next," Walker said, placing a hand on the old man's shoulder.

"She made me open up the lorry."

"She made you? She threatened you with her knife?"

"No, no, no, not at all, she begged me. I didn't really think the knife was for me. It was for her, for all of them, for their protection. They were more bloody terrified than I was. In fact, as soon as I told 'em that the police were coming, they all put down their knives and just sat there, just like that, without a care in the world."

"OK, thanks, Mr Edwards. Just wait for our colleagues to arrive."

"Do you think she, you know, killed him?"

Walker smiled sincerely. "It's unlikely. None of their knives or clothes have any blood on them. A neck wound like that ... there'd be blood everywhere."

"Yeah, I saw it all over the windscreen."

"It'll get better, Mr Edwards. Over time."

Walker's smile was fake now. He was lying. Both men probably knew that.

The police constable joined his partner behind the lorry. The wind was bitingly cold. Henderson was still eyeing the women, passing the time by giving each one an internal score, a mark out of ten for their imagined performance in his dark fantasies. There was nothing else to do at this time of the morning.

"Any luck?"

"Nah, not a word from any of 'em. Not surprising, is it? They always shit themselves when we turn up. Probably can't speak proper English anyway."

"Nor can you," Walker said, climbing into the lorry.

"Here, what are you doing? You gotta wait for forensics."

"He's not dead in here, is he? I'm not disturbing anything in the back of the lorry."

Walker sat beside the woman in the crop top and high heels. "This is the one that ran out to the old man?"

"Yeah, the fit one."

"So she does speak some English." Walker smiled at the woman. She wore too much make-up to hide puffy eyes and a lack of sleep. Her coarse features couldn't entirely hide the fragility. "I wonder why she ran out for help?"

"She was scared."

"Or she's the leader. She looks older than the others. It's worth a try."

Walker tapped his notepad. She shook her head. The other women didn't move.

"It's OK. I'm here to help. Really. I just want to help."

Walker meant it, too. He was grateful that the women were still alive. He had attended enough manslaughter cases on Essex industrial estates.

He waved his pen in the air. "What is your name?"

Nothing.

"Where are you from?"

Nothing.

"Who sent you here?"

"You're wasting your time, Stu. They won't talk to us. Leave it to the translators."

"Low."

Her soft voice surprised both men. Walker looked for guidance. Henderson shrugged his shoulders. Neither officer had a clue.

Walker leaned towards her. He had the boyish, kinder face. "What's Low?"

"I speak to Inspector Low."

Her English was surprisingly good. But her words made no sense.

"We don't know an Inspector Low at our station,"

Walker said, quietly and carefully, not wishing to antagonise her.

"He's in Singapore."

"Ah that's great," Henderson said. "Our only lead is some geezer in China."

Chapter 2

Detective Inspector Stanley Low checked his pistol. He didn't recognise it. The Singapore Police Force had recently replaced his trusty Taurus with a Glock. Apparently, his previous weapon was out-of-date and obsolete.

He knew the feeling.

Low examined the faces hurrying into Parklane Shopping Mall. They were much younger now. They stopped at the escalators and checked their pistols too, mimicking their inspector, following the leader, as always, the Singapore way.

Low checked the deserted mall one more time. This side of Selegie Road was a sweaty, neglected place at the best of times. At 2am, the officers had cooks, street walkers and the odd rat for company.

Only the rats lingered.

The Parklane Shopping Mall was an architectural relic, still trapped in the 1970s. Even the smells belonged to Low's childhood. Cooking oil and musty carpets filled his senses. Guitar shops, nail salons and TCM outlets catered to those hoping to recreate their past, to look and feel younger, happier. Sexier.

The Classic Doll KTV Lounge took care of the lot. Stretched across the third floor, the walls were blacked out, covered entirely by a large, tacky print of a flying horse. Low's team moved quickly along the print, their shoulders brushing past the wings of the magnificent beast.

"Why they always have a horse *ah*?" Xavier Ng asked, wide-eyed and jittery.

"Superstition. They think business will be fast, like the horse. Now shut up *lah*."

Ng was the latest junior detective assigned to Low in CID. The inspector usually got the kids now. Being a legendary babysitter kept him on the payroll, but out of harm's way.

"I think it's time to go in sir," Xavier Ng said.

"Wait *lah*." Low tapped the glass door. "It's quiet inside. No singing. They're drinking. You wanna surprise them or not?"

"Yes, sir. You're right, sir."

The other sheep bleated in agreement, raising their alien pistols and waiting for further instructions, always waiting for orders.

The sudden blast of Mandopop from inside the KTV lounge made them all jump, including Low. A male voice warbled tunelessly on the other side of the door.

"OK, good, they're either singing or shagging. Remember, we've got our guns out. They've got their cocks out. No need to shoot anyone, OK? Right. Go."

Low kicked the door open and crouched along the long, dark corridor. The smell of overpriced booze and stale sex filled the air. Low's team moved swiftly towards the violin strings of a weepy Mandarin ballad, just a little further ahead, on the other side of a locked door. His boot took care of the bolt. The butt of his unfamiliar gun took out the overweight Chinese minder.

The sound of a large man's nose breaking and the sight of half a dozen armed detectives triggered the screaming. Skinny, semi-naked women reached for their clothes. Fat, semi-naked men concealed their erections. The small, dank room was filled with sofas, bottles of cognac, used condoms and aroused men and women running around a table in search of their underwear.

On the huge TV, a young couple expressed their love for each other from the top of a Chinese mountain as the lyrics scrolled across the bottom of the screen. The surround sound speaker system amplified that deep love, filling the room with soaring vocals.

"*Wah lau*, somebody off the bloody TV."

Low's orders were drowned out by the teary-eyed singers on screen so he pulled the plug himself.

"Eh, who switch off my KTV?"

A large, angry Chinese man ambled into the room. His stomach appeared to spill over in several different directions, covering the waistband of his shorts. He took a moment to digest the chaotic scene of men and women being handcuffed and turned on his slippers.

"No, no, no, brother, you stay."

Low hurdled the table, narrowly missing two Chinese women shouting at his junior colleagues and grabbed the fleeing man by the back of the neck.

"Don't leave your own party, Ah Meng."

Ah Meng made the mistake of taking a slow, lazy swing at his captor. Low ducked and decided a controlled head-butt would bring an end to Ah Meng's resistance.

Ah Meng wiped the blood from his nostrils and swiftly agreed.

"Eh, sorry, *ah*, Inspector Low, I didn't know it was you."

"Didn't know it was me? Balls to you." Low shoved the

heavier man onto a crowded sofa. "You always get *chee ko pek* look like me, is it?"

"You do have one of those faces."

"Shut up, *lah*."

Low was tired. Raiding KTV lounges was beneath him. He was catching nothing but headlines. He watched the others eagerly handcuff sex workers, punters and pimps, almost impossible to distinguish one from the other. They would all be faceless in the next morning's media photos, deliberately pixelated, supposedly for their protection. But the altered images were for Singapore's protection. Low knew that. These people had to stay invisible to maintain the illusion that they didn't exist. Low and his team were the pied pipers of pointlessness. Catch a few. Release a few. It didn't matter, as long as there were arrests, headlines and photos with no faces.

"You never bother me last time." Ah Meng wriggled forward on the torn sofa, pushing a sex worker to one side. "Last time you never disturb."

"Last time you never got greedy."

"I not greedy, *wha'*."

"No *lah*, Ah Meng. You kept the doors open, right or not?" Low pointed at the sex workers, pulling up their knickers. "You kept them shagging. Forgot about the social distancing last time. You were supposed to close your property, Ah Meng, remember? Property owners who allow their premises to be used for vice-related activities can face a jail term of up to five years or fines of up to $100,000. Remember that one, *ah*? Those who knowingly allow their premises to be used for vice-related activities will be prosecuted under the Women's Charter. Repeat offenders can *kena* fine $150,000, jailed seven years some more. Remember that one, *ah*?"

Ah Meng's arms flapped in their air. "I'm not the property owner, lease only."

"Right, well, those who live off earnings from prostitutes can face a jail term of up to seven years . . ."

"And get a $100,000 fine, *lah*. You were funnier when you were a fake gangster."

"Balls to you. Eh, how come you change the picture outside? Now got a galloping horse. Last time you had a flying dragon, right?"

"Dragon lousy for business," Ah Meng grumbled. "Had to change *lah*."

"So the horse is better for business?"

"Where got better? You bastards are here."

Low only realised he was giggling with Ah Meng when he caught the rest of his team staring at him. They knew his past. They didn't know how much he still missed it.

The inspector and the brothel owner only stopped laughing when they heard the crying next door.

Chapter 3

L ow realised his mistake immediately. Rookie mistake. The kind of blunder he'd expect from new recruits like the doe-eyed Xavier Ng, but not from himself. Never himself. He'd castigate himself later for such a gross error of judgement, another chance to self-flagellate and feed that internal loathing, but not now.

Now he needed to recover. Make amends. Follow the fireworks.

His mind always overcompensated in such moments. The self-hatred fuelled the anger. The anger triggered the fireworks, the explosions of coherence that made the internal shit just about worthwhile.

The crying came from the room next door. There hadn't been a room next door. During previous raids, the KTV lounge had one ugly main room, with microphones for the singers and hidden cameras for potential blackmailers later. But there was no additional room with an adjoining door.

Low was already pointing his gun at Ah Meng. "You built a secret room after the pandemic."

"What? No *lah*." Ah Meng looked for help around the room. None was coming.

Low tapped Ah Meng's forehead with his gun barrel.

"Bullshit. You bastards didn't play fair, not during the pandemic. Everyone else did, but you kept opening for shagging sessions. After that, no one liked you anymore. Everyone fed up already. No more closing one eye to KTV pimps like you. No more tolerance, right or not?"

"Talk cock, *lah*, Low."

Low waved the gun in front of Ah Meng's face. "You put in secret rooms that the public cannot find, for your special customers and their extra-special service."

"I never."

"Give me the key or I'll shoot you in the balls," Low said wearily.

Ah Meng did as he was told. Low instructed everyone else to stay put. He didn't need backup. He had two clear advantages. A gun. And focus. The guy in the next room had neither. Low moved quickly, picking up two faint voices. One distinct, in control, the other distant, in pain.

"You like it, right?"

"Please.

"Stop crying *lah*."

"Please. *Don't*."

Her tone destroyed Low. She wasn't asking or even pleading. She was resigned to her fate.

The inspector didn't bother with the key. Bullets were quicker. The naked man made the mistake of rolling off the sofa and jumping to his feet. He had a tattooed web on the left side of his neck, stretching across the jugular. He was facing Low, but still off-balance, confused and uncertain, presenting the inspector with an obvious and prominent target.

Low couldn't miss.

The naked man dropped to the floor, squealing in agony. "She let me do it. She let me do it."

A second kick was necessary.

"I don't cheat her, OK. I always pay."

A third kick broke whatever remained of the naked man's defiance.

"Yeah, OK, OK, don't kick me anymore."

"Then say sorry."

"What?"

"Say sorry."

"Sorry, *lah*, officer."

Low stood over the crumpled heap on the floor, lying in the foetal position, clutching his testicles. The inspector's shoe prodded the groaning's man thigh. "Not to me. To her."

"But I paid her, *wha'*?"

A fourth kick changed the naked man's perspective.

"Sorry *lah*, *wah lau*, don't kick me again, *basket*."

Xavier Ng arrived in the doorway, respectfully keeping his distance. "Shall I take him outside, sir?"

"Yeah. And don't let the fucker get dressed."

Ng dragged the whining man away. Low gently pushed the door towards the splintered frame. He picked up the woman's clothes and handed them over, his back turned, avoiding eye contact.

"Here. The aircon outside is damn cold."

She turned away and dressed in silence. Low examined the empty bottles on a cheap, IKEA table. The curled $2 bills. The upturned mirror. The powder. The residue. He heard the groan, too, a spontaneous, unwanted confirmation of pain. "We can take you to a doctor," he whispered.

"Don't want."

"That arm looks painful. You should see someone."

"No need."

"He's too violent."

She pulled on a T-shirt. "My pimp."

"So he can be violent?"

"He can send me back. So you, *ah*, cannot . . ."

"Press charges," Low interrupted, rubbing the stubble on his cheek. "Yeah, OK. So how?"

She tied her hair into a ponytail. "Like that *lor*."

"Yeah. Like that *lor*," Low muttered.

He turned to face her. She looked even younger fully clothed, too young for this life and too pretty to be allowed to escape it. He managed a weak smile and thought about his team outside, making arrests and collecting statements. They still believed that their work counted for something.

She reached down for her high heels. "They look uncomfortable," the inspector said.

"Make me tall. He like tall ones."

"What's his name?"

She scowled at his naivety.

"Yeah, all right," Low said, feeling sheepish. "What's your name?"

"Janice."

"Real name?"

"Today, it's Janice."

"And tomorrow it's whatever you need it to be."

"Yah." She tightened the buckles on her high heels.

"Surname?"

"Janice good enough."

"OK, Janice Good Enough. Take care *ah*."

She left without bothering to reply. She was a foreign woman in Singapore. She had no status. The inspector couldn't guarantee her safety and there was little to gain in either of them pretending otherwise.

Low sat on the edge of the massage table and listened to Janice slam a door outside. He still didn't know how to speak to women.

Chapter 4

Detective Inspector Ramila Mistry hated speaking to women's groups. She struggled with the tokenism. She was successful. She was attractive. She was British-Indian. She was a high-profile officer in London's Metropolitan Police Force. But some audiences recoiled at her impressive resumé. She didn't fit their ingrained expectations. In public settings she was either admired or alienated. On this occasion, it could go either way.

Mistry waited for them to take their seats: mostly white, nearly always middle-class, those with the time and affluence to champion the causes of the downtrodden. She was the daughter of Gujarati immigrants and raised in a Dagenham corner shop, selling cigarettes to angry teenagers in the vague hope that she might not be called a 'paki' that day. She didn't have time between homework and helping in the family shop to read *The Female Eunuch*.

But she empathised with the fury. That was shared ground for speaker and listener. These women knew that they couldn't walk home safely after dark. Growing up, Mistry just couldn't walk home safely.

She sipped the cold tea from a polystyrene cup and waited for the red-faced latecomers to settle. The paper plate filled with cheap biscuits only underlined the sad, feebleness of it all. They were armed with a half-empty community hall in East London, dreadful tea and dark chocolate digestives to take on the shit outside. They didn't stand a chance. Mistry could only play pretend.

"I am a copper. Please don't hold that against me," she began, pausing for the polite laughter.

"But I am also a woman. When I'm walking home alone, this doesn't do much for me." She held up her police ID and appreciated the respectful nods.

"At work during the day, this is power. At night and off-duty, this is a piece of paper. It offers no physical protection. You know that and so do I."

Mistry placed her car keys between her fingers and raised her fist to the small audience. "Come on, admit it. Who's done this walking from the car?"

She laughed, genuinely, when almost every hand in the room went up. "Of course, we've all done it, right? Every advantage. Every edge. Every possibility. We weigh them up every single time we walk from A to B, especially when it's dark. We consider every angle. How close can I park to my destination? Which is the brightest side of the street? Will the shops still be open to give us more lights, more potential eyewitnesses and support? Every footstep. Every glance. Every sound. We're always on alert, always asking questions. Why is he wearing a hoodie in warm weather? Did he cross the road to be on my side? Should I cross over? Walk quicker? Phone someone? Start running? Or should I rely on our tried and tested fallback of stabbing him to death with the keys to a Honda Jazz?"

There was less laughter now. Mistry's speech was too close to the bone for many, too accurate. They wanted solutions, not graphic depictions of daily scenarios.

"Yeah, OK, bad joke," she acknowledged. "None of this is funny. I'm guessing you all know why I was invited here, apart from the obvious. I have a vagina."

Mistry was taken aback by the warm giggling. She would remember the improvised line about her vagina. She took another sip of the bloody awful tea. What was it with community hall meetings and crap tea?

"Two years ago, my family were attacked. I'm sure you read about it."

The awkward shuffling in plastic chairs confirmed that her audience had pored over every lurid detail.

"A serial killer came after me and my family. My little boy almost lost his life. We survived, but the trauma took its toll. It almost cost me my marriage. It certainly cost my little boy his innocence. But we got through it. We got through it because police officers solved the case. Police officers did their jobs and justice was served. We are not perfect. There will always be bad apples. There are still lessons that need to be learned and mistakes that cannot be forgotten. But equally, I cannot forget that day. And I cannot forget that my first instinct, as a woman, as a mother, was to call the Metropolitan Police Force. It was the right instinct. And I still hope that every mother, every woman, would do the same."

The applause was generous but confused. The women sympathised with Mistry's horrific story but doubted the sincerity of her convictions. And so did she. For a start, she knew that she was partially lying. London's Metropolitan Police didn't save her son. She did.

But *he* had helper her.

Local officers didn't crack the case either.

He did.

That only made her more irritated. She didn't want to be thinking about him.

Fortunately, there were enough raised hands and disgruntled women in the room to keep her occupied. She
picked a woman of a similar age, early to mid-forties, in the
front row, smiling kindly, in the hope of a benign question.

"Why are you defending a misogynistic organisation?"

"I don't think that I am. I'm an Indian girl from an
Essex housing estate, who rose from a uniformed officer at
a Dagenham police station to a detective inspector, leading
my own major investigation team at Charing Cross Station.
And I would say that . . ."

"You are a direct beneficiary of affirmative actions,
which is great. We all support that. People of colour should
be represented in all major institutions, especially women."

"Thank you. I appreciate that." Mistry's tone was sarcastic. Lectures on inclusivity from people of racial privilege
still rankled.

"But the patriarchal structure endures. Less than two per
cent of reported rapes lead to a charge. And when we do
report something terrible, we suffer the victim-blaming bit.
We shouldn't have walked down that street. We shouldn't
have worn that skirt. We shouldn't have gone to that bar
or had that much to drink. We shouldn't be sex workers.
We're blamed for the perverts and porn addicts that are still
being employed at the highest levels of society, in politics
and in your police force."

The spontaneous applause was louder and more sustained
than anything that Mistry had enjoyed. She wasn't angry.
She mostly agreed.

"I know, I know," Mistry said, holding her hands up.
"I've had my arse pinched at staff parties. Didn't complain.
When I was in uniform and on the beat, walking those
freezing streets in a thin white shirt, the blokes would go
on about seeing my nipples. Didn't complain. But then,

you know what, a dick pic turned up in my email and I did complain. Took it to my DCI and the idiot faced a disciplinary hearing."

Mistry's interrogator raised her hand again. "But is he still in the job?"

"Yeah."

"Well, there you go."

The murmurs of dissent spread around the room. Mistry was at risk of losing the room. She decided to give a lost cause one more shot.

"Look, I'm not going to lie to you. We've still got a long way to go. Women need greater protection, on the street, in the workplace and even within the police force. I've worked with a few dodgy guys. We all have, in every workplace. But I've also worked with some great policemen too, inspirational blokes, decent, kind, positive people. Not every copper is rotten."

An hour later, Mistry regretted her words when she discovered that the only lead in an Essex murder case was the pain in the arse that had saved her son's life.

Chapter 5

Mistry didn't want to go back. The brick building reflected its surroundings. Dagenham Police Station was a dreary, functional relic of a neglected past. Everything seemed smaller than she'd remembered. The windows. The rooms. The ambition. Everything had shrunk.

Mistry had left the station and the town behind years ago. She had no intention of hanging around. Nostalgia was for the elderly, the nativists and those who didn't want too many looking like Mistry in their beloved country. Nostalgia was for the threatened and the vulnerable. Mistry insisted that she was neither.

She took a seat in the waiting area and pretended to be deaf. It was an instinctive act of stress relief. She was an Indian woman. Selective deafness was a vital life skill. So she just watched.

"Is that her then?"

The questioner leaned over the station counter, leering at his colleague. They were both young, uniformed officers, probably in their mid-twenties, Mistry reasoned, stocked up on youthful bullshit and local stereotypes.

"Yeah. She knows this Low geezer, apparently. Seems all right."

"Yeah, not bad." He glanced over his shoulder, casually, but still too obvious. "I wouldn't say no."

The detective inspector rose to her feet. "I'm flattered, PC ... What is your name?"

"Er, PC Henderson, ma'am." He stood up straight. "I didn't mean to ... I didn't know that ..."

"I'd be listening? How could I hear anything, being in the same room and sitting a few feet away. Clearly, I'm invisible. I'm just grateful that you acknowledged me, for a second or two. I'm so privileged that you deem me worthy of your erection."

"No, he didn't mean that, inspector," PC Walker said, playing the diplomatic duty officer.

Mistry joined them at the counter. "Do you know what always gets me? It's not your everyday misogyny. It's the presumption of my consent. The idea that I'll be happy to let you give me one, that I'd actually ask you first, beg you by the sound of it, putting you in such a tough position, where you've got to actually take a moment, and give me some serious consideration before deciding that, if you had time in your busy schedules, you'd probably do me a favour and give me one."

Henderson looked up at the ceiling. He saw the omni-present eye in the sky. Bloody cameras. In the corner, above the duty desk, on their chests, everywhere. Coppers were monitored, day and night. They really couldn't say anything anymore. The PC in his title meant something else entirely now. His career was in those cameras.

"Sorry, ma'am. I didn't think you could hear me."

"Of course I could hear you." Mistry eyeballed the junior officer. "We can always bloody hear you."

Walker cleared his throat. "Would you like to register a complaint, Inspector?"

Mistry sighed at the shrivelled men. "What would be the point? What would it achieve? Yeah. Exactly. Shall we just crack on? Why am I here?"

Henderson stepped up, eager to make amends. "We found twelve women in a lorry at Rainham Marshes, all alive, which was lucky. But the driver, an IC5, was found dead in his cabin."

"An IC5?"

"Yeah, Chinese," Walker interjected. "No ID yet. Doing a fingerprint check, but might be an illegal, so that'll take time. His throat was slashed with a large blade. Early pathology suggests it was swift, one slash, not a frenzied attack, quite deliberate, almost professional. They had little penknives on them, but too small to do that. Anyway, there was no blood on any of them."

"Obviously, the murder isn't on your patch," Walker continued. "Not anymore anyway."

"Yeah, I heard you grew up around here," Henderson remarked eagerly.

Mistry ignored him. "Carry on, PC Walker."

"Yeah, right, so we've tried to interview all twelve women. But none of them are speaking, not one. We've had in all kinds of Chinese translators, but nothing, not a single word, except one."

Mistry nodded. "The one who mentioned Low's name."

Henderson and Walker exchanged nervous glances. "Yeah, well, after what happened before, with your family and that, our guvnor got in touch with your guvnor at Charing Cross and that was it. We don't really know what else to do at this point."

The interview room was grim. Mistry adjusted her skirt beneath the table. She was surprisingly nervous. She had buried her past life at the police station for a reason. There were always too many like PC Henderson and not enough like PC Walker.

On the other side of the table, the Chinese woman's appearance surprised her.

The woman was still attractive, despite the scrubbed, tired face and the borrowed clothes from a local charity. But she was older than they usually were. Illegals were younger, stronger and more eager to make any kind of living. This woman was around Mistry's age. Her long black hair flowed down her back. Her nails were recently manicured. Even her eyebrows had been threaded. She chewed gum continuously. She was too polished for a sex worker and too old to fit the Asian village girl archetype. The image was jarring. Nothing matched.

Mistry gestured towards the other, much younger Chinese woman sitting at the table. "Well, we have a translator who speaks both Mandarin and Cantonese, am I right?"

The younger woman nodded proudly.

"But I'm told by the other officers that you understand English, which is great. So let me give you the good news first. You are not in trouble. The knives that you all had in the back of the lorry are too small. They are not the murder weapon. Plus, none of you had any traces of blood or any evidence to suggest you'd even been near the driver's cabin or his seat. There is a possibility of all of you seeking asylum status in the UK, if you meet the criteria, though the criteria seems to change on an hourly basis. But you had no passports with you in the lorry and you're all refusing to speak. We can't identify you. We don't know who you are. We can't help unless you speak."

The Chinese woman folded her arms. Her translator

muttered advice in Mandarin. She shook her head. Mistry checked her watch. She had promised to pop in and see her father on the way home. He lived nearby; the last connection to a distant past.

"I know Stanley Low," Mistry said.

The Chinese woman stopped chewing. She was finally paying attention to the Indian copper.

"Detective Inspector Stanley Low. He works for the Singapore Police Force, right? I've known him for many years." Mistry's words sounded confessional, almost remorseful. "I've known him since we studied at university together in London. At least twenty-five years. He's my friend. Was he your friend in Singapore?"

"Last time."

The voice terrified Mistry. It wasn't her words. It was her accent. The woman sounded liked Low.

"Oh, he was your friend last time. That's great. That's really great. And why do you want to speak to him now? Do you think he can help you?"

"His people send me here." She tapped the table hard.

Mistry couldn't hide her confusion. "Policemen? Policemen sent you here?"

"Pimps." The Chinese woman spat out the word. "Low was a pimp last time."

Chapter 6

Dr Tracy Lai noticed a change in appearance. Low had made an effort. The stubble and unkempt hair were still there, as always, but the inspector had at least graced their appointment with clean clothes.

"You look well." The psychiatrist wasn't lying.

"What can I say? Life's been good to me."

Lai always found her patient amusing. His intellect was a polarising, divisive quality, but his mood had improved of late. The wearying, misanthropic sarcasm had almost given way to self-deprecation. Almost.

"I raided an illegal KTV lounge this morning. Arrested half a dozen sex workers, a few pimps, some punters and a CEO from a well-known multi-national corporation," Low said, counting off the arrests on his fingers.

"Sounds interesting."

"Sounds like a dull Monday morning in Singapore." Low stretched his legs. He hadn't bothered with sleep. He needed to come down first.

"You seem bored."

"I am bloody bored. I was doing this shit twenty years ago and I'm doing it again, wasting my time, sweeping up piles of ants. Next week, there'll be another raid, another pile. I don't work for the police. I work for Rentokil."

Lai had noted some time ago that her patient's rage often gave way to a degree of resignation, even melancholy. That could be worse from a medical standpoint. The anger gave him a target, a focus. Now he didn't particularly care.

"We talked about this before, keeping perspective," Lai said softly, straightening her skirt. "Two years ago, your career was done. You said so yourself. They had put you on some speakers' circuit, to get you out of the way, according to you. And then you got involved with that London case and everything changed."

"Yeah, I saw her again."

Low always saw her. Now she was in a psychiatrist's office, sitting across from him in an executive leather chair. Perfect hair. Impeccable dress sense. Taking notes. Judging him.

"I know. You told me."

"She reminded me of you."

"You've told me that, too."

"Or you reminded me of her. I knew her first, right? Anyway, you both have a lot in common."

"Such as?"

"You don't put up with my bullshit. That's the first thing."

"You like independent women?"

Low considered the question. "Nah, too obvious. Bit too textbook for you, that one. It's more than that. You don't *need* me. I almost forget what that feels like."

"I don't understand."

Hunched in his chair, Low peered up at his confidant. He was no longer obligated to see a psychiatrist. He was no longer working undercover. The original order, from

30

an old boss in the corruption unit, lapsed years ago. But he had nowhere else to be.

"A woman was raped this morning."

Lai couldn't hide the horror. She was trained. Instructed. Never look away. No clues. Open face. Blank canvas. But Low saw it in her eyes. He usually did.

"Yeah. I know," he continued. "But she *wasn't* raped, not in a legal sense. There was consent. Sort of. There were pre-existing conditions, to use the popular phrase. She's a foreigner working illegally as a KTV hostess, whatever that means. And he was her pimp, whatever that means."

"What does that mean?"

"It means we ignore her and he owns her. She doesn't exist. She isn't real. And if she isn't real, he can do whatever he likes. Play out his Pornhub fantasies whenever he likes. He beats her. She bleeds. She wipes away the blood and they start again. That's the agreement. And I sit here with you, two elite-school kids, sharing my first world problems about an ex-girlfriend like a needy teenager."

"So you have to save a rape victim to feel needed?"

Low almost laughed at Lai's bluntness. He pointed a patronising finger at her instead. "Now that one was good. That's why I come here, to get the juices flowing. Yeah, I need rape victims to play the great male saviour, right? That's good. I'd probably reach the same conclusion in interrogation. But that's the difference between your world and mine. You still think these people can be saved. She knows she can't. I could've destroyed him. But she wouldn't press charges, wouldn't even tell me his name. So, no, I don't want to save rape victims to feel needed." Low looked away. "It would be nice just to feel needed."

Now it was Lai's turn to lean forward. "That sounds like self-pity."

31

"No, it sounds like a sleep-deprived detective who spent the early hours kicking a rapist in the balls."

The psychiatrist offered a kind smile. "Well, I hope you found the target at least."

"Every bloody time," Low said, appreciating the levity.

"Do you still miss her? Ramila Mistry?"

"Wow, that was a punch in the face. You even said her full name, too. Double jab. Bang. Bang. I'm impressed. You go subtle with the balls joke, lull me into a false sense of security, and then you kick *me* in the nuts."

"Metaphorically speaking."

"Yeah, well, metaphorically speaking, no, I don't."

"You don't miss her?"

"No, I don't miss her." Low registered the surprise. "You don't believe me?"

"Did I say that?"

"Your raised eyebrow did."

"We often end up talking about her. You just said I reminded you of her."

"You also remind me of an old auntie who never gave me *hong bao* at Chinese New Year and I don't miss her either."

"But you still remember her?"

"Of course. Her breath stank of durian and she always kissed me on the lips. You'd remember her, too."

Lai chuckled. "And she didn't even give you *hong bao*?"

"Gave me nothing. Just sat in the corner with her soggy lips playing mahjong."

"And Ramila?"

"She never had soggy lips. Or played mahjong."

"How do you feel about her now?"

Low scratched the back of his head in irritation. "I feel like she's happily married with a cute kid and an idiot husband. Why would I begrudge her that? She's settled over there. I'm raiding KTV lounges over here. Everyone has moved on, except you and your A-level psychiatry."

Low almost believed his words, too. He believed them when his phone buzzed in his pocket. He believed them when he swiped the screen. He believed them right up until the text message appeared.

It's Ramila. It's urgent. Call me now.

"Oh, fuck," Low said, already on his feet.

With a heavy sigh, Dr Tracy Lai closed the door on her lost patient.

Chapter 7

Heathrow Airport was always cold, especially at dawn. And the road outside was full of startled Singaporeans struggling with the cold. Low watched them all, throwing suitcases to the floor and scrambling for extra layers. He saw himself doing the same, a quarter of a century ago, in a different life.

Faces changed. Behaviour didn't.

Singaporean travellers still arrived wearing the wrong clothes at the wrong time of day. Those raised in an air-conditioned nation struggled with any temperature that couldn't be controlled.

Low stomped his feet and pulled on his hoodie, but it made no difference.

England still got into his bones.

"No loitering. No loitering."

The voice was grumpy, a walking, talking hi-visibility vest ushering guests away from the road and out of the way. His message was unequivocal.

Welcome to England. Now piss off.

Low identified with the bluntness. It reminded him of Singapore.

While those around him hurried to follow orders, Low

gripped his tea and waited. He savoured the cup's warmth. He wasn't sure how much he'd get from her.

He didn't even recognise her initially. Different car. Different haircut. Same face. There was only so much she could change.

He threw his overnight bag into the back seat. No child seat. Time had passed.

Low opened the passenger door and hesitated.

"I think you can sit in the front," Mistry said, looking up at him. "Hurry up, before I get a ticket."

Low was still tugging on his seatbelt when she roared towards the M4. "How was the flight?" She asked, changing lanes, looking only in her mirrors.

"Ah, you know, the usual chicken or fish and no sleep."

Low rubbed his eyes and watched the dark clouds drift towards the motorway. "Why is the sky always so low here?"

"We're closer to God."

Low laughed politely. "Oh yeah, I forgot. How's your boy?"

"Good, yeah, really good actually. It was tough at first."

"I bet."

"But in the last few months or so, he's really started to flourish in school."

Mistry honked her horn. The car in front had changed lanes abruptly, but not dangerously. She wasn't really lashing out at the driver.

"Dad's struggling though. Wants to retire. He's had enough."

"Can imagine."

Mistry briefly examined her passenger. Low didn't look any worse, which was progress of sorts. He was still a human collage, all mismatched clothing and unbrushed

35

hair, thrown together and mostly missing. She was pretty sure he was wearing the same jeans and hoodie from two years ago. The eyebags were deeper and his face more hollowed out. But he seemed less volatile. He looked spent.

"You didn't have to come back. We could've done this on Zoom or something."

"She would never speak to me on Zoom. Anyway, it's only a couple of days and my boss didn't mind. Actually, my boss didn't care. Told me to interview the woman. Deport her if necessary and that's it. Heck care *lah*. My numbers are good."

"Numbers?"

London's greenery rolled past the window. Low still found it extraordinary that a city so dense could be surrounded by such a timeless hinterland. Even the sea couldn't stop Singapore's building blitzkrieg. Land was reclaimed and the cranes marched on. But London's M25 divided two worlds, one green, the other full of concrete. Singapore had no hinterlands, only the concrete.

"My number of prostitutes. Sorry. Sex workers. I never do get the terminology right. Sex workers. I'm in vice now, raiding KTV lounges, massage parlours, all the glamorous shit."

"Christ, you're back where you started."

"Yep." Low stared at the passing trees. "Aren't I lucky?"

"Why vice?"

"Politics. KTV lounges didn't behave themselves during the pandemic."

"I don't get it."

Low sighed. "While everyone else was social distancing and closing businesses, the KTV lounges sneakily stayed open. Singaporeans kept shagging during the pandemic.

"The public didn't like that. So the government told us not to like it either."

"Didn't like what? The shagging or the staying open?"

Low laughed. "Both. In a controlled nation, all must be controlled. We get very vindictive when people don't do as they're told."

"Singapore has always had dodgy KTV lounges," Mistry said, changing lanes again.

"Public less tolerant now. So they let me out to clean 'em up. Then they'll hide me in an office again."

"Nothing changes, eh?"

"Never. How's your husband?"

"Not a copper anymore."

"Oh." Low rested his chin on his hand. "That's a shame."

"Yeah, right. Don't pretend you care."

"I don't. But you obviously do. What's he doing now?"

"Lecturing. Criminology."

Low clapped his hands together. "Ah, that's brilliant. Criminology. That's where we met at LSE. The irony, eh? Does he know I'm here?"

"Of course he knows. We're grown-ups. Have a look in there."

Low grabbed a brown folder off the dashboard and went straight for the mugshots. The women's faces surprised him. "They're not all Chinese."

"No and seeing as they're not saying a word to us, we're reduced to racial profiling."

"Cannot say that in the next diversity seminar."

"Sod off. Anyway, we reckon they're mostly Chinese, China Chinese, except your girl, who seems to be Singaporean, which makes no sense at all. And there could be one or two from Indonesia and a few in there from further north, maybe Burma. It's hard to tell when they won't speak. Someone has scared the shit out of them."

"A guy with his throat cut will do that."

"We're doing fingerprint checks, but we don't even have their passports or their backgrounds. Reduced to checking CCTV at the airports and docks. Looking for needles in haystacks because we've got no idea when or how they arrived in the UK."

"Her name is Grace Chen," Low said, holding up a photo of the Chinese woman. "She's Singaporean, a bit younger than us, around forty, forty plus, but definitely too old to be part of a sex trafficking operation."

"You could've told me her name before you got on the plane."

Low grinned. "Wanted to make sure I got my UK holiday first."

"Bastard. Is that what she was before?"

"Yeah, a long time ago though. Worked for Tiger. Most of them did."

"That makes sense. She said you were her pimp."

Low laughed loudly. "I wasn't her pimp. I'll *tekan* her for that."

"Well I know what you were." Mistry wouldn't look at him. "You don't have to hide anything from me."

"Yes, all right. It's seven o'clock in the morning and that was eight cases ago. Don't need another psychiatrist. Got one already."

"How's that working out?"

"Expensively. Look, I was never a pimp for Tiger. But I knew Grace quite well. I liked her. She was sweet."

Low turned the mugshots over. He didn't need to see Grace Chen's face anymore.

"Especially to me. She was really kind to me. Considering."

"Considering what?"

"I almost had her killed."

Chapter 8

Low watched the fog drift across the M25 as they passed a sign for the Harry Potter studio tour. He used to think London was magical. The city with silly names. Potters Crouch. Abbots Langley. Bricket Wood. He remembered being a student on the National Express bus, laughing at the absurd *ang moh* place names. They tapped into a Singaporean visitor's escapist fantasy, a whimsical land of village greens, cream teas and a splash of casual racism.

Back then, Low had wanted from London what every tourist expected from the Harry Potter tour now. Red buses. Black taxis. Old mailboxes. That was the truly magical bit, to feed one's nostalgia and make the past look better than it ever really was.

The inspector understood that now.

"Grace knew that I was an undercover cop," he muttered, staring at the misty fields.

Mistry was surprised at the revelation. Low was flawed in all aspects of regular life, except one. He was never exposed as an undercover operative because there was nothing to expose. Quaint notions of morality were for lesser coppers. Low was whatever he needed to be. Simplistic lines of right and wrong were not ignored or crossed. He rarely saw them in the first place.

"That's not like you," Mistry said. "You don't usually get caught."

"I wasn't caught. I was seen, coming out of CPIB." Low noted her confusion. "The corruption unit, when I was undercover as Ah Lian."

"Yeah, you can skip that bit."

"Hey, they teach that case at LSE now, in our old criminology class. Maybe your husband will give out my Tiger case as coursework."

"Get on with it."

Low smirked. Her feistiness still amused him. "I saw Grace in the CPIB car park," he recalled. "It was late, dark, no one around. She was giving a blow job to my superior officer."

"Clean and safe Singapore, eh?"

"Sunny island in the sea."

"So she blackmailed you?"

"No, he did."

"Your old boss? Why?"

"Gambling debts. What else? This is before we had the respectable casinos. So respectable senior officers had to place their bets with illegal bookies. I don't think he knew that he had debts with Tiger, not directly. I certainly didn't, not until I caught him in the car park with Grace."

"Did Tiger know your boss was a copper?"

"Of course. The old bastard loved it. Once he knew, he went all in. Set the detective up with Grace in a KTV lounge and then he had everything. Photos. Videos. Debts. A complete insurance policy against a church-going, family man in the corruption unit. But Tiger couldn't help himself. Started to squeeze my boss for more money, wanted his condo, his car, just because he could. Tiger didn't need the money. It appealed to his perverse righteousness, putting a god-fearing detective out on the street."

"What happened?"

Low wiped the condensation from his window. The fog was dissipating. The grass verge was full of litter.

"My boss retaliated. He tried to set us all up. He wanted me to see him with Grace. He set up the blow job in the car park. He wasn't stupid. He wanted me to know everything so I could fix it."

"How?"

"I had to persuade Tiger, as Ah Lian, that CPIB had too much evidence. He had to back off. Forget my boss' debts and let him go. And Tiger had to take care of Grace."

"Kill her?"

"No, take her to get her legs waxed. Of course, kill her. And if I didn't, my upstanding boss, a government scholar no less, was going to tell Tiger who I really was, blow my cover, all because he couldn't say no to a bloody bet. Every option seemed to involve someone dying. And I liked Grace. We made each other laugh."

"So what did you do?"

"A day later, my boss shot himself."

Mistry saw her knuckles turn white as she gripped the steering wheel. "Jesus Christ."

"Yeah, they found him at East Coast Park. Service revolver. A single shot to the head. No suicide note."

Mistry turned to her passenger. "Did you?"

"You're not seriously going to ask me that, are you?"

"No. I suppose. Did you speak to Tiger though?"

"The night before."

"What did you say?"

Low focused on the hypnotic patchwork of stone walls,

farms and hedgerows. He still loved the orderly shapes of England's greenery. "What does it matter? I was a better liar than my boss. I lived and he died. We make our choices. But I was still screwed if Grace gave me up to Tiger, but she never said a word. Never told anyone that she saw me in the CPIB car park. Never said who I really was. I owe her for that."

"She still called you a pimp."

"Ah, that was Ah Lian," Low said, grinning at Mistry. "She liked Inspector Low."

An hour later, Low and Mistry were ushered into the dingy interview room at Dagenham Police Station. Low was shocked at Grace Chen's appearance. She looked haggard. Her eyes darted around the room. She was petrified.

"Hey, Grace, good to see you again," Low said, taking a seat.

He meant it, too. Old faces from the past reminded the detective of who he once was. He liked that. "Never thought we'd meet in a shitty London police station, eh?"

Chen wasn't interested in small talk. She was already crying when she grabbed Low's hands.

"They try to kill us, Ah Lian. They try to kill all of us."

Chapter 9

Low tried comforting a woman he hadn't seen in fifteen years. He sensed Chen's fear. He recognised the discomfort. She was a foreigner, an Asian, an alien. She was never going to feel secure around these people.

The Singaporean inspector examined the leering uniform standing over Chen's shoulder. Overbearing. Intimidating. Uncaring. The constable's crispy face and sharp haircut revealed too many trips to the tanning salon and the mirror. He also wore a watch that was beyond his pay grade.

Low could only be in Essex.

London's next-door neighbour benefited from the proximity but lacked the cosmopolitanism. There was a tendency to overcompensate with superficial displays of wealth. In his short sleeves, the copper even had the tan lines of a weekend golfer, strolling across fairways to emphasise his acquired status. Low smiled. Essex people reminded him of Singaporeans.

"What's your name?"

"PC Henderson." The much younger man flashed the brightest teeth that Low had ever seen. "I'm the one who found 'em."

"*Women*," Mistry said, sitting beside Low. "You found twelve women."

"Yes, ma'am. My partner and I found twelve women. She was the one who ran for help and then asked to speak to you." Henderson nodded towards Low.

"Yeah, that's great. Thanks. You can leave now," Low said.

"My guvnor asked me to stay."

"And we politely asked you to leave," Mistry said. "I don't need to pull rank, do I?"

"No, ma'am. But I've been ordered to stay here."

"That *ang moh* said he'd fuck me." Chen glowered at the tanned officer. Her anger caught everyone off guard, even Low.

"What?"

"He think I *blur* one. Talking with the other *ang moh* before, saying I was the best, right or not?"

"No, no, I never said that," Henderson said,

"Why would she lie?" Mistry patted Chen's hand. "Would you like to make a statement?"

"A statement about what? She's lying. This is ridiculous. I'm calling in my guvnor." Henderson reached for the door handle, but never quite made it.

"She's not lying. I know she's not lying for two reasons."

There was something about the Chinese copper's voice that stopped Henderson at the door, something authoritative, absolute even. "Yeah? Like what?"

Low waited for the police constable to make eye contact.

"Well, PC Sun Burn, the first thing is, Grace lies for a living. But she's not working now. She's got no reason to lie now. Plus, she's never lied to me. And second, that white line on your ring finger."

Henderson examined his left hand. "What about it?'"

44

"You've taken off your wedding ring. So maybe you're divorced. But you put it back on when you play golf or sit in the garden with your family, which has given you the tan line. So maybe you're not divorced. You just lie about being married. Either way, you take it off when you're on the hunt. That white line is a beacon for all the ladies."

"Including me," Mistry said.

"Really *ah*?" Low was almost giggling.

"Yeah, he was telling his mate that he'd give me one, too. You and I are in privileged company, Grace. We're both worthy of *this*."

The two women smiled at each other.

"Ah, that's hilarious, PC Sun Burn," Low said, clapping his hands. "Well played. You should come to Singapore and teach us men how to interact with women. We're always bringing *ang moh* experts to Singapore to teach us how to communicate with each other. But I do have one more question."

Low rose to his feet. "Would you shag me?"

The question unnerved Henderson. "What?"

"Would you shag me, PC Sun Burn? Your wife has either left you or she's not giving you enough, so you're clearly desperate. You don't stop talking about all the women you're gonna shag. These two here. The girls on the truck. You're not fussy. It sounds like anyone with a pulse and an orifice will do. I think I've still got both. So, would you like to shag me?"

"No." Henderson was incredulous. "You're mental."

"Well, that's settled then. The three of us don't want to shag you either. So, if you wouldn't mind, *ah*, fuck off."

Henderson slammed the door on his way out. Low rubbed his hands gleefully as he returned to his seat. "I actually enjoyed that," he said, looking straight at Chen. "Now, who's trying to kill you, Grace?"

Chen focused on the Indian copper.

"*Ah*, she's OK. Seriously," Low said. "Inspector Mistry and I have known each other for many years. She even came with me to Singapore last time, right?"

"Get on with it," Mistry whispered.

"She contacted me and got permission for me to be here. I wanna help you Grace. You helped me last time. Remember?"

Chen seemed to nod in recollection.

"OK, then. Then you gotta help me now. How did you get here?"

"Fly."

Mistry frowned. "On a plane? Seriously? We need you to tell the truth, Grace."

Chen turned to Low for an explanation.

"Pimps don't pay for chickens to fly to England, Grace. No need. Got enough *ang moh* sex workers, from here, from Eastern Europe. No need for Asians. They can make money in Asia. Plus, hookers don't leave Singapore to make money. Hookers go to Singapore to make money. They don't fly sex workers to the UK from Singapore, Grace. You know that. Come on *ah*. You need to help me here."

Chen jabbed a manicured finger at Low. "You help me first."

"Of course. I'm here *wha'*."

"I never want to come here. You bring me home."

"To Singapore? Yeah *lah*. Can. No problem. That's why I'm here, Grace, to help you. Now you help us."

Chen's bloodshot eyes peered into the detective's weary face. "You sure or not?"

"You saved Ah Lian last time. My turn now."

Chen nodded, seemingly satisfied with the answer.

46

She picked at the chipped tabletop with a long fingernail. "Chickens."

"Yeah, I know," Low said.

"No, *chickens*, chickens."

"Understand. But why bring chickens to England?"

"No, *lah*, not those chickens, real chickens."

"I swear if one more person says 'chickens'," Mistry said. "What are you two talking about?"

"Sometimes sex workers are called chickens in Singapore," Low said quickly, eager to move on.

Chen slapped the table. "Not chickens. We pull chickens. The real one *ah*. Cluck-cluck. We come to England to pull chickens, OK?"

"Pull chickens?" Mistry sought an explanation from Low. He shrugged, equally clueless.

"Pull chicken *lah*, you know, cluck-cluck." Chen flicked out her arms, miming poultry. "Pull out the feather one."

Mistry leaned in. "You've been brought over to work on a farm?"

"Ah, this one gets it." Chen sat back in her chair and showed off her false fingernails. "*Ang mohs* expect me to pull chickens with these. Idiots."

Mistry finally understood, shaking her head at the realisation. "We don't have enough foreign workers in the farms. So they bring her over to pluck chickens . . ."

"And turkey," Chen interrupted. "Turkey also got."

"So they bring over chickens to pluck chickens to save your roast dinners?"

"That's how we're making England great again," Mistry said.

"Unbelievable. And you agreed to this, Grace?"

"No choice. I owe money and too old to fuck men already. So I fuck chicken."

"*Pluck*, Grace. The word is *pluck*."

"*Aiyoh*, pluck, fuck, heck care *lah*. Still got shitty job."

"So how is working for Old MacDonald gonna get you killed, Grace?"

Chen took a moment before answering. She eyed the female detective. Mistry had a kind face. Chen seemed relieved.

"At the airport, they put us inside the truck. Damn smelly. We drive first. One hour plus. Then they stop. Open the truck. Place damn ugly. Lots of trucks and garages."

"Like an industrial estate?"

"Yah, exactly," Chen agreed. "Like Kranji. First, the China driver tells us to get out. Go pee. Then this *ang moh* come, quite fat one, very fierce. He locks us inside again. Shouts at the driver. Tells him to go somewhere else. Rain something."

"Rainham. Rainham Marshes," Mistry said.

"Whatever *lah*. We don't drive for long. We stop and then nothing. For a long time. Then we hear the driver screaming to someone. He was shouting. *I won't. I won't.* Then nothing again. Then we hear him on the phone."

"The driver?" Mistry asked.

"No. His killer."

Chen's eyes looked off into the distance. "He was outside one. Heard his breathing. Heard him speak on phone. *It's done,* he said. Then he listen some more. Then he say something else. *The women, too?* That's it. He just say that. *The women, too.*

"We never moved. We heard his footsteps. I take my knife. The other girls follow me. We were so confused. First, they give us knives outside airport. For protection, they said. Now they want to kill us. We heard the keys. He was opening the truck. So I scream and bang on the wall. Bang. Bang. Bang. Bang. Bang."

Chen's fist pounded the table. "Everyone copy me. We bang and bang and bang. And I bluff him some more. I keep screaming the same thing ... *Got secret phone. Call police already.*"

"That was really smart, Grace."

"Yeah, it was," Mistry agreed. "Saved your life."

Chen shrugged. "Must make noise in my job."

"And then what happened?"

"We heard him run away. I wait first. Then I look outside. Take my knife. I close the girls inside. Keep them safe first. Then I find that uncle. Mr Alan. Nice man."

Low sat up. "The fat guy at the industrial estate. Did he say anything else?"

"The *ang moh* one *ah*? No *lah*, just complain, complain. Too many women. Not enough drivers."

Mistry glanced over at Low. "Lorry company."

Low nodded. "That's great, Grace. Anything else?"

"His accent. Like that arsehole outside." Chen pointed at the door. "Same accent."

"Henderson? That's a local, Essex accent," Mistry said.

"Whatever *lah*. Maybe he's called Steven."

"Why do you say that?"

"When they open the truck to go pee, I saw another truck outside. It said Steve's Transport and ... something ... something beginning with H."

"Haulage?"

"Don't know. Maybe."

Low could've hugged her. The years had passed, but Grace Chen was still helping her fellow Singaporean.

Chapter 10

S teve Robertson took his time along the fairway, waving to his staff and their young families. One of the kids ran towards him. "Can we fix it?"

"Yes, we can," Robertson shouted, ruffling the giggling boy's hair.

Robertson had pulled out Bob the Builder this year. Last year, he was lumbered with the Peppa Pig costume, which had covered his head.

Bob the Builder was better. The costume didn't obscure his face and Robertson liked to be seen. His face was his passport around Essex. Everyone knew his story. From stacking supermarket shelves to stacking pallets on one of the largest haulage companies in Europe.

Steve's Transport and Haulage Company. *His* company.

"Come on Stevie, you fat bastard."

Robertson tipped his yellow hardhat to the puce-faced heckler as he made his way to the eighteenth green. The Castle Point Golf Course was always going to be his choice for the company's annual family fun day. As a kid, he'd pinched the club's golf balls and sold them in school. As a self-made millionaire, he was a revered, lifetime member. He had arrived. So he had paid for the lot, the course fees, the clubhouse grub, the fancy-dress costumes, everything.

Everyone else needed to know that he'd arrived, too.

But the location was also symbolic. Built on the banks of the Thames Estuary, the golf course allowed Robertson to wander near the river that had made him rich. His cargo flowed out of Essex and across Europe. Further opportunities flowed back again. The tides guaranteed money at both ends.

But he prided himself on still being one of the lads, one of their own. Everyone called him *Steve* on site. Everyone knew where they stood with him, even the sunburnt heckler. "Piss off, Shaun," Robertson said, removing the yellow hardhat to wipe his brow. "I'm sweating like a nun in a knocking shop here."

Shaun roared with laughter. His cheeks developed a purple tinge as he swigged from a lager bottle. Others in the crowd tittered politely. Robertson paid their wages.

Only one woman frowned, folding her arms to emphasise her displeasure. "Language please. Remember the kids, Bob the Builder."

Robertson waved apologetically at his wife. "Sorry, love. Forgot where I was."

"Well, stop milking it and hurry up. We're all starving," Emily Robertson said. Her frown quickly gave way to something warmer, kinder. She was proud of their success.

As always, Robertson obeyed his wife's instructions and lined up the putt. He was within two feet. It was a gimme. But he dithered anyway, playing to his crowd.

"Right, who fancies a flutter? Fifty quid says this goes straight in. Anyone?"

"This is a family day, not a gambling event," his wife said. "Remember that."

"Ah, you're a miserable lot."

He sank the putt and set off around the green. His portly frame struggled beneath the cloudless sky, but the perspiration was a badge of honour. Sweat and toil had taken him to the eighteenth green of his beloved golf club. Robertson had earned this.

"Can we fix it? Yes we can!" he cried, basking in the applause. No one was going to enjoy his family fun day more than his family. He was paying for it.

A scowling Chinese bloke and a tasty Indian bird were waiting for him outside the clubhouse.

"Nice costume," the woman said.

"Never met a murderer dressed as a cartoon character before," the bloke added.

Robertson stepped away from the clubhouse, making sure to close the door behind him. He took a moment to soak in the surroundings. Hadleigh Downs always looked lovelier on a sunny day. Other golf clubs had superior postcodes, but never a better view.

He pointed westwards. "Grew up over there, near Canvey Island police station, funnily enough."

"Yeah, we know," Mistry said.

Robertson gestured towards the other direction. "That's Leigh on Sea over there. Posh. My parents used to tell people we lived near Leigh on Sea, not Canvey Island. But I've never been ashamed of where I grew up. Proud of it."

"Yeah, that's great. Can we save the 'working class hero' bit. I've only got a couple of days here," Low said.

The inspector was testy. He needed another lead, a breakthrough, anything to delay the sense of impotence. He had secured an initial lead from Grace Chen and promised to get her home to Singapore. His work was almost done. Mistry wouldn't need him anymore.

Robertson sneered at the Singaporean. "Look, what do you want, mate? You're not local police and I still haven't forgotten your dig about me being a murderer. I'm being polite. I'm helping you out because I've got a clubhouse full of my staff and their kids and I don't wanna make a scene. But don't take the piss. If you've got something to say, just say it."

"Fair enough, you're right," Low said, holding his hands up. "I'll go first. Why do white men always wear ankle socks with white trainers?"

"I'm going back inside." Robertson headed for the clubhouse.

"Why was a lorry driver killed doing a job for you?" Mistry asked.

Robertson stopped. The source of the accusation confused him. He thought more about the questioner than the question. Her confidence threw him. She was an Indian and a woman. The demure appearance, brown face and ballsy attitude didn't add up.

"None of my drivers have been killed. They're all in there, dressed like Captain America and Barney Rubble."

"It does look like a fun day for all the family," Low muttered, peering through the clubhouse window.

"You didn't hear about the lorry found at Rainham Marshes? It was only up the road from your company," Mistry said.

"Didn't have my name on the side, did it? Not my lorry. You do know there are haulage firms from Barking to the Dartford Crossing right? We tend to stick our supply chains near rivers and ports. I heard the Romans did the same round here."

"The Romans didn't stick twelve women in a lorry and stab the driver."

"Neither did I."

"I think that's true," Low said, turning away from the clubhouse window, as if finally ready to pay attention. "Well, half of it's true. The other half is probably bullshit."

Robertson took off his Bob the Builder hardhat to wipe his balding head. "What's he going on about?"

"Yeah, what is this, Stanley?" Mistry asked.

"It didn't make sense. It didn't make sense coming over here." Low paced along the gravel footpath. "You don't shit on your own doorstep. You don't bring a potential murder target into your own workplace, one of your own drivers, in front of dozens of street cameras and then send him away to have his throat cut."

"Yeah, exactly," Robertson said, cuffing his sweaty chin.

"You don't let people you intend to kill see your face, your workplace and your name on the side of your trucks. And you don't let them out to pee in your site toilets."

"That's because I didn't."

"Oh shut up, Bob the Builder. You knew they were in the back of your truck, even if you've deleted the CCTV footage on your site. You saw them. Grace doesn't lie. And you locked her in the back of a truck and sent her off to be killed. So we'll get you for trafficking. Maybe you knew what was planned. Maybe you didn't. But someone told you to send that driver to the marshes, which makes you an accessory to murder."

Robertson unbuttoned the drenched shirt of his Bob the Builder costume. "Let's not get carried away, eh? Yeah, I told the driver where to go. But it's not what you think."

Chapter 11

Robertson almost laughed in their Asian faces. One brown. The other, well, Robertson had no idea how to describe the other one. Dirty, perhaps. One brown. One dirty. Both judging him. A white man being tried in the court of Asian opinions, at his beloved golf course, during his family fun day. The world really had spun off its axis.

He sensed their indignation too. He saw it in their dark, smug faces, looking down at him for lacking the empathy and liberalism that only comes with university educations and multicultural upbringings, apparently.

They really had no idea.

"So I guess I'm a people smuggler now."

"We don't know what you are," Mistry said.

"Oh, I think I've got a vague idea," Low mumbled.

"Look, nothing I do is illegal, all right?"

"Well, in a literal sense, locking twelve women inside the back of a lorry is illegal, so you're wrong already," Mistry made little effort to conceal her anger.

Robertson spotted it and turned on the woman. "Oh, I get it, now. I'm a white van man, right? You've already got me pegged. I love a full English, hate foreigners and wish they'd all piss off back to where they came from, right?"

Mistry tugged on her cuffs. "If the cap fits."

"You're way off the mark, love."

Mistry stepped close enough to smell the Stella Artois. "Don't call me love. You call me 'Detective Inspector'. And, no, I'm not way off the mark. This area voted to get them out. And it all went tits up. So now you've got to sneak the foreigners back in again, in one of your bloody lorries."

Robertson took a step towards Mistry. His cheeks reddened, the broken blood vessels betraying too many last orders in dying pubs.

"Oh, because I voted leave? You see a white, working-class bloke so I must be a raving right-winger. Look. I built my company in the 1990s, love, I mean, Detective Inspector. Most of my drivers came from Eastern Europe. My best drivers were Polish and Romanian. We celebrated all our drivers' national and religious holidays in my firm and gave them extra days off. Do you know why? They bought my house in Chigwell. They also bought my Spanish holiday home. You know what my British drivers do? Scratch their bollocks all day. So I'm not exactly running around my yard singing *Rule Britannia*."

Low leaned forward. "The driver was Chinese."

"Yeah, I saw the news."

"The driver was Chinese," the Singaporean repeated, as if reassuring himself. "Truck drivers aren't Chinese, not here. We buy and sell the shit in the back of the trucks. We buy and sell the people stuck in the back of the trucks. But we don't drive them, not around here. In Chinatown, sure. London, Manchester, Liverpool, the main cities, I can see that, maybe, but this is white man's land. Where got Chinese drivers?"

Low marvelled at the dancing fireworks. He followed their dizzying trajectories, channelling them. "No EU drivers. Not enough British drivers, too expensive or not trained, so someone gave you Chinese drivers. Always got enough Chinese. We're everywhere. But there was a trade. Must be a trade. Always a bit of bartering with the Chinese. The world is our *pasar malam*. Give and take. We give you drivers. You take our women. Right or not?"

Robertson took in the sweeping Hadleigh Downs. His associates often mocked his golf course, but he wouldn't be a member of any other. On a clear day, he could just about see where he grew up. He liked to be reminded of his roots.

"Do you know anything about the driver yet?"

"He's from China," Mistry said. "No ID yet."

"They called him Cheng. But no idea what his full name was. No papers." Robertson shook his head. "I've got no idea about any of this. It's a nightmare, to be honest."

"So who's the connection?"

"I just wanted decent drivers."

"And one of them had his throat cut. Who got you the drivers?"

A breeze drifted across the golf course. The salty air kissed Robertson's cheeks. He could practically taste the Thames Estuary.

"I've got a mate," he sighed. "We meet socially round here. His missus gets on with my missus. Village fetes. All that crap. I think he's bit of a prat to be honest. But he likes to sniff around my money and his influence comes in handy for me, I suppose."

"He's Chinese?"

"Nah, but I think his mate is. Well, he must be. He's something to do with the casino we go to. Anyway, my mate came to me and asked if I needed drivers."

Low wasn't convinced. "Just like that? You're playing blackjack and he suddenly says, 'oh by the way, would you like some truck drivers?'"

"No, I was just telling him how hard the business was with the supply chain crisis, petrol prices and the driver shortage and he said his contact might be able to help."

"What's the name of the casino?"

"Genting."

Low turned to Mistry. "Malaysian Chinese. Makes sense. The connections there give you a pipeline to all that exploitable cheap labour, right? You've got access to whatever you need in South-East Asia, truck drivers, sex workers, bloody chicken pluckers, you've got an endless supply, right?"

"No, it weren't like that," Robertson said, pacing up and down. "There's nothing dodgy here. I wanted drivers. My mate wanted a taxi service, someone who could get workers to local farms. And what's wrong with that? Do you know how many farms there are in Essex? Have you seen the news? We're short of everything. It's not like we were sticking them in meat lorries and letting them freeze to death. Everything was straight. They came in on planes, not boats. I sub-contracted the pick-ups."

"Because you didn't want your bloody name on the side," Mistry said.

"Yeah, all right, but did your kids get their toys last Christmas? Did you get your French cheese and your bottles of wine in the supermarket? Of course you did. And you didn't give a shit how it got here. We're just keeping the supply chains going."

"Wow, thanks. Maybe you'll be knighted in the New Years' honours list," Mistry said. "You're gonna tell me you had no idea where the women were going?"

"I knew it was mostly manual labour."

"Mostly?"

"I didn't ask. I just had them dropped off at different

addresses. Their jobs and paperwork were handled by someone else."

"By your mate?"

"Look, I don't feel great about it."

"We're sorry if we pricked your conscience," Low said.

Robertson wiped his sweaty chin on his chequered Bob the Builder shirt sleeve. "I'm just a bloody taxi service, all right? I get these women where they need to be. Safely, too. I give them food, a chance to have a quick wash and brush up on my site. I even gave them little penknives. Did you know that? Me. I slipped them to one of the women when they went for a slash. I'm married, too, for fuck's sake. I don't know where these women are gonna end up or what they're gonna do."

"You just take their money," Mistry said.

"No, I just take the drivers. Pay them the same rate. Chinese, off the books, British, on the books, same rate. My conscience is clear."

"One of your drivers is dead."

Robertson threw his yellow hardhat to the floor. "Yeah, and I feel shit about that. But I barely knew him. I've got dozens of foreign drivers, all over the place. They hardly speak a word of English. I don't know them and I didn't know Cheng. I'm gutted what happened to him, but I had no idea."

"So what happened?"

"That night, Cheng was told to bring them to my firm. They usually split them up in the yard and move them on. Farms. Factories. Whatever. But this Cheng then made a call and said there was a message to go somewhere else. That's it."

Low tried to keep up. His thoughts were too fast to catch. He glimpsed only fragments. He saw a self-made millionaire. Proud. Upstanding. Boastful. That seemed to matter. Robertson wallowed in his self-importance, demanded it from the fairway. He organised charity events in the community. He was a local public figure, a well-respected man. His reputation was everything.

"Too much risk," Low muttered.

"What?" Mistry recognised the jittery behaviour in the Singaporean. "What's a risk?

"The whole thing. He lost some European drivers. So what? He'll survive. Lose some money, but he'll survive. But now he'll lose everything. If this goes public, he'll lose everything. For what? A few China drivers? Not worth it. His reputation means more than a few China drivers. Look at him. Mr Family Fun Day. Bob the Builder. And Bob the Builder doesn't stick women in his truck. Not worth it. Doesn't need the money. Can retire already."

Low spotted a flicker. An eye movement. Barely perceptible. But it registered.

"It's leverage. Where's the leverage? He's doing it to make money? No, not enough money to make on a few China drivers. He's doing it to make back money. The casino. Owe money. Pay money. Simple *ah long* economics. But he cannot pay the money. So they make him pay. That's the leverage. Pick up our women. We'll give you help with the casino. You take on their women. They take on your debt. I'm even a bit impressed. This is old school stuff."

Mistry frowned at the freewheeling Singaporean. "That's a bit of a stretch. If he owes the casino, then he can just take time to pay it back. He's a bloody millionaire."

Low shook his head. "No, that'd mean telling the only person that he listens to, the one person who's been with him since the beginning and tells him not to swear in front of the kids at a charity event and he obeys. It's why he closed that clubhouse door just now, so she wouldn't hear. It's why he agreed to bring in those women and close one eye to everything else, so she wouldn't find out about the debt."

"Well, you're a cheerful bastard, aren't ya?" Robertson blew hard, trying to stop the tears.

Low empathised, to a degree. He understood addiction better than most. "How much?"

Robertson wiped his eyes, but said nothing.

"Your wife. She's just inside," Low said. "How much do you owe?"

"She doesn't know," Robertson whimpered.

"How much?

"About one and half."

"Million?"

Robertson nodded and turned away from the detectives. He didn't want his wife to see the tears. Mistry took out her notepad. "Who's your mate, Steve?"

Robertson wiped his nose on his sleeve. "Nah, I can't."

"Yeah, you can," Low whispered. "Don't make us tell your wife."

Robertson faced the cold, dispassionate Chinese inspector. "You wouldn't."

"We've got a dead driver, Steve. We almost had twelve dead women, too. And maybe your penknives helped to save them, gave them confidence to scream and shout and bang on the sides of the truck. I don't know. Maybe you can live with that. But I can't because one of them is my friend. Grace Chen. My friend. On the back of your truck. And I owe her my life, Steve. So, yes, I'll tell your wife. I'll put an ad in your local newspaper to tell your wife. I want the killer."

"That's not my mate."

"That's for us to decide. Give me his name."

Robertson hesitated. He took in the uplifting vista of the eighteenth hole, just one more time. He loved this golf course. But he loved his wife more.

"Nigel Fielding," he mumbled.

"Are you serious?" Mistry's reaction surprised Low.

"You know him?"

"Everybody knows him." Mistry was already tapping her phone. "He's the local MP."

Chapter 12

Nigel Fielding adored constituency events organised by the Women's Institute. The attendees were his demographic. And they always baked the best cakes. The bunting was a bit much though. Union Jacks, balloons and party poppers felt a little excessive for a fundraiser on food poverty.

But the lemon drizzle and strawberry cream sponges usually made the trip worthwhile and the photos generally made the local newspaper. Besides, the setting was undeniably gorgeous. When the sun was shining, an Essex village looked positively resplendent, a timeless utopia of freshly cut greens, yellow daffodils and beaming white faces.

His constituency was proof that a civilised existence was still possible on the outskirts of the M25, the ring road that divided his people from the barbaric philistines currently destroying London from within. His people still believed in simple family values and basic decency; qualities that had once defined a nation. Sneering liberals mocked his people for being old-fashioned and intolerant, but he wasn't sorry for what he had accomplished in his constituency. Nor was he embarrassed for achieving huge majorities at consecutive elections. He was immensely proud.

The MP for South-East Essex paused his speech, but not merely for dramatic effect. He wanted to breathe in his accomplishments. He watched the children running freely and safely around the church's grounds and gardens. He saw the women in his audience—caring and dutiful—coming together to help the less fortunate in society. He took in the pastries and sandwiches—all homemade of course—and their immaculate presentation on decorated tables. And he saw a civic-minded community with fine traditions. His traditions. His people.

Fielding clapped his hands together. "So I want to thank you for all the work you've done in making our church fete such a huge success. Father Hodgson is being a little coy in the exact number. But I'm told it's in the hundreds, hundreds of pounds, that you've raised today with the bake sales, the raffles and the water dunking. Yes, I've been asked to spend a few minutes in the dunking chair. And if I've learned anything, it's that you never say no to the Women's Institute."

Fielding waited for the applause to subside.

"But you are making a real difference here today. I've visited food banks in cities across the country. They need our help."

Fielding sensed the audience's restlessness. He understood immediately. There was no need to mention food banks on such a lovely, sunny day.

"And I need help grabbing a slice of Mrs Travers' lemon drizzle."

The women's cheering and Mrs Travers' blushing brought the audience back on side.

"So I'll leave you in the capable hands of Father Hodgson, who'll briefly talk about an upcoming fundraiser for the church roof. Now, where's my lemon drizzle?"

Fielding made a scene of dashing through the women seated on the lawn. He held a slice of cake in the air as if it were Liberty's torch. The MP for South-East Essex was reminded, yet again, of his addiction to political theatre. He still needed the audience's applause.

"Arsehole," Low said, standing at the back of the church garden.

Mistry looked on as Fielding worked the crowd. "You're surprised?"

"Only at the lack of self-awareness. They're not keen on irony around here, eh? Or dark people. We look like two turds in a bag of golf balls."

"It's little England," Mistry said.

"It's lost England."

"What's the difference? Come on."

The detectives waited for Father Hodgson to wrap up his rambling speech about repairing timber beams in the church roof and then made their way through the gushing women balancing paper plates with plastic cups of warm prosecco. The crowd parted for them, but slowly and reluctantly.

Low and Mistry were not local. Obviously.

Fielding was holding court with a couple of ruddy-cheeked women. "So I said to him, I'll attend your meeting, as long as we don't call it a party and there's no cake."

The women roared with laughter, almost spilling their prosecco.

"And that's probably why I'm still a backbencher," Fielding added, noticing the unfamiliar faces. "Oh, hello, thanks for coming. Do you live round here, too?"

"No." Mistry flashed her ID card. "I'm Detective Inspector Ramila Mistry."

"You're not from our station."

"No, I'm based in Charing Cross. And this is Detective Inspector Stanley Low of the Singapore Police Force."

"Wow, that's even further afield than Charing Cross." Fielding shook their hands while shooing his female constituents away with a polite flick of the head. Low admired the practised effortlessness of such a casual dismissal.

"Yeah, a little bit," Low said.

"I went to Singapore once, as part of a parliamentary committee, visited your parliament. It's very . . . what's the word? . . . Efficient."

"And clean and safe. We usually get efficient, clean and safe."

"Right." The MP swivelled his body away from the weird Chinese guy and towards the one with actual influence. "So Inspector Mistry, why is an officer from Charing Cross gracing us with her presence here today?"

"We're just conducting preliminary enquiries about the murder of a lorry driver at Rainham Marshes."

"And the trafficking of twelve women," Low said.

Fielding didn't know what to make of either of them. "Right, yes. Well, I'm obviously familiar with the case. It was unspeakably awful, but it happened in another constituency at least ten or fifteen miles away; an opposition constituency I believe."

"There may be a connection, sir."

"To my constituency?"

"No, to you," Low said. "How's the cake?"

Fielding turned his attention to Low. The Chinese copper's expression unnerved him. It was contemptuous, which was common in educated foreigners. They hadn't gone through Britain's class system. They didn't necessarily know their place.

"I'm sorry. I'm struggling to make sense of any of this. And I'm not sure about a Singaporean police officer . . ."

"Making fun of you for eating cake? Suggesting your involvement in a trafficking operation? Which one are you not sure about?"

Fielding knew that everyone was staring at him now. In fact, the MP for South-East Essex paid so much attention to the gawping members of the Women's Institute that he hadn't noticed the lemon drizzle had slipped off his paper plate.

Chapter 13

The spring sunshine poured through the stained-glass window. Low had no idea who the depicted figures were, but they glowed across the nave. The parish church was elegant but deserted. More than eight hundred years of history was no match for a bake sale. There was little chance of their conversation being interrupted.

Fielding sat back in his pew and peered up at the roof. "You can still see remnants of the original hammerbeam roof. What an architectural feat that was. Look what the English Medieval carpenter achieved with the tools at his disposal."

"Yeah, I just see an old roof," Low said. He stood in the aisle, refusing to join the MP and Mistry on the long, varnished bench.

"Not a lover of classic architecture then, Mr Low."

"I'm Singaporean. We live in concrete boxes. Why did you set up Steve Robertson in the people trafficking business?"

Fielding looked to Mistry for support. "He's blunt, isn't he?"

"Yes. But according to Mr Robertson, you helped him with his gambling debts by putting him in contact with a third party to import cheap migrant labour. A lorry filled with twelve women was found in a boggy swamp after their driver's throat had been cut. And, no, they weren't found in your constituency, sir. But the driver was one of those cheap imports, according to Mr Robertson, so I really would answer Mr Low's question, *sir*."

Fielding had met so many like Ramila Mistry. They were young, idealistic and foreign in their thinking, still believing that things moved in simple straight lines. He usually met them in social services, not so much in the police force. But then, there weren't many coppers like Mistry in his constituency. His voters were not interested in box-ticking exercises.

"Yes, yes, I'll answer your question. There's no need to be quite so melodramatic." Fielding's exasperated voice drifted towards the cherished hammerbeam roof. "Although it sounds like our mutual friend has already gone overboard with the amateur dramatics. Had he been on the sauce?"

"I'm sorry?"

"Where did you meet him?"

"At the golf course. He had a staff event."

Fielding was already shaking his head. "Steve loves a bevvy, as he likes to say. Had he simply conformed to cliché, he might have made all our lives easier. You know, get drunk, go home and assault the downtrodden wife. But, no, Steve adores his wife. When he gets pissed, he heads to the casino instead. The self-made millionaire from the council estate was always intent on showing us tossers from Eton what balls he had. I'm paraphrasing. I didn't even go to Eton, but you get the drift. Of course, if the buffoon drove a lorry like he played poker, he'd be at the bottom of the Thames."

"We know most of this already." Mistry jabbed the arm of the pew with her fingernail. "Where do you come in?"

"He was running his business into the ground. He was either half asleep or half cut. He'd already lost most of his European drivers, obviously. Now he couldn't keep his British ones. It's a driver's market. With such a labour shortage, they could pick and choose. His drivers are my voters. His suppliers, customers, wives and families are all my voters."

"I don't quite see how a few disgruntled lorry drivers are going to determine the next election."

Fielding struggled to hide his disdain. Bleeding hearts were such fools.

"May I share a quirky fact about my constituency, Inspector Mistry? Do you know that we have one of the highest car and home ownership rates in Essex?"

"Good for you."

"And yet we have one of the lowest university graduate rates in the whole of Britain. What does that tell you?"

"Your *blur* residents steal more cars and rob more houses."

"No, Mr Low. We are a community of self-made men like Steve Robertson. Small and medium enterprises dominate here. And recent political events are slowly taking that away. They feel impotent. Angry. Their supply chains are directly impacted. If goods and services get affected, then the pain literally hits the doorstep. My voter's doorstep. So I help. It's my job to help, to connect people within the community. I met someone at a casino charity event. A Chinese investor. He mentioned something or other about being involved in haulage and suggested he might be in a position to help with the drivers' shortage so I introduced him to Steve."

"Just like that?" Mistry leaned towards the MP. "You didn't ask any questions?"

"First, I didn't need to ask any questions. That was

for Steve to do later. Second, I met the guy for all of five minutes. Do you have any idea how many local and international businessmen I meet at charity events, all promising something in return for some kind of political patronage? One or two are genuine. The rest are charlatans. That's for others to decide. I just make the introductions."

Low laughed. "So was it money or blackmail?"

"I beg your pardon?"

"A random Chinese guy offers you lorry drivers during a national supply chain crisis and you just accept them?"

"No, I passed his contact along to Steve. And then he accepted them."

"But a Chinese guy just pops up here, in this toy village, out of nowhere."

"It wasn't here, Mr Low, as I said, it was at a casino charity event." The MP spoke slowly, as if explaining simple instructions to a child. "And excuse the apparent absence of political correctness, but if you want to find a Chinese person in the UK, either go to a takeaway, a university or a casino."

Low chuckled. "Hey, I like this guy. So it's money then. You get a finder's fee, is it?"

Fielding checked his Rolex. "Mr Low, I am the director of a large brokerage firm. Money hasn't been a concern since I graduated from Oxford thirty-five years ago."

"It wasn't for him. It was for the party," Mistry said.

Fielding nodded in appreciation. "The penny drops. Well, I couldn't possibly comment about the private contributions made by those looking to make positive changes to our country. And I don't recall his name."

Fielding got up to leave. He didn't wait to be asked. He didn't typically wait for anyone. "Well, if there's nothing else."

"You really don't give a shit, do you?"

"It's a human tragedy, Mr Low. And I sincerely hope you bring the killer to justice. But please remember this. I met the Chinese businessman at least a year ago now, maybe more. That means Steve Robertson was doing whatever he was doing with him for more than a year. I met the guy for all of two minutes."

The detectives watched the MP stop at the altar and cross himself.

"So why did he mention your name?" Mistry asked.

"Because he's desperate. Because I'm an MP. Or perhaps, Inspector Mistry, because he's a lying bastard."

Chapter 14

The barking dog made Low jump. Mistry ignored both as she opened the iron gate. Every industrial estate in Essex seemed to come with a barking dog, usually chained, hungry and vicious. The snarling canine set the tone for unwelcome visitors. And most visitors were unwelcome. The high fences and barbed wire were not really to keep out thieves. They kept in the thievery.

Declaring everything was optional in the haulage game. Illegals and a dead driver were certainly kept off the books. In a fractured supply chain, full transparency was bad for business.

The two detectives moved quickly between a pair of lorries, making use of their cover as they headed for the site office. Avoiding detection was relatively easy. Steve Robertson's Transport and Haulage Company boasted a fleet of lorries, covering almost every pothole on the property. Any remaining spaces were filled with puddles and drying dog shit. In the darkness, it was difficult to spot either.

"*Chee bye*," Low hissed, scraping his shoe against the tarmac.

"Shut up," Mistry said, gliding along the side of a lorry.

"Why doesn't anyone clean up this shit?"

"You're not in Singapore. We clean up after ourselves here."

"I've just stepped in Alsatian shit."

Mistry stopped beside the lorry cab. They were about to lose their cover. She checked the CCTV cameras. There were two, hoisted high on scaffolding poles. Both scanned the forecourt outside the site office. They would be spotted.

"It's a German Shepherd," she whispered. "We don't say Alsatian anymore."

"What?" Low was now scaping the sole of his shoe against the lorry's tyre.

"The guard dog was a German Shepherd. You stepped in German Shepherd shit."

"Christ, when did that happen?"

"What?"

"When did Brits start knowing more about dogs than people? When I was at uni here, a dog was something you took for a walk once a day and gave it a tin of cheap meat. Now, they're dressed up like toddlers and expected to sit at the bloody dinner table."

"Yeah, it must be hard for a Singaporean to understand. Has your government had all the dogs shot yet?"

"Not yet, but I've volunteered," Low said, lifting his shoe in the air. "Can you still smell dog shit?"

"Will you piss off." Mistry brushed him aside. "I'm trying to concentrate. His wife said he was still here. So we get him quietly. Take him in for questioning. I don't want him buggering off. Why are you being so weird?"

"What do you mean?"

"I don't know. You're a bit too ... happy. It's annoying."

"Are you kidding? It's cold and damp. We're wandering around looking for an *ang moh* in a murder case. All I need now is popcorn."

74

Mistry stared at the peculiar man as he gleefully blew on his hands to keep warm. "Is it really that bad in Singapore?"

Low took a while to answer. He considered lying, but only briefly. She'd seen through him years ago. "Well, I told you I was back in therapy," he said finally.

"Does it help?"

"It doesn't hurt."

"What do you talk about?"

"You mostly."

A torchlight silenced them. They squatted beside the lorry cab. "It must be a security guard," Mistry said. "And yes, I can still smell the dog shit."

"Bastard Alsatian."

"It's a German Shepherd."

"That doesn't really help me, does it?" Low gestured towards the site office. "And that's not a security guard."

The torchlight moved across the window of the site office quickly, almost frantically. "Robertson wouldn't walk around his own office in the dark."

Mistry was already running. Low wasn't far behind, savouring the adrenaline. He knew the clock was against him. He knew Singapore's conformity and irrelevance was waiting for him. He knew that the only woman he'd ever loved was currently two steps ahead of him, almost within his reach, but forever beyond his grasp.

But in the moment, it didn't matter.

Someone was ransacking the site office. Their identity was of no real consequence to Low. The chase gave him a purpose again, a reason to exist. He could hold off the feeble nihilism until the Heathrow departure lounge at least. He was chasing something illusive. He knew that. But the chase kept him alive.

"You're not armed," he said to Mistry, matching her stride for stride and tugging at her elbow.

Low's sudden empathy surprised her. He was addressing Mistry's vulnerability.

"I know that," she said, struggling to keep up with Low.

"They know we're coming, Ramila. They're checking for a paper trail."

"Yes, I went to police college, too."

Low reached out and grabbed her elbow. "It could be him. He's already a murderer. He's got nothing to gain from letting us live."

"Or it could be Robertson shitting himself and shredding anything incriminating."

The torchlight went off. Low and Mistry appreciated the protective darkness, but not the uncertainty. Low considered their options. The site office was still twenty metres away, maybe more. The detectives had a numerical advantage, but no weapons. There were too many maybes. In the past, that was never a problem. Low went into every case with nothing to lose. But Mistry had a son, a family and responsibilities beyond silencing a contemptuous, internal voice.

"We should wait," Low whispered.

"For what?" Mistry pointed towards the site office. "That's Robertson in there. He used a torch to avoid being spotted on CCTV. He's destroying evidence about those girls. *Your* girl. Grace. Come on."

The detective didn't get very far before a door slammed shut. Distant footsteps found the puddles and woke the barking dog. The booby traps of every industrial estate in Essex responded accordingly. The howling of a German Shepherd accelerated the splashing footsteps. The violent rattling of a railing fence and the dramatic roar of a motor-cycle engine completed the aural journey.

The intruder had left the premises.

"Ah, that's bloody great," Mistry said, switching on her phone light.

"We were never going to catch him, even with you sprinting like a lunatic."

They checked every step on their way to the site office, hoping for clues, but finding only excrement. Over by the fence, the damn dog had stopped barking.

Outside the site office, Mistry peered through the window. Low wandered off behind the building.

"The place is a mess," Mistry said.

She leaned back and shouted into the night air. "We're gonna have to call in the local station to go through this place. Then get a warrant for Robertson. He and his wife are probably halfway to Spain."

"He's not." Low reappeared at the front of the site office. "He's around the back."

"Have you detained him?"

"No need."

Chapter 15

Mistry was no stranger to death. Corpses became commonplace years ago. She didn't even dream about them anymore. There were too many to count, too many to remember. Arson victims were generally the worst, but stabbed teenagers occasionally lingered in the memory. Their tender, decomposing faces preserved the horror. In such cases, Mistry preferred to arrive before the flies went to work on the rotting flesh.

She had seen many things. And still, she was not prepared for Steve Robertson.

His throat had been cut. His right eye bulged through its socket. His swollen, bloody face resembled a slab of butcher's meat. There was a puddle beneath his feet, a foul mix of blood and urine, because Steve Robertson was still standing up.

His arms stretched across the pallet, which leaned against a tall, clumsy stack of pallets. The congealed blood around his palms almost covered the nails pinning him to the wooden slats.

"He's been crucified," Mistry said.

"Yeah, I think we can rule out suicide."

"Piss off, Stanley. This is not even in my jurisdiction, let alone yours."

Low wasn't listening. He was already on the move, scanning the muddy floor for clues. Death always made him feel alive.

"He was dead before we arrived. No time to do all this after. The guy kills him, does all this, then goes inside to check the office. Crazy."

Mistry used her phone light to examine Robertson. "Yeah, this would've been noisy too. Risky."

"Unless the bigger risk was in there." Low directed the light towards the window. "Killing him was less important than whatever was inside the office."

"So they're desperate."

"Or powerful. Your MP for Little England gave him up, the poor bastard."

Low pointed at Robertson. The dead man's head drooped. Decomposition would soon be on its way.

"I thought he was a prick, but he didn't deserve this."

Mistry began to dial. "Nor did his wife. We should offer to break the news."

Low seemed surprised. "Why?"

"Because I'm struggling with the bloody guilt here. It's the least we can do."

Low decided not to speak, for once. He thought the idea was terrible.

The detective stood by the crucified victim, pleased with his self-restraint, until the German Shepherd arrived and quietly lapped the bloody water around Robertson's feet.

Emily Robertson had earned her glass of pinot grigio. She hadn't stopped all day. Nails in the morning, teeth whitening in the afternoon and then a quick dinner with the old man before he'd dashed off into the night, another lorry crisis to fix. He was rarely home these days. And when he was, he wasn't his usual self.

The charity golf day had been different at least. He was the old Steve again, the cheeky one she'd fallen in love with all those years ago, when he'd bought her cod and chips with loads of salt and vinegar on Clacton Pier and promised her the world.

And the stupid sod had somehow kept his promise.

He gave them a detached house in rural Essex with a gravel driveway and a couple of stone lions, to really underline the accumulated wealth. Rural Essex was full of old money, farmers and commuting stockbrokers. But the Robertsons were new money and proud of it. So they pinned St George's flags in every one of their windows during the World Cup to underscore their patriotism and irritate their pretentious neighbours. They hosted boozy parties on Saturday nights and loud outdoor barbeques on Sundays. Unlike their entitled neighbours, they had earned their money.

The name of the company was Steve's Transport and Haulage, but Emily Robertson had managed the accounts from the moment her husband bought his first second-hand Ford transit, right up until the job became bigger than both of them.

But the business was consuming him. As the orders shrank, he shrivelled, too, in more ways than one. But they didn't talk about that. She didn't even care about that. She just wanted her cheeky chappie back, the one that had popped in briefly at the charity golf day. She wanted him to make her laugh again.

A large pinot grigio might do the trick. She took a second glass and poured generously, before settling onto their sofa. Her trash TV was starting shortly, the one about New Jersey housewives. They usually watched that one together. He loved taking the piss out of the characters. She grabbed the remote control. She'd record it for him. Some trash TV and a bottle of pinot grigio would do the trick.

He'd make her laugh again.

The doorbell surprised her. He was earlier than expected. Plus, he had his own key. What was the silly sod doing?

Emily Robertson's toes found her favourite carpet slippers. Marble floors were expensive, but cold, even in the spring. Though the weather was definitely improving. They could host another of their rowdy, outdoor barbeques. He always loved those.

The doorbell rang again.

"Use your bloody key," she shouted, tightening the belt of her dressing gown.

She never bothered with the peephole. Force of habit. Besides, they had paid for that force of habit. Their long gravel driveway, electronic gates and security systems rendered such paranoia unnecessary. So did their postcode.

They were too posh for peepholes.

So she never bothered with the peephole. If she had, she wouldn't have been so shocked when her husband didn't appear on the doorstep. She wouldn't have been so confused at the sight of a haunted Indian woman and a rough Chinese man.

And when she heard the news, she wouldn't have screamed and slapped the Chinese man across the face.

Chapter 16

Emily Robertson had insisted on making them tea. It wasn't about the slap. She didn't care about the slap. It was the patronising tone. The weird Chinese bloke and the annoying Indian spoke to her like a child. Robertson had grown up on a dying housing estate. Her father had left as soon as the nappies had needed changing. The option of being treated like a child was never available.

She wasn't going to be treated like one now.

"Thanks for the tea," Mistry said, gently placing the mug on a coaster, on the John Lewis side table. "I would've been happy to make it for you."

Robertson smiled at the imbecile sitting on the Laura Ashley sofa.

Yeah, not in my house, you don't.

"I've always made the tea," Robertson said, cradling her mug in her manicured hands, grateful for the only genuine warmth in the room.

"He loved his tea."

"I can imagine," Low said, rubbing his red cheek.

"Sorry about the slap," Robertson said.

She wasn't.

"Don't worry about it."

She wouldn't.

"We're really sorry to bring you such awful news. We know how you must feel right now," Mistry said, reaching for her tea again.

This time, Robertson made no effort to hide from the two children in the room. "Really," she scowled. "How do you know?"

Low moved aside one of the matching Laura Ashley cushions. "Er, Inspector Mistry suffered a terrible family incident herself a couple of years ago."

"Yeah? Did anyone die?"

Neither detective answered. Robertson went for her tea again. "Then you don't know how I feel, do you?" She blew the top of the cup. "How come you two found him?"

Even Low was shocked at the question's bluntness. It was perceptive, too, a legitimate line of enquiry, coming from a woman widowed only minutes earlier.

Low turned his mug around. The Hammers made him smile. In Singapore, the crossed hammers were the symbols of the leading opposition party. Their profile had increased, but they were never destined for real power. In England, the Hammers were West Ham United, a football club with an increased profile, but never destined for real power. Low loved the absurdity of life's freak coincidences. They didn't exist in his job.

"That's a fair question," he said. "I'm guessing you saw us at the charity event? At your golf club?"

"You know I did."

"Well, we are investigating a tragedy that had links to your family's trucking company."

Robertson sipped her tea, but stared off into the distance, past the 80-inch monstrosity projecting images of bickering housewives. "But you're not from round here."

"No, I'm from Singapore. There may be a Singapore connection."

"Yeah, he'd started to use more drivers from China."

"Singapore's not actually in ..." Low stopped himself and smiled broadly instead. "I believe there are other officers on the way. Local officers. We should really let them conduct formal interviews. We know you have no children, no next of kin and we just felt that ..."

Low turned to Mistry. His eyes pleaded for some help. The delicate part should not come from him, a stranger, a foreigner, a man.

Mistry returned her mug to the polished table. "They will probably ask you to formally identify your husband. And we were wondering, Mrs Robertson, if there was anyone who might do it for you."

"Why?"

"In my experience, it's too much, the news and then the formal identification, it's just too much, too soon."

"You've seen him." Robertson cut them off. "You've seen the state of him and you don't think I should see him."

"Something like that," Mistry said, smiling awkwardly.

Robertson almost wobbled. The tears almost came. But she wasn't wasting them on these two. When she was alone, with him, they could share their final moments on this earth together. She would grieve for her Steve then. She owed him that at least.

"No, I'll do it." Robertson's toes were already edging across the wool rug, in search of her slippers. "But I'll have to get changed first. He wouldn't like it if I came in my dressing gown to the ... where is he anyway?"

"He'll be at the police mortuary," said Mistry. "I can accompany you in there."

"Why? You didn't know him. No, I'll throw on some

84

decent clothes and I suppose I'll have to take the other car. He'd have taken the other one to the site office."

Low watched the bereaved woman pull the slippers over her tanned feet. Her robotic behaviour confused him. It wasn't the rhythmic nature of her actions. That was normal, predictable even. Shrinks called the first stage of grief *denial*, but shrinks didn't break the news to dead victims' relatives as often as Low did.

Denial was too simplistic. He usually saw suppression, a return to default mode, a human brain frantically trying to restore factory settings and start again. Simple routines. Brainless routines that required no deeper thought beyond their execution. Stand up. Make tea. Sit down. Drink tea. Find slippers. Get dressed. Identify body. Identify battered body. Identify the bloody husk of a lost life. Identify two lost lives, one dead, the other suppressing everything beyond the mundane tasks of existence.

And then the revelation comes.

And then the denial takes hold.

But this wasn't denial. It wasn't quite suppression either. To Low, it looked more like confirmation.

"Nice slippers," he muttered.

"Yeah, Steve got them for me last Christmas. Very comfy."

"Mrs Robertson, forgive me, but you don't seem very surprised."

Low felt the sudden revulsion in the room. He was aware of the risk he was taking.

Robertson stopped fiddling with her comfy slippers. "What?"

"Don't do this now," Mistry said, under her breath, but possibly loud enough for Robertson, subconsciously expressing solidarity with the other woman.

"Ah, it's probably nothing."

Robertson sat back on her expensive armchair and tightened the belt on her dressing gown. "No, go on. How would you like me to be?"

"No, just ignore him," Mistry interjected, starting to get up. "It's been a traumatic evening. I'll make a call to see who is on their way to join us. They will advise you about all the counselling services."

"Sod the counselling services. I'm talking to him." Robertson pointed a long, red fingernail at Low. "Why am I not surprised enough for you? Would you like to me cry my eyes out? I'm not doing that in front of you. Would you like me to smash up my own house? What would that achieve? Come on. Tell me. How would you like me to deal with the news that my husband is dead?"

"You're too methodical." Low's voice was barely a whisper.

"I'm what?"

"When I see delayed shock, I see a shutdown. I see a zombie. They can still function. But you're not just functioning. You're reasoning. You're questioning. You are making the tea and laying out all the mugs neatly on the table. You're consciously deciding not to grieve in front of us, making a choice. And your only real question to us, after hearing that you've tragically lost your husband, is how did we find him? How come we were the people on the site at this time of night? Those are the questions of a detective. You were practically interrogating us. You knew, didn't you, Mrs Robertson? You already knew that your husband was dead."

Chapter 17

Emily Robertson wished she had slapped the Chinese detective even harder now. He had an alien smugness to him that irritated. The racial profile and the arrogance didn't match. Chinese faces usually bowed in gratitude when they were ordered to pick up a load at Dover. They didn't challenge authority.

But the freak sitting across from her, in her living room, sipping her Yorkshire tea and leaning forward on her custom-made sofa, was questioning her behaviour. He was unshaved, like a tramp, rather than a hipster. He dressed like a teenager, in jeans and a hoodie, but had the eyebags of an old man. He was an infuriating contradiction.

And the widow had just about had enough.

"Right, get out."

Robertson was already on her feet.

"Go on, get out. The pair of ya."

Mistry stood up. "Mrs Robertson, we cannot leave you alone. We will wait until uniformed officers arrive and then they will have a chat with you about counselling services."

"I'm not having him in here, accusing me of this shit. Go on. Piss off."

Robertson waved the detectives away, but Low didn't

move. She stood over the Singaporean, looking down at the ridiculous hoodie. "I said, 'get out'."

Low reached for his mug of tea. "Yeah, the histrionics don't help you either. I actually think this outburst is genuine though. Your first real emotion is being directed towards me. Actually, it's your second. The first was when you slapped me at the door. That was a real emotion, but it was the wrong one." Low sipped his tea, then shook his head. "No, it was the right emotion for you. But the wrong one for anyone else." Low returned the cup to the table. "I've been doing this for most of my life, Mrs Robertson. Given bad news a hundred times. Never been slapped in the face before. It's not the instinctive, natural response. The usual response is to recoil not lash out. But you lashed out because you were angry. You were not sad about your husband dying. You were angry with us about your husband dying."

"Well, you shouldn't have poked your nose in, should ya?" Robertson was shouting now. "It was none of your fucking business."

Mistry returned to the sofa. Two things immediately horrified her. First, Low was right about Robertson. And second, the Singaporean was revelling in the psychological destruction of a widowed woman. His eyes sparkled. His feet twitched. His knees bounced up and down. He lived for the dark shit that he unearthed in others, an archaeologist rooting around in other people's misery.

"What was none of our business?" Mistry's voice was flat and calm.

"You kept on at him, didn't ya?"

"Who did?"

"Him, sitting there drinking my bloody tea. He kept on at Steve about the gambling, didn't he?"

Low was surprised. "You knew?"

"Of course, I knew. How could I not know? I did the books for the company for years and I was his bloody wife. But they think we're all fucking stupid, don't they?"

Robertson found support in Mistry, who nodded in agreement. Robertson slumped back into the armchair. "I didn't know how much. I guessed it was quite a lot, the way he kept sneaking out to the casino, or the office, at all hours, either spending it, losing it or trying to bloody hide it. And then there'd be calls to the house. He'd say they were about work. But I knew."

"Why didn't you say anything?" Mistry wondered.

"I should've done. But I knew what it would've done. He was proud of himself, self-made man and all that, and he could see that he was losing it."

"From the gambling?"

Robertson glared at the ignorant foreigner. "No, from the bastard European Union. He only started gambling, seriously gambling, when he started losing his drivers back to Europe. And then he started losing big contracts. And then every load got more expensive, more paperwork, more visas, more fuel costs and then our old clients started leaving us altogether. He never really got over that."

"Because he voted for it," Low sighed.

"Yeah, all right. We both did. Can't say that though, can we? Otherwise, we get the 'told-you-so' merchants in our faces, so we just got on with it, like everyone else. We just wanted to have safer streets and less of, you know."

"People who look like me," Mistry said.

"No, I didn't say that," Robertson said quickly. "We just didn't want them coming in on bloody boats."

"But they can come in your husband's trucks."

"I didn't know about that."

"Yes, you did," Low snapped, savouring the tracks clicking into place, one straight line, all the way home. "Yes, you did know."

Low lifted his empty mug. "A perfect coaster for your perfect tea, on a perfect table, in front of a perfect sofa, in a perfect house, street, car, postcode, whatever. This isn't a home. It's a mission statement. Look what we did. Look who we are. Look at the sacrifices we made to get here. We'll do anything we can to keep this for us and to keep others out. So you voted to keep them out. But it didn't keep them out. It kept you in. It cut you off from the rest of the Europe, left your shiny fleet sitting in muddy puddles, doing nothing, except costing you money. Every day, they're sitting there idly, doing nothing, the Robertsons are losing money. The proud Robertsons. From council house to country estate. Look at this. It's a palace. And you did it. Both of you. And you wanna keep it, no matter what. So he gambles. He's desperate. But the odds are shit. The house always wins, right. You need better odds. Bigger numbers. Like foreign labour. There are millions of us in Asia, right? Millions of poor bastards who look like us and are desperate for any other life. We don't want a house like this. We just want a job. And your trucks can help make that happen. So you closed one eye and opened up your trucks at Heathrow and it all went to shit, didn't it?"

Now, finally, there were tears. Robertson wiped them away.

"We were only taking them from the airport to wherever they wanted them," she said.

"They were people smugglers," Low said. "Snakeheads. Organised gangs. Whatever. Using your trucks for cover. You never wondered where the girls might end up?"

"We didn't ask."

"Yeah, I get that. Your house is *very* nice."

Mistry allowed the seething to settle before continuing, slowly. "From this point on, you might want to speak to a lawyer, Mrs Robertson, get some legal advice. Do you understand what I'm saying here?"

"Why? We didn't do anything wrong. We were a taxi service."

"Yeah, your husband said the same thing. Nice line. Hope it made you both sleep better. When did you know things were getting out of hand?"

"You don't have to answer that," Mistry added.

"Why? I didn't do anything wrong and nor did Steve. I was just told that you two were asking about the murder in the truck, which had nothing to do with us. It wasn't even our truck. We didn't know anything about it until we read it online."

Low sat up. "Who told you about us?"

"What?"

"Who told you about us investigating the murder in the truck?"

"It hasn't got anything to do with him either."

"He? Who's he? Who warned you about us?"

"He didn't warn me. He just told me not to get involved."

"For god's sake, how much do you really want to pay for this beautiful house. Who told you about us?"

Robertson leaned back in her armchair. The copper had finally said something agreeable. She really did have a beautiful house.

"Nigel Fielding, our MP," Robertson said. "He just wanted to help. That's his job."

Chapter 18

Father Hodgson stood outside a temple to England's glorious past; a time of piety, patriotism and entrenched inequality, a better time for his congregation.

He was careful to stand beside the round, blue plaque. He was proud of the church's heritage, though the flint-rubble exterior needed urgent restoration.

Besides, the parishioners were always keen to shake their priest's hand on their way out, hoping for a bit of store credit. They improved their chances with baked donations. Father Hodgson's sweet tooth was well known.

But his flock still hovered, even after the handshakes and blessed farewells, waiting for the star attraction.

Nigel Fielding and his gleaming family were usually the last to leave the service, making a point to circulate among constituents. The MP had married well and the couple had been blessed with photogenic kids, one of each, covering all aspects of their demographic. So the Fieldings were happy to oblige the many selfie requests in the church garden. Local elections were coming.

Fielding was posing with a vanilla sponge when he spotted the two of them, loitering among the crumbling gravestones like homeless miscreants in search of a cider bottle.

With a heavy heart, he noticed that the disturbed Chinese one was already on his way over, sidestepping the graves, showing no respect for the dead. The MP was not surprised. He had visited Singapore before. They didn't even bury the dead. No class.

Fielding eased himself away from the cooing crowd that had gathered around his family and Father Hodgson, touting their baked offerings to church and state, stopping only when he was sure he was out of earshot.

"What an unexpected surprise," Fielding said. "Inspector Mistry and Mr Low, good morning to you both."

The MP placed special emphasis on the '*mister*', to underline the imbalance of power.

"If it's a surprise, then of course it's unexpected," Low said. "There's no such thing as an expected surprise. Why did you tell Emily Robertson about our inquiries?"

Fielding examined the dishevelled foreigner. Low really was an incongruous presence. His accent was neither British nor Chinese and he had no grasp or respect for established boundaries and structures, which was most unusual for a Singaporean.

"Mr Low, it's a Sunday morning. This is family time for me. Can we do this on Monday morning or at a time at your convenience?"

"Absolutely. It's a convenient time for me to do it just over there, in front of your wife and all your voters, and ask you about your friend being crucified."

"You are blasphemous."

"No, I went to an all-boys' Catholic school. I'm just juvenile. Why did you tell her?"

Fielding looked to the other copper. At least she was British, sort of. "Must I answer these questions, Inspector?"

"No, not at all. But as you are directly involved now,

we can ask you to come down to the station and conduct a formal interview."

"And these things always leak," Low added. "Imagine if it leaks out that you knew about a man being nailed to a pallet."

Fielding suddenly felt uneasy on his feet. His hand found a nearby bench for support. He noticed his wife looking at him across the church garden, a sudden flash of concern. He mustered a wave in her direction but turned away quickly.

"I didn't know that. I'd heard, obviously. I've had his wife on the phone to me, screaming at me. But I didn't know that he was ... my God."

Mistry decided to get into the MP's face. "He was battered so severely, his eye was popping out of his head like a tennis ball. His throat was severed, cutting through both carotid arteries. He was already dead before someone took a nail gun and pinned him to a wooden pallet. This was an execution. He was crucified to silence him. So, we are going to need something on the record. But in the meantime, let's start with Mrs Robertson. What are you trying to hide here?"

Fielding gripped the bench frame. He felt a splinter jab the side of his palm. "There's no grand conspiracy theory. Do not go looking for things that are just not there."

"So what is there, Mr Fielding?"

Fielding decided to sit down, wiping fluff from his trouser leg and straightening the creases. Old habits. Impeccable grooming.

"Look, I called Emily to tell them both to keep their story straight. Just tell the truth. They didn't know anything about that lorry murder. No one does. I wish your lot bloody did. Do you think I need this? A murder connected to one of my local businesses? My electoral majority is owed, almost entirely, to families like the Robertsons. I need them. Half of this town is farmers and landowners. They'll vote for a pig in my colours. Yes, I've heard all the jokes. The other half is the white flight crowd, the working-class escapees from London's housing estates, self-employed men made good. Men like Steve Robertson. All I did was help a voter, a wealthy local businessman and the occasional party donor. Steve was all of those things, yes, and he asked for my help and I facilitated. That's it. Do you think I'm happy about any of this? My political future is entrusted to these people."

Mistry joined Fielding on the bench, "Surely, these people are your people, too."

"We share a postcode," Fielding fixed his tie.

"What does that mean?"

Fielding almost laughed. Young liberals never understood politics. It's why they usually lost. "Look. I recently got attacked by the lefties for the public library cuts. Do you know why?"

"Because you were responsible for the public library cuts?"

"No, Mr Low. Because most of my voters never used them. We gave them grants for university education for decades. Did they use them? No, they drove white vans instead. We gave them the internet. We gave them access to the kind of knowledge that Einstein could only dream of. What do they do with the internet? Use it for porn and betting sites. And then, despite all of that, one breaks through and becomes a self-made millionaire. And what does Steve Robertson do? Does he become a role model for the community? No, he pisses it all away in the casino. I saw him in there so many times, destroying one of the most successful blue-collar industries in my constituency.

What was I supposed to do? The working-classes and their age-old vices made this mess. I just tried to fix it."

Low almost envied the politician. Fielding was so polished and self-assured, swathed in a security blanket of entitlement. Besides, the MP was right.

"Yeah, it's about weakness," Low muttered. "Robertson's weakness was the casino. He kept going back. It's plausible. That's why you kept focusing on it in your little speech just now, rehearsing it no doubt as we wandered through the churchyard. It makes perfect sense. Pisses it all away, you said. Deadbeat gambler. Heavy debts. Blackmailed by traffickers. He might talk. Traffickers kill him. Nothing to do with you."

"It wasn't."

"So why were you there? At the casino. You said, you saw him in there so many times. The Genting Casino. But you do not gamble. You hold no accounts there or anywhere else, right, Inspector Mistry?"

"No, we checked."

"So why is a local MP being seen so often at the casino?"

"It's a major employer in my constituency."

"Yeah, so is McDonalds, but you don't spend your days flipping burgers. And I bet if we called the casino, asked for their CCTV, we'll find you popping up all over the place."

"Let's not be naïve, shall we? It's a casino. It's where the wealthy people go. My job is to connect influential constituents."

"And possible party donors. Yeah, we know all that. But how important are you? You're just a—what they call it here—a backbencher? You're nothing. *Ikan bilis*. I know it's an Asian casino, but no Asian billionaire is gonna waste time with you, a nobody MP from a tiny town. Network with you for what? No need. Go straight to the ministers.

One phone call. You go for something else. You got no vices. Sundays, go to church. Take the whole family. You wave at her just now, but cannot look at her. Never mind. Keep up appearances. Go to the casino, then pray in church. You spend, then must pay. But not money. *Women*. Casino always supply women to people like you. Nice women. Not old women baking cupcakes, but nice women, young women, free sex for you, free MP protection for the casino. And then they got greedy, got extra protection, right?"

Fielding decided to stand up, taking a couple of steps away from the small crowd fussing over his family. "You've got it all worked out, eh?"

"What was it? A waitress? Croupier? Sex worker?"

Fielding could no longer look at them. Mistry's scornful gaze, in particular, really bothered him. "I believe she was a sex worker," the MP muttered.

Mistry was incredulous. "You believe? You don't know?"

Fielding turned back. "Oh, that's right, because I'm a degenerate politician, cheating on my wife with another woman. No." He pointed at Father Hodgson's church. "I was married in there. Our vows are sacred."

Low began pacing, circling the bench. "You believe she was a sex worker," he said.

"That's what I heard."

"Yeah. Probably. Plenty around a casino."

Mistry looked for a clue from either man. "What's going on?"

"Robertson," Low said. "Robertson and the sex worker."

"*Voila*." Fielding raised his hands appreciatively in Low's direction. "I believe she was the proverbial shoulder to cry on. Couldn't tell his wife about the debts, for obvious reasons, so he confided in a casino sex worker. Puerile pillow talk when he was three sheets to the wind. Of course, he was terrified that his wife might find out, about the debt, the affair, everything. I kept getting drunken, weepy calls after every casino visit. I told him to speak to his wife. Not me."

Low stopped in front of Fielding. "And they black-mailed him."

"That appeared to be the gist of it, according to his intoxicated rants. They took some photos. Threatened to send them to his wife. They wanted his entire company."

"Who are they?"

"I've no idea. He would ramble on about Chinese men at the casino talking to Chinese men on his site. And, you know ..."

"We all look the same?"

"No, Inspector, that's a rather tired stereotype. I never saw faces. I just endured Steve's long, weepy confessions on the phone."

"I didn't ask for faces. I asked for names."

"I never heard any."

Low was in Fielding's face now. "No, let's try again. You put them together. At the casino. You introduced them. Give me a name."

"I don't know the middle men."

"Then give me the top man."

"I only met him briefly."

"I'm not writing his biography."

"He's a party donor," Fielding whispered. "He supports us."

"Then you should be able to remember his name then."

"I really can't."

"Fine. We'll give what we know to the media, about your late-night conversations with a crucified *ang moh* and see if they can give us a name."

Fielding noticed a robin's nest in a tree hollow. He loved his quiet corner of England.

"Patrick Lin," he said softly.

As the MP scurried back to his restless constituents, Low took Fielding's place on the bench to ponder life's vicissitudes. He had hoped that a fresh lead might prolong his stay. Now he was almost certainly on the next plane back to Singapore.

Chapter 19

Detective Chief Inspector Charlie Wickes continued to waver on his retirement plans. His promised pension was more than decent. His garden was waiting and it was planting season. He was ready to devote his remaining years to natural life. He had given enough time to unnatural death.

It wasn't just the murders. It was the certainty of future murders, the futility of his profession. Nothing was certain except more death.

And if Wickes needed a further reason to call it a day, Stanley Low of the Singapore Police Force was only too happy to oblige. Sitting on the other side of the chief inspector's desk, the Chinese detective looked craggier than before, but strangely happier. He didn't dress like regular detectives and certainly didn't belong at Charing Cross Police Station. But then, Low didn't seem to fit in anywhere.

"I thought you'd retired already," Low said, grinning at the older Englishman. He liked Wickes.

"I'm working on it."

"Your hair is whiter than last time."

"Yeah, you did that. How have you been?"

"Surviving. You?"

"Bloody retiring, I hope. Are you sure about this, Ramila?"

The chief inspector often deferred to Mistry. He had nurtured her, trained her to shake off the insecurities of being a minority in a conservative profession. And she had become one of Wickes' most reliable officers.

Mistry managed a rueful nod.

"Shit." Wickes returned to Low. "All right, tell me about him."

The Singaporean leaned forward. His right leg fidgeted beneath the desk. He struggled to sit still.

"Patrick Lin is one of Singapore's richest men, a motivational speaker's wet dream. Born poor. Son of a hawker seller. Brilliant at maths, but a lousy education. So he quits school and works for a loan shark. He's great with numbers, but a terrible gangster, not a tough guy. So he gets caught, right? He's sent to a boys home, but it doesn't help, makes him worse. He just makes more gang connections. Ends up in Queenstown."

"Queenstown?"

"Remand prison. Short sentence for illegal moneylending. Comes out and works at his father's hawker centre during the day and does night classes in trading. Becomes a broker, reads the market like Rain Man and somehow makes a fortune in the Asian Currency Crisis. He's a millionaire in his twenties, a billionaire in his thirties, invests all over the world and promises to give everything to charity before he dies. A national hero."

Wickes caught a glimpse of the clock on the wall. He wanted to pop into the garden centre after work. He also wanted both detectives to go away. He turned to the rational one.

"You seriously believe this guy is involved in the murders?"

Mistry shrugged. "I don't know, sir. One of his companies does have an interest in the casino in Essex, where Fielding supposedly introduced him to Robertson. And he has visited both the UK and the casino several times in the last year or so, though he wasn't in the country at the time of either murder."

Wickes tapped his thumbs against the table. "But even if he was, what has the case got to do with me, or you for that matter, Ramila? This is not our case. The murders weren't even on our patch. I agreed to let Stanley act as, I don't know, a go-between because of your connection to him and his connection to one of the girls, but I think we've covered that one now. Let the Essex teams take over. And I'm sure Stanley will follow up in Singapore."

Low chuckled at the suggestion. "I won't be allowed to do that."

"Then it becomes someone else's problem."

"Oh, no. I'll definitely follow up."

"You're still a pain in the arse then."

"I still haven't been fired."

Wickes sat back in his executive chair. He needed the extra cushion. The persistent backaches had finally ended his golf weekends. He wasn't giving up on his garden just yet. He was stubborn, like the man sitting opposite.

"So what are you thinking, Low?"

"What am I thinking? I'm thinking all sorts of things. I'm thinking you need to see a chiropractor about your back because you wince every time you move without realising it. The expensive chair is making no difference. I think you keep checking the clock because you'd rather be anywhere but here. I think you've only agreed to see me out of a sense of loyalty to Ramila and you just want me and the case to piss off back to Singapore as soon as possible."

Wickes managed a smile. "Yeah. That's about right."

"But I also think that Lin is using his *ang moh* businesses to bring in cheap, illegal labour. For what, I don't know. Makes no sense. He doesn't need the money or the risk. Maybe blackmail. Maybe this driver, Cheng, asked for more money or threatened to go public. And Robertson knew about Cheng's killing and thought he had some leverage."

"Bit of a stretch, isn't it?"

Mistry shook her head. "No. Robertson was being blackmailed. He was having an affair with a sex worker at the casino."

"Christ." Wickes ran his hand through what was left of his hair. He considered his retirement, his pension and dusky evenings on sun loungers with his wonderful wife. He tried to think about his beloved garden. But he couldn't quite see it. The image was fading.

The chief inspector had served for almost thirty-five years. He had avoided the corruption scandals that had plagued other stations and departments. He didn't want an asterisk after his name now.

"Fielding said all this in a statement?"

"No, *lah*. Everything off the record. Patrick Lin is a party donor."

"Oh, for fuck's sake."

Wickes made a point of not swearing in front of his junior officers, especially on duty, but Low had that effect on people.

"All right, so he's a party donor. Fielding is cagey. Robertson is dead. What's any of this got to do with me? Or Charing Cross? Or Mistry? It's not our case. If Fielding wants to go on the record with his local police, then that's his funeral. It's got nothing to do with me."

Wickes still had time to pick up some fertiliser. His wife would be waiting with a cup of tea and a plate of chocolate digestives and then he could briefly enjoy a simpler world without sex, blackmail and murder.

"I want to go to Singapore."

Wickes was surprised at both the request and Mistry's tone of voice. She sounded flat, almost resigned to her fate.

"What? Why? He doesn't need you there. You have nothing to offer over there."

"She's a solid detective," Low said.

"You don't have any detectives over there?"

"Not like her."

Low's deference caught Wickes off guard. But he meant every word. Singapore had decent detectives, but they were identikit officers. They didn't understand Low. They respected the work, but loathed the man.

Low didn't take it personally. He often felt the same way.

"Do you even want to go, Ramila? What about your boy?"

"It'll just be for a week or so. His dad and grandad could look after him. It'll be good for them. I need to do this, sir."

"Because he helped you out before?"

"Because he saved us, sir. My family."

"And we're all grateful. But this is not some quid pro quo arrangement."

"He did it for me." Mistry eyeballed her boss. "And he caught a serial killer for you."

Wickes took a moment to reflect on Mistry's version of events. Her analysis was fair. "It can't be official," he said finally.

"I'll take leave, sir. I fancy a short holiday in Singapore."

Wickes had read Steve Robertson's file. They were both working-class kids from single-parent households. They had taken different paths, but Wickes didn't judge Robertson's choices. His job didn't allow it.

They had simply taken different paths.

"Robertson was really nailed to a pallet?" Wickes asked, as if seeking clarification.

"He was crucified, sir. His head was essentially cut off."

Wickes took a final look at the clock. He'd never make the garden centre now. But he could always go tomorrow. He still had a choice. He still had his garden. His home. His wife. Robertson did not.

"One week's leave. That's it," the chief inspector said. "We didn't speak. I don't need to know anything. No direct involvement, no crime scenes, just give him a bit of moral support, a sounding board, whatever, just exorcise your bloody demons and get back here."

"Thanks, sir."

"Yeah, thanks, chief," Low said, shaking the chief inspector's hand.

"Try not to kill anyone. Or each other."

The detectives laughed politely, but Wickes wasn't sure if he was joking or not.

Chapter 20

The phone was ringing.

He didn't appreciate being woken up. He switched on the ornamental lamp beside the bed. It was gold plated. A gift. He received so many gifts, an irony that occasionally tickled him. People with nothing always gave to those with everything.

And he had everything that a man could need in life.

He didn't need gifts from poor people. The work fulfilled him in every way.

But the ornamental lamp kept him focused. It was a nightly reminder of his responsibilities to others.

During the day, he had the side table itself. Another gift. Another token of appreciation from grateful strangers. The side table was handcrafted with sustainable materials, a symbol of Mother Nature's fragilities.

And he loved his side table. And the ornamental lamp. And the paintings on the walls, and the plaques and the paperweights and the accolades and appreciative letters in the cheap frames, he revered them all. Their cost was unimportant. The gifts were tributes to a life well lived, a life devoted to others.

He needed to see those gifts now. They comforted him when his work ventured into less salubrious areas.

He ignored the ringing phone for a moment and picked up a simple drawing on the side table. Another gift.

The crude artwork always invigorated him. There were two stick figures, holding hands, beneath a rainbow. The simple illustration conveyed a sense of hope, of innocence even. The picture calmed him.

He sat up and placed the drawing on his lap. He was ready to answer the phone. "Yes?"

A gruff voice coughed a couple of times, before replying. "Oh, did I wake you?"

"Yes."

"Oh, I am sorry. I really am. But I didn't think it could wait."

He filtered out the grovelling coming down the phone line and held up the drawing again. Why did they always paint the sun in the top, right-hand corner? It was so bright and vibrant.

"What is it?" He asked.

"The inspector is heading home."

He put down the drawing. "Low? Already? Did he find anything?"

"No, not really."

"Then he won't find anything here," he said, still staring at the drawing.

"Yes, I'm sure. Well, I thought I should let you know anyway, just in case."

"OK. I must get back to sleep. Busy day tomorrow."

He hung up the phone and took a final look at the drawing before switching off the ornamental lamp.

The use of crayons was undoubtedly clumsy. But the sun shone so brightly.

Chapter 21

Mistry marvelled at the sarong kebayas as the flight attendants sauntered through the cabin. Singapore Airlines always offered a little primer of island life before arrival. The batik uniforms were tasteful, conservative and practical. They pleased the eye and offended no one. The Singapore Girl was the poster girl for the Singapore way.

But Mistry had gone her own way.

She didn't conform to Asian stereotypes. Or maybe she did: the restless, ambitious child of obedient immigrants. Even her accent stood out on the flight, a brown face with London's rough edges wrapped around every vowel.

Low always stood out, even on his national carrier. He slouched in his aisle seat, his unwashed jeans occasionally obstructing the stewardess' trolley bringing him another vodka. He spoke loudly. He fidgeted. He clenched his fists every time the passenger behind kicked his chair. Low was the only Singaporean that looked like a foreigner on a Singapore Airlines flight.

He found the stewardess' button in the arm rest. He needed another drink. The mania had driven him through Steve Robertson, Nigel Fielding and even DCI Wickes to a degree. But the self-importance was giving way, inevitably, to self-doubt as his homeland approached on the flight path screen in front of him. Years of therapy had encouraged him to put the past behind him.

Now he was bringing her back to Singapore.

He pressed the button repeatedly.

"You'll break it," Mistry said, raising her voice over the infernal hum of the engines.

"I need a drink to help me sleep."

"You don't need a drink to sleep."

"That a Jedi Mind trick?"

"No, but I'd rather you weren't pissed when we get to Singapore."

Mistry looked around the darkened cabin. Asian families slept or watched movies. The Caucasians sipped from their plastic glasses.

"Every flight out of London is full of pissheads and the one time I'm on a quiet plane, I'm stuck next to the only pisshead."

"I'm not pissed." Low felt the back of his chair being kicked. He started to turn. He felt her hand on his.

"Don't," Mistry said.

"Don't what?"

"I know you."

"Yeah, you know me." Low threw his head back and shook the last dregs of vodka into his mouth. "That's why you left me."

"I'm here now."

Low gave up shaking the plastic cup. There really was nothing left. "Yeah, I know. Means a lot."

Mistry smirked. "Did that hurt?"

"Like a kick in the balls."

They both giggled. Mistry was a little light-headed too. The cabin pressure and the extra wine at dinner hadn't helped. She leaned back in her seat, tilting her head towards him. "What happened after me?"

"Work happened."

"No, come on, what about women?"

Suddenly, Mistry appeared incredibly naïve to Low. She was Asian. She knew Singapore. And she knew the man sitting beside her, demanding more vodka.

"Did your Dad want you to marry me?"

"What?"

"Did he?"

Mistry didn't answer.

"Yeah. Exactly. Now imagine he's Singaporean in the 1990s, typical *kiasu* father, follows every word of our great leader Lee Kuan Yew. Graduates must marry graduates. You know he actually said that? Graduates should only marry graduates. We got state-sanctioned match-making in Singapore. Sheep marry sheep. We're writing our own Animal Farm and we marry accordingly. Women look up for their partners. Not down."

"You're also a graduate."

"Yeah, got a criminology degree on my resumé and *parang* scars across my back. Spent my best years with gangsters and hookers. I think women swipe past me on Tinder."

Low prodded his forehead. "And then there's this. Who wants to take this home to meet the parents? I don't even wanna take it home."

The back of Low's chair was kicked again. He jolted forward. Mistry held his hand, pressing it against the armrest, just in case. "So there were no women? In twenty odd years? No women at all?"

"Of course there were women. Women like Grace." Low pushed the stewardess' button again. "Where's my drink?"

"What's wrong with women like Grace?"

"Nothing. That's the point. We're the same. Me and Grace don't get to see when a man loves a woman. We get to see what a man does to a woman. It's not an aphrodisiac."

The stewardess arrived with a drinks trolley. Her hair was swept back in a ponytail. Her make-up was perfect and her smile genuinely warm. She was also Indian. She reminded Low of the woman sitting beside him, only twenty-five years ago, the woman who had left him behind.

The stewardess poured a large vodka and raised the bottle.

"No, thanks," Mistry said. "He's drinking for both of us."

"Thank you *ah*. I promise not to pester you for at least five minutes."

The young stewardess moved on quickly. Her training had taught her to brush off flirty drunks.

Low raised his glass. "To Patrick Lin. We're coming to get you."

"Well, you are. I'm a tourist. I'm coming to take some photos of your weird Merlion."

Mistry stretched out and closed her eyes. "Wake me up when we land."

Low nodded and pursed his lips in anticipation. One more for the road.

An unexpected jolt sent him lurching forward. The vodka dribbled down his chin.

"Fucking *chee bye*."

Low unbuckled his belt. He spun around to face a large, tanned man, watching a movie in the seat behind. "Eh, Ronaldo. Can stop kicking *ah*?"

The man removed his headphones. "What did you say?" His accent was European and affluent.

"You been kicking me the whole flight. Just stop."

Low turned away, impressed with his composure and self-restraint.

"Can you say 'please?' I know there's not a word for please in your language, but there is one in mine."

With a weary sigh, Low turned back. "Oh, 'cos I'm Chinese, right? Actually, we do have a word for 'please' in Chinese. It's *qǐng,* but it's used a little differently so I can see where the misunderstanding comes from. You didn't know the word for 'please' in my culture. You do now. And I didn't know what a cunt looked like in your culture. I do now. So we've both learned something on this flight."

Low swivelled round and pushed the stewardess' button again.

Snuggled in her seat, Mistry opened one eye. "Feel better?"

"Absolutely," Low said, rubbing his hands together. "Let's go catch a billionaire."

Chapter 22

They stood in rigid lines and stomped their feet. Happy clappers in green blazers, waiting for the man to come. Hormones raged across the hall. Puberty confused them. Their teaching controlled them. Lifted them. Inspired them.

He had shown them the way.

He had proven, beyond all doubt, that his path was the righteous path, the only path.

On stage, Madam Cheong was trying and failing to muster a sense of order, committing a basic error, a public speaker misreading her public.

The sex education teacher raised her hands. "Girls. Please."

But the chanted continued. They would not be silenced, not today. He was about to give them meaning, validation and something beyond their teenage grasp. He was going to give them certainty.

Still, Madam Cheong endured, wilfully ignoring the crowd, determined to get through any other business at the beginning, rather than the end.

"Girls, please, I don't mind you standing to welcome our special guest, but I have to make a couple of announcements first. Please sign up for the talk on abstinence. We will be bringing in an outside speaker for this delicate topic. She's a wellness coach, an expert, though some of you may recognise her from her Chinese TV dramas.

"And there have been complaints, again, of foul language, overheard in the classroom. That is not who we are. That is not who you are. Action will be taken so mind your language in public places, please."

Madam Cheong had made her point. No one in the audience was listening, but she had ticked the boxes in front of her principal. She had conveyed a sense of order, discipline and self-control. The girls had been told, even if none were listening.

They never seemed to listen anymore. That was the tragedy for Madam Cheong. Instead, they chanted the name of that wealthy ruffian, turning the school assembly into a tacky cheerleading session.

Clap. Clap. Clap, clap, clap. Clap, clap, clap, clap ...
"Patrick Lin!"
Clap. Clap. Clap, clap, clap. Clap, clap, clap, clap ...
"Patrick Lin!"

Madam Cheong watched them, hands above heads, applauding the grinning guest waiting at the side of the stage. It was all too *western* for her taste. Western influences were diminishing Asian values. Later, she would pay close attention to the attendance figures at the abstinence talk.

Generally, teenage pregnancies happened to other races and religions in Singapore, but one could never be too careful, even at a prestigious academic institution. They were already cheering and whooping like *ang mohs*. Whatever next?

She ushered the guest onto the stage. He was strikingly handsome. That would hardly help. His polished black trousers and crisp white shirt, open at the neck were almost too much for an all-girls' school.

Madam Cheong might need a word with the principal about the attire of guest speakers in future, whomever they were.

As his heels tapped across the polished timber of the elevated stage, the cheerleading gave way to something more instinctive, more sincere, a roar that exceeded euphoria. It was orgasmic.

Madam Cheong made a mental note to make the talk on abstinence compulsory for all students in the upper levels. Enough was enough.

"Well, ladies, you are clearly excited. So I'll pass over to Mr Patrick Lin."

He offered his hand. She shook it. His gleaming eyes beamed at her. For a moment, and it was just a moment, she enjoyed his attention, felt a deep gratitude for it.

She was disgusted with herself.

She would make an appointment with Father Fernandes to discuss her puerile behaviour towards that man at the lectern.

Even now, shamefully, Madam Cheong still envied him.

Patrick Lin succeeded where she had clearly failed with her own audience. He raised a hand, a single hand, and grinned. "Girls. Thank you. I'm overwhelmed. But no need to stand for me."

The green blazers dropped to the floor, as one, without a murmur of dissent.

"Believe me, I remember these 7am school assemblies. At least, you've got air-con."

Lin waited for the inevitable laughter to subside. The joke wasn't funny and he wasn't a particularly funny man, but he was a billionaire.

"I want to thank Madam Cheong for that lovely intro-
duction and your school for this honour. It's unbelievable.
I cannot believe that I have an entire building named after
me. And I hope the students pay more attention at the
Patrick Lin Humanities Block than I did at school, which
was none, because I was never really there."

He wasn't surprised by the sincerity of the laughter that
time. A frisson of rebellion was always gleefully leapt upon
by single sex schools.

"But you know my story. It's often called the Singapore
story, but that's not my story. I didn't go from Third World
to First World. That's Lee Kuan Yew's story."

At the side of the stage, Madam Cheong struggled with
the juvenile giggling in the crowd. Some of it was coming
from the other teachers. Money really was the root of
all evil.

Lin gripped the sides of the lectern and edged forward.
"But my story is actually our story, isn't it? It's His story,
isn't it?"

Lin pointed at the sculpture on the wall, looking down
upon all of them. "He found me and I found a purpose.
I'm good at making money, yes. But what does that really
mean? It means I'm good at making money for those who
can't. I can help those who cannot help themselves. That's
going to be my Singapore story. And I hope it's going to
be yours, too. Go find your purpose. Go find your cause.
Go out there and make a positive difference, to yourself
and others. I wish you the best of luck. Thank you, again,
for this wonderful honour. Now, go and write your own
Singapore story."

The green blazers were back on their feet.

The standing ovation accompanied Lin off stage, down
the steps and through the giddy crowd.

The standing ovation accompanied Lin all the way to the back of the school hall, where he was met by two unfamiliar faces.

"*Wah*, nice motivational speech," the smirking stranger said. "You can use it in prison."

Chapter 23

L in stopped his security team from intervening. In truth, his team consisted of a former nightclub doorman and his Bentley driver. Security was a rare threat in Singapore and a negligible one in an all-girls' secondary school. A compliant population served only money and ministers. Lin had acquired plenty of both. He was a cherished and protected species.

Besides, he finally recognised the stubbly Singaporean.

"Ah, Inspector Low," he said. "The man behind the Tiger."

Mistry was impressed. "You know about him and Tiger?"

Lin examined the Indian woman. Her accent was the obvious giveaway. But her comportment stood out, particularly in a crowd of conformist green blazers. Without introducing herself, she had jumped in with a personal question that wasn't quite impertinent but wasn't entirely polite either. She hadn't gone through the training like the gawping girls around them. She wasn't Singaporean.

"Everyone knows about the Tiger syndicate," Lin said. "It was the biggest criminal case since independence and this guy brought them all down."

Lin bowed his head towards the Singaporean. "Everyone knows Inspector Low."

"Yeah, it's screwed my undercover career. We need to talk."

"And who is we? I don't think we've met before."

Lin spoke softly. Force of habit. Rich men talked. Everyone else listened.

"I'm Ramila Mistry, sir, a detective inspector with the Metropolitan Police Force. In London."

"In London?"

"The school hall has an echo," Low said, his impatience growing. He was aware of the audience. They needed privacy. "She's just an observer. Can we talk outside?"

Lin raised an eyebrow. "Do I need my lawyer?"

"Only if you've killed someone."

The school garden amused Low. In forty years, they had never changed. A small, rectangular patch of grass, squeezed between three-storey buildings, a utilitarian nod towards Singapore's transparent attempt to be a city in a garden.

This particular school was an elite institution, so there was a koi pond. A small, stone bridge added to the Asiatic flavour. A bed of soil had been fenced off for younger students to plant vegetables, a tokenistic, green gesture for a wealthy country that couldn't feed itself.

A butterfly passed their table as they sat beneath a shade sail.

"They're growing *kai lan* over there," Lin said, pointing at the vegetable soil. "Can tell by the leaves. I worked in a wet market last time. Queenstown. It's gone now. Every day. *Kai lan. Cai Xin. Kang kong.* First time I earned my own money."

Lin appeared to enjoy the memory.

"Was that before you become a gangster?"

Lin smiled. "No *lah*. I was more of a pretend gangster. Like you."

"Eh, who says I pretend?"

"And it worked, right? You caught Tiger. I'd love to hear that story."

"I wouldn't," Low snapped.

"Nor would I," Mistry said, checking her phone. Her son would be sleeping now. She already missed him. She was eager to get this over with. "We just have a couple of very quick queries, Mr Lin. Back in the UK, I was working on a case, a murder case actually."

"That's unfortunate," Lin said, waving to a gaggle of sniggering sixteen-year-olds, flapping from the third floor of the new humanities building bearing his name.

"Yes, it is. And, well, I don't really know how to say this, Mr Lin, but there were two victims and both appear to have had connections to you, or your companies at least."

Lin turned up the cuffs of his white shirt. The heat was stifling beneath the shade sail. The morning sun had risen over the school buildings and was now making its way across the garden. There was not enough protection for the Chinese vegetables.

"They should put a net over that vegetable patch. Leaves can burn, especially if they're wet. Must always water before sunrise and after sunset. My father taught me last time. He kept a stack of plants along the HDB corridor outside our rental flat."

"Could you answer the question, please, Mr Lin?"

Lin finished his cuff rolling. "There was no question to answer, Miss Mistry. You made a statement. You didn't ask me a question. Just as you didn't show me any identification in the school hall. You didn't explain to me what your role

120

is here, as a British police officer in Singapore. You didn't do anything except make a joke about me being a gangster."

"Yeah, that was me," Low said, resting his head on his hand, enjoying the billionaire's little speech.

"The only reason I'm speaking to you out here was to avoid a scene in there."

Lin started to get up. "Speak to my legal team before you speak to me."

"Your companies are linked to a couple of murders."

"And that's tragic. But my companies employ hundreds of thousands of people. They probably commit dodgy crimes in dodgy places every day. And they'll be brought to justice, I'm sure. But I can't be blamed for every crime in every factory, hotel and business in which I have a financial interest."

Low raised his arms in the air. "He who blames others has a long way to go on his journey. He who blames himself is halfway there. He who blames no one has arrived."

"What's that?"

"Chinese proverb. Read it on Google. Why did you blackmail an *ang moh* truck owner for shagging one of your casino girls?"

Lin returned to his seat. He didn't speak. Low leaned across the wooden table. "Maybe your gangster not so reform one, *ah*? Maybe you can switch back, any time, like me. It's in our blood, right or not? Chinese. Gambling. *Kelong.* It's like, I don't know ..." Low pointed at the koi pond. "It's like running water for us. Can switch accents, can switch personalities, can switch from poor to rich, but *we* cannot switch, it's what we are, right?"

Lin sighed, as if bored. "Can I speak now?"

"Sure, *ah beng* billionaire. Tell me your story."

"It's that Essex one, right? The Robertson guy."

"Yeah *lah*, Steve Robertson, former owner of Steve's Transport and Haulage Company, last seen crucified. That one *ah*."

"Yah, him and the other one. The MP."

Mistry leaned forward. "Nigel Fielding?"

"Yah, met them both. First, that Fielding fella. Met him when we needed planning permission, for the casino. I went down, with some of the Malaysians, straightforward pitch. Everyone was on board. Local council. Local politicians. Once we showed how many jobs there'd be for the community, everybody was happy. Plus, we also made a promise to make regular contributions to local charities and social enterprises."

"Now that you've seen the light," Low said.

"But then this guy *ah*, he's like a relic from the British empire. He thinks we all still pull rickshaws and he's working for the East India Company. He wants extra all the time. Help this one. That one. Then he tells me about Steve Robertson. Big-time local businessman. Turnover of several million." Lin almost laughed. "And this Robertson supports the local MP, whatever *lah*. The MP kept pestering me, telling me they had a driver shortage in his constituency. Supply chain problems. So I ask recruitment to follow up. Small issue."

"*Wah* so helpful."

"Not really, Inspector Low. The casino is one of the community's biggest employers. But gambling always polarises and we're sensitive to local needs and interests."

"Sorry, Mr Lin, but I have to ask."

"Then ask, Miss Mistry."

"You didn't really address Inspector Low's question just now. He suggested that Mr Robertson was having an affair with a sex worker at that casino—your casino—and was being blackmailed. Do you know anything about that?"

Lin rubbed his forehead. "Wow. OK. Right. Out of respect for Inspector Low's accomplishments, I'll answer the question. You are living there right, Miss Mistry? In the area? What do you know about our Essex casino?"

"Nothing much."

"Ever hear anything negative?"

"Not really."

"No. Thank you. We follow our Singapore casino model. Quiet. No fuss. No publicity or self-promotion. Just pay competitive salaries, make our money and give back to society."

"Never heard that in your school speech," Low said.

"Look. If someone inside the casino was blackmailing the poor man, how would I possibly know. The place employs dozens of people."

"That's impressive."

"It's the truth, Inspector Low."

"Yah, it's also true that you provided a steady flow of drivers to cope with their supply chain crisis over there. One of those drivers, Cheng, a China guy with a dodgy visa, is now dead. And the trucking boss who told us about this illegal labour force is also dead."

Lin shook his head in exasperation. "I don't know what you want me to say. We've had illegal workers at our Singaporean casinos. We've had people die at our Singaporean casinos. We've had prostitutes and pimps and other filthy businesses operating inside our casinos. I believe you've investigated some of them over the years. Does that make me personally responsible?"

"So you didn't put Robertson in touch with a snakehead?"

Lin looked straight at his fellow Singaporean. "A people smuggler? Why? Where's the financial or political benefit for me? Why would I possibly risk my portfolio and my entire business for a few illegal workers, when I have access to thousands of legal and trained migrant workers across Asia?"

Low had nothing. No comeback. No fireworks. The *towkay* was right. There was no angle, no obvious gain.

"Yeah, OK, you can go," Low mumbled. "Thanks for your time."

Lin stood up and gestured towards the woman at the table. "It was a pleasure to meet you, Miss Mistry. Enjoy your stay in Singapore. Inspector Low, I hope you find what you're looking for."

"Yeah? What's that?"

"I'm not sure. Inner peace?"

"Nah, lost that years ago."

Low's sarcasm was wasted on Lin. The revered billionaire had returned to his obsequious hosts. The two detectives, sweating beneath the shade sail, had already been forgotten.

Chapter 24

The rundown shophouse was too sweaty and their skirts were too short. Too obvious. Too unseemly. He would pay a visit to the Salvation Army at Changi North in the morning. The charity shop was usually stacked with yesterday's trendy items and tomorrow's junk.

In such a sadly superficial and consumerist society, the waste appalled him.

But there would be clothes. Long skirts would suffice, but trousers and jeans might work better, considering the change in climate.

He certainly didn't blame them for their tasteless sartorial choices. Mini-skirts and crop tops were cheap, less than five bucks a piece at Lucky Plaza. The poorly-made clothes were usually dumped in large trays outside shops for the girls to ransack on their rare days off, like rats through a rubbish chute.

Plus, the extra flesh on show made the moonlighting more profitable. He understood their choices. Fate had dealt them an unfair hand. They were trying to survive.

Moving quickly through the squalid living room, he passed around the Maggi noodles, chicken or curry. They couldn't have both. His instructions were clear. One packet per person. He had already supplied the kettle for boiling water and his funds were limited. Besides, they wouldn't be staying long.

After the phone call, he had decided to accelerate the process.

The women clasped his hand in theirs, often refusing to let go, treating the processed noodles like spiritual offerings. They bowed their heads in gratitude, muttering something in Tagalog or Bahasa, giving thanks to whatever deity had dumped them in a neglected shophouse off Jalan Besar.

But they had food and water and the faint hope of something better. They were the lucky ones, huddled together on the living room floor.

Still, their appreciation was humbling.

"Eh, *basket*, give them maggi mee, for *wha'*?"

The uncouth *ah long* with the web tattoo moved around the living room in his slippers, stepping over sleeping bags and snatching yellow noodle packets from shaking hands. "Wanna make them fat, is it? Bloody hell. How to sell if fat, fat one? They want fit one, OK?"

He inhaled slowly, before stepping between the foul-mouthed fool and the terrified women. "They need to eat," he said calmly.

"Make them all *ah pooi*. How to sell *ah pooi*? Might as well sell *ah kua*. Cannot."

"They need to eat," he repeated, softer this time.

He took back the noodle packets from the gangster, who offered no resistance. He returned the food to a woman sitting on chipped tiles. Legs crossed. Eyes down. Her hair covered her face. She nodded in gratitude.

He grinned at the gangster, pointing at the younger man's neck. "Why a spider?"

"Where got spider? It's a web *lah*."

"Why?"

"I like Spiderman."

"The movies?"

"No, the comic books. Stole them from Bras Basah last time."

He giggled at the insouciance. "What's your name?"

"Shumai."

"Like a dumpling?"

"*Yah lah*, last time I also fat one."

"But you're so slim now. Did you change your diet?"

"Prison change my diet."

Shumai scratched his testicles. His shorts and T-shirt were loose-fitting, but the airless living room was stifling. "No air con, *ah*?"

"Unfortunately, no. But they won't be here for long. Maybe we can bring in a fan. Would you all like a fan?"

The women never spoke. They sat in a loose semi-circle, huddled together, staring at noodle ingredients written in a language most didn't understand. It didn't matter. Avoiding eye contact did.

"Maybe get them a fan. I'll look in the Salvation Army, when I pick up some clothes."

"No need *lah*." Shumai was restless. He was eager to return to the KTV lounge. Since the restrictions on social gatherings had been lifted, business had never been better. His girls had never been more grateful for the extra work.

But Shumai wouldn't be sad to see these ones go. They had never been grateful.

"They got clothes already," Shumai snarled.

"Clothes for Singapore, not clothes for cold weather."

"Can buy when arrive *lah*."

"No. We can buy for them now."

Shumai didn't argue. He never did really. He liked to talk cock, especially in front of the women. He had to keep face.

But he mostly understood the hierarchy. Once the hierarchy had been explained to him several times.

A woman screamed. Another leapt to her feet.

"*Relak lah*," Shumai said. His slipper found the cockroach at the fourth attempt.

Shumai dropped the dying insect into the nearby toilet. The oily gangster then pulled down his shorts and relived himself, urinating on the floor around the toilet bowl. "Eh, sorry, *ah*, cannot see in the dark. One of you come clean."

But the other man headed off to the kitchen instead. He returned with a mop and bucket and stood in the toilet doorway, waiting for Shumai to finish. The two men passed each other in silence.

And then he went to work, wiping away the puddle of urine.

When he was finished, he washed his hands and returned to the living room.

"I'm sorry. You should not have witnessed that." He glared at Shumai. "We will have this place cleaned properly. And we must do something about that smell."

He wandering around the living room, passing each woman sitting on the floor, sniffing the air, in search of the alien odour. Mould had spread through the cracks in the walls and ceiling. Mustiness was common in most inter-war shophouses in Singapore, even those with no furniture. The humidity was merciless.

But this was something else, something *personal*.

He hovered above a couple of women. The smell was overpowering. He crouched before them. "Is it that time?"

One was Indonesian. The other was probably from Myanmar. Neither responded. He understood. Maybe they spoke English. Maybe they didn't. But they had been trained to be docile.

He joined them on the floor, crossing his legs. "Could you look at me, please?"

The girl from Myanmar did as she was told. Or maybe she didn't know what she was being told. She was younger, a teenager, and still eager to please.

The Indonesian woman was a little older and presumably wiser. She probably understood every word. She was also crying.

He cradled her chin in his thumb and forefinger and gently tilted her head upwards. With his left hand, he pushed her long black hair away from her face. Her brown, tear-stained eyes were rather beautiful.

"What's your name?" His voice was soft.

She looked at him and then across at the Chinese gangster. She would not answer.

He continued to rest his hand under her chin. "It's OK. Tell me your name."

"Dewi," she said finally.

"Ah, Dewi. The goddess. A lovely name." He offered a kind smile. "Is it your period, Dewi?"

She nodded.

"And you do not have anything."

She shook her head.

"I'm sorry. I'm so, so sorry. We will take care of you." He stood up. "Shumai. Come."

The gangster dragged the mop bucket towards them, cursing under his breath.

Chapter 25

Deputy Director Anthony Chua hadn't finished his chicken rice. The phone call had ruined his appetite. His reaction irritated him almost as much as the news. He was still afraid. Despite his position, authority and experience, he was still afraid of a scolding from the Minister. He was still Singaporean.

But he was also afraid of Low. An underling. An irrelevance. The fading inspector lived off a distant past, clinging to a job that was leaving him behind.

And Low still didn't behave like a Singaporean. His antics baffled Chua. The inspector had no interest in a career path, salary or social status. He took nothing within the walls of CID seriously. Meetings, planning sessions and staff appraisals were for others. Minions. Nobodies.

Criminals were the priority. Catching them was the obsession. And they couldn't be caught at a staff appraisal. So Low ignored the mundane trivialities of internal police procedure and interrogated prominent philanthropists instead.

Low had harangued Patrick Lin at a school ceremony, an elite school, for heaven's sake, and Lin's people had called the Minister.

The first call was always going to be to the deputy director's office. The director was playing golf with private secretaries from the Ministry. A buffer was usually maintained, should plausible deniability ever be needed.

And the deputy director's first call was always going to be to his incorrigible inspector.

Chua sat back and watched the circus play out through his glass partition.

Low swaggered through the office, dressed in his provocative hoodie, hands in pockets. Every expression was an aggressive one. He scowled at the other officers, cowering in their cubicles. The contempt was mutual.

Chua smoothed his tie and checked his shirt for stray grains of rice. He was a messy eater and Low noticed every imperfection.

The inspector flopped into the chair across from his boss, legs apart, scowl firmly fixed in place. "Not hungry is it?" Low pointed at the open polystyrene container. "Can I finish? No time for *makan*."

Chua nodded. Low tucked in, using the same plastic fork and spoon, slurping loudly. The Hainanese soup stock filled his senses. "Missed this in England. Cannot get chicken rice like this over there. It's like fish and chips over here. Not the same."

Chua eyed the detective with a curious mix of disdain and uncertainty. Something was off. He didn't expect a contrite Low. But a defiant Low was almost too much.

"What are you doing?"

Low peered up from the rice, holding a spoonful to his lips. "*Makan*."

"No, all this," Chua gestured at the other man's appearance. "And all this." He waved his hands at the chicken rice.

"All what?"

"This isn't you."

"Why?"

"Normally, you come inside, screaming and shouting, but now you're like a teenager, like a fake *ah beng*, putting on a show. But no one else is here. Where is the other one?" Chua checked the notes on his desk. "This Ramila Mistry?"

"She's back at my apartment." Low shovelled in another mouthful. "Got jetlag."

Chua pondered the inspector's behaviour. Low's rebellion usually had a purpose. The idiot eating leftover chicken rice wasn't a rebel with an actual cause. He was acting.

"You don't have anything."

Low stopped chewing. "What?"

"You've got no leads in your case."

Low dug the spoon into the rice. "I spoke to the big shot just now."

"And he gave you nothing."

"Well, of course," Low said, wiping his mouth. "He's not going to confess inside a bloody school, is he? Break down in front of schoolgirls. But he's involved."

"In what?"

"The trafficking case, the murders, I told you. Two murders. A China truck driver and an *ang moh* owner of the truck company. They are smuggling girls into England."

"I know. You told me. On Singapore Airlines, right? Can they keep the air miles?"

"Eh, they're getting sent over as forced labour."

"Yah, you told me that also, to work in factories and farms, plucking chickens."

"Eh, balls to you."

"Remember the rank, Inspector Low. Remember the rank."

Low threw up his hands. "OK, balls to you, Deputy

132

Director. This Lin got a stake in the casino. Genting some more. He also got the trucking company."

Chua picked a rice grain from a tooth. "He's also got a stake in the cruise company here. Took my wife on that cruise. She got food poisoning. Too many king prawns. Should I blame Patrick Lin for the buffet?"

Low couldn't control his foot-tapping. His right knee was thumping the underside of the deputy director's desk. "So why did the *ang moh* MP give me his name then?"

"To get you out of his face. To get you out of the country. And it worked." Chua was surprised that he was the angrier of the two men. "Look at you. You walk in here dressed like your old gangster. But he's gone. You should've retired after London last time. Or do lecturing. I offered you the lecturing."

"Talk to greasy undergrads for what?"

"To stop you chasing this woman all over the world."

Low's eyes brightened for the first time. He was focused, dangerous even. "You think I went to England for her? I went to help Grace Chen. A Singaporean."

"Please *lah*. Some old sex worker says your name? Heck care *lah*. They all knew your name last time. Did you help them in the old days? You didn't get a bus to Balestier to help them last time, but this one you fly all the way to London? Rubbish. You went there for the other one. The British one. This Mistry. And now you bring her here. For nothing. You're not chasing a snakehead. You're chasing a ghost."

Low looked down at his right foot. The tapping had stopped. There was no point in pretending anymore.

Chapter 26

Dr Lai noticed the stillness. Low wasn't fidgeting. The irony of her patient's physical ticks wasn't lost on either of them. The inspector read other people for a living. But he was an open book. Normally.

Today, he was frozen, unmoved in every sense. He sat across from her, hunched in the chair, waiting for the mania that would not come.

"You're not saying much," she began.

"Not much to say."

Low rubbed the stubble on his chin. Jetlag was a temporary irritation. The lethargy never really left him, a by-product of his condition. He had recovered briefly, in England, convincing himself that the case was triggering him.

But it wasn't really. Mistry was.

"Why did you ask to see me urgently then?"

"No choice. My boss."

Lai was taken aback. "No one from your department contacted me."

"My boss hammered me just now. Ripped my case apart. I'm not thinking straight, he said, because of her. Said she was distracting me."

"Any truth in that?"

"She's been distracting me for twenty-five years. But I still solved cases. Still did my job."

"Not with her standing beside you."

Low's right foot started tapping. "Ah, so that's why I'm going nowhere with this case, is it? She was standing next to me in her father's mini-mart when I saved her kid's life. I saved the whole bloody family. And where did it get me?"

Lai always felt a tad guilty for the internal rush of euphoria. Her job was vampiric. She had hit a nerve. He was shouting. She was winning.

"That sounds a little like self-pity. Do you feel there's a lack of gratitude?"

Low rubbed his forehand hard, leaving a deep, red mark. Weak analysis annoyed him. "Don't be ridiculous. They're grateful. They could take ten lifetimes saying thank you and it'd still never be enough for them. I saved their son. I saved their everything. So, no, I don't feel a lack of gratitude."

"So are you yearning then? Yearning for something you do not have?"

"Are we on TV? Is this psychology for soap operas? I don't want her kid, her family life, her home or her cheap bloody car. She's happy. And she deserves that happiness."

"So what is it then?"

Low could see the different colours slowly returning. He visualised fireworks to explain the mania, to rationalise it and channel it towards something productive, something other than self-harm.

"I'm weak around her. It's like, I don't know, she's turned into this fucking kryptonite. I took her to this *atas* school, to interrogate a suspect, this *towkay*. And I should've realised straightaway that he's not really a legitimate suspect, too implausible. But I wanted her to see me in action in

Singapore, my *kampong*, the local hero taking down the bad guys."

"It's not an unusual scenario."

"It's a childish fantasy. I was a like twelve-year-old boy trying to impress the pretty girl with my breakdancing. Feeble. Pathetic. Sitting there with this businessman, watching him brush my questions aside, like I'm a mosquito. And I was ... I was nothing, this fucking big."

Low made a tiny gap between his thumb and forefinger. "Why? Because I'm trying to show off in front of a girl."

"So you still have feelings for this woman?"

"No. Well, yes, but not in that way." Low acknowledged Lai's quizzical expression. "Please. Leave the non-verbal interrogations to me, OK? It's not about her. It's me. It's what she does to me, up here."

Low prodded his right temple. "She wipes this out. She's like a history button. She clears my browsing data, all the disgusting shit of the last twenty-odd years is gone. All the cases are gone. Ah Lian is gone. Tiger is gone. It's like I'm reset, back to the beginning. I'm not this guy anymore."

Low tucked at his hoodie. "I'm not Inspector Low with her. I'm Stanley. "

"She's not a portal for your nostalgia," said Lai.

"That's good. You should write that down."

Lai ignored the goading. "You can't use her as a course correction for your life. She's not a functionary for your conscience."

"Wow, you're on fire today." Low stretched out his legs. "Do you know what's really depressing?"

"Go on."

"I need her to go back to England. But not for the reasons you think."

"You don't know what I think."

"Yeah, I do. I can't be stuck in the past, right? She's happily married. She's never coming back. Yeah, I know all of that. The truth is, I can't be Stanley. Simple Stanley. Happy Stanley. It doesn't work. I can't be *blur* like *sotong* because I'm trying to impress her all the time. I need my inner bastard. She has to go back home so I can go back to being the only thing that I'm good at. An arsehole."

"You are very good at that."

They both chuckled. The respect for the other person's intellect was mutual, but only one of them danced along the edges of insanity. Deliberately.

Low sat up straight. "I bought her a china Merlion today."

"They have a Merlion in China?"

"No *lah*, a china Merlion, made of china, not in China. *Wah lau*, you're supposed to be the *cheem* one."

The psychiatrist was overcome by a fit of the giggles. "Oh dear, I'm sorry. Shouldn't laugh. Very unprofessional. Yes, you bought her a Merlion. That's nice."

"Yah, it was one of the first places I took her when she stayed with me in Singapore, in the nineties. She thought it was the weirdest thing ever. Took those vomiting photos that every tourist takes."

"That's a nice memory."

"And that's all it is now." Low slapped his thighs, preparing to get up. "Right, I've ordered *makan* for her from Gokul, best North Indian in Singapore. Gonna have a last meal tonight, a bottle of wine and then I'm gonna send her back to her family."

"That seems like a really positive move."

"Yep. And then you'll be the only one stuck with Inspector Low."

"Can't wait."

*

Mistry had made an effort to tidy the apartment, but Low's home needed a serious makeover. His crumbling HDB flat had never been renovated. The original breezeblocks poked through the living room wall. At least he occupied a high floor.

She savoured the breeze as she pinned a damp cloth to a bamboo pole. Leaning out of the window, she found the metal slot and hung out the pole.

The view was uniquely Singaporean.

The surrounding HDB blocks looked like they had been attacked by spears. Bamboo poles jutted out from beneath every kitchen window in neat, straight rows. Even Singapore's washing habits followed a fiercely conformist model.

Beyond the HDB blocks, the treetops of MacRitchie Reservoir dominated the dusky skyline. Mistry made out a flock of whitish birds flapping from one high branch to another in the distance, squawking loudly, possibly cockatoos.

Mistry had always assumed that cockatoos were native to Australia, but it made sense, really. Singapore imported everything.

Many years ago, the island had almost imported her. In a different life.

The brusque knock at the door interrupted her reminiscing. She welcomed the distraction. Unlike Low, she had no interest in wallowing in the past.

"Delivery."

Mistry smiled as she made her way to the door. No hello. No feigned politeness. Just a direct, literal utterance of intent. Singapore was still a direct, literal kind of country.

"Hang on." She fumbled with the door lock. "Is it the Indian food?"

"Yah."

"Fantastic."

She opened the door. Guy Fawkes stepped forward and punched her in the face.

Chapter 27

Mistry was aware that she was falling. So she made a promise to herself, instinctively, defiantly. She was not going to pass out.

She saw her boy running towards her, little Ben, his legs scampering, arms stretched out, ready to butt her in the stomach.

But it was not her boy.

It was a man, his stubby legs scampering through the doorway, making his way into the apartment.

On her way down, Mistry took a quick inventory. Short guy. Muscular. Black T-shirt. Blue shorts. White trainers. Guy Fawkes mask.

Guy Fawkes mask.

He was wearing a Guy Fawkes mask.

Mistry was hallucinating. Her mind was winding down, inviting her to sleep. The garish, cracked blue tiles of Low's living room floor were on their way. She tensed, bracing for impact.

But she was not passing out, not for her boy, or for Low, or Singapore or for a fuckwit in a cheap Halloween mask.

Mistry adjusted her body, turning to the side, away from the door, away from Guy Fawkes. Her shoulder smashed into the grubby tiles, tearing her rotator cuff, but shielding her head. She would not lose consciousness.

Instead, she curled into the foetal position, returning to a blissful childlike state, hoping it might be over quickly, allowing for a possible rebirth later.

Her hands covered her ears and face, but she could still hear him.

"Fuck you, bitch."

His kicks found the sides of her stomach. She winced. But the immediate pain bothered her less than the internal gurgling sensation.

The fear of the unknown somehow streamlined her thinking.

Organs. Internal bleeding. He's going to kill me.

He's going to kill me.

Her son appeared again, but he was no longer running towards her. He was waving. Saying goodbye. Fading away.

Mistry reached out to him, rolling onto her stomach, crawling towards him, dragging her bleeding body across those shitty tiles. Guy Fawkes stomped on her thigh, but the pain was no longer getting through.

Mistry was trying to get to her son. The wounded mother had transcended pain.

She grabbed the leg of a wooden chair and pushed it aside. Low's cheap IKEA dining table offered sanctuary.

But he was still coming. He grabbed her ankles and pulled hard. She dug her fingernails into the tile grooves, but they offered no resistance. Instead, she heard the nail from her middle finger being torn from its nailbed. Her other fingers slipped in the fresh trail of blood.

"Indian bitch."

Guy Fawkes dragged her out from under the dining

table. She seemed lighter this time. Her resistance was faltering, and she knew it, too.

Mistry's hands flailed around in search of one of the table legs, but her fingertips caught the edges of something else.

Guy Fawkes flipped her onto her back and leaned into her face. His breath reeked of cigarettes and fish head curry.

"That's it," he whispered. His hands were around her neck, squeezing quickly. "Go quiet, OK?"

He shushed her. Comforted her. Death was on its way. No need to make a fuss.

Mistry's body agreed, falling limp, surrendering. She raised an arm, either in resignation or defiance. He wasn't sure. But he liked it.

"Quite cute," he said. "Come. Put it down now."

He leaned across Mistry's weary body to lower her left hand and then he couldn't see.

The hissing confused him. The pain disorientated him. The screaming weakened him.

She had never screamed.

When his fist opened her nose, she had not screamed.

When his foot found her ribs, she had not screamed.

And when he tried to kill her, she had not screamed. Not once.

Now he was screaming.

"It hurts, eh? It really fucking hurts." Mistry took aim at his puffy, weeping eyes and squeezed again. "Do you like that? Fucking piece of shit."

Guy Fawkes tried to find his footing but stumbled backwards. His screaming had given way to the wailing of a cornered animal. He fell into Low's cheap IKEA dining table. But there was no sanctuary.

There was only Ramila Mistry. Detective Inspector. Wife. Mother.

There would be no forgiveness.

She was on her feet now. Revitalised. Ready for what needed to be done.

"You think you can do this to me?" Her bloody right hand grabbed the back of his head, finding clumps of oily hair. She noticed the missing fingernail. Strangely, this pleased her. She wiped the blood from her eyes. "You think you can do this to me?"

She found the necessary strength. Guy Fawkes's forehead found the corner of the dining table. Now he was on his hands and knees, scampering across the blue tiles, blood streaming down his face, a blind mouse with nowhere to run.

Mistry stood over him. "Nobody gets to do this to me again. You understand? Nobody gets to hurt me again."

Her kick found his balls, emasculating him, finishing him.

"Never fuck with a mother," she said breathlessly.

The insect repellent bottle clattered against the tiles and rolled across the floor. It had done the job.

"Eh, you're very noisy, you know."

The voice came from the next-door neighbour, banging on their shared wall.

Mistry kicked Guy Fawkes aside and slumped into a chair. "Sorry."

"That house got policeman, you know."

"I know," Mistry shouted back, picking up her phone. "I'm calling him now."

While she waited for Low to answer, she made the decision to identify Guy Fawkes cautiously. He was drifting in and out of consciousness, but she still had the insect repellent.

"Hey Stanley, it's me," she said, slowly lifting the

weeping man's mask. "No, the food hasn't come yet. Someone did try to kill me though . . . Don't know . . . But he's got a web tattoo."

Mistry dropped the phone. She was spent. Finished. She knew what was coming. And she was prepared. These final moments were going to belong to the people that mattered. She closed her eyes and saw her son.

Ramila Mistry's beautiful boy was scampering towards her, arms outstretched, ready to welcome her home.

Chapter 28

Xavier Ng stared at the tattoo. The rookie detective admired the artistry. He knew little about tattoos, or spiders' webs, but he recognised quality craftmanship.

"That's a nice tattoo, Mr Lee."

"Shumai."

"Sorry?"

"Everybody call me Shumai."

Ng tapped the file on the table. "In here, it says you are Lee Hong Weng."

"Out there, I'm Shumai."

"A dumpling?"

"That's why."

Shumai folded his arms. He tried to stay relatively still. The rustling of the surgical gown was annoying. Nothing else concerned him. He had been here before, sort of. The room was sparce. The air-conditioning was too high. The steel table was drilled into the concrete floor. Different police department. Different time. But Singaporean inter-rogation rooms had never really changed. There were no concessions for suspects. Shumai had the right to be intim-idated, but little else.

But Shumai refused to be cowed by his environment.

As a short, fat kid, he'd had his lunch money taken in his Yishun neighbourhood school. Every day.

Now he took money from much bigger men. Every day.

He feared no one.

"Why you bring me here?"

"How do you mean?" Ng scrolled through his phone. Killing time. Staying calm.

"This one *ah*? What you call it? Specialised Crime Division. What's that *ah*? Last time, I go Corruption division. Now send me here for what?"

"Don't know. Don't care."

"*Wah*, tough guy *ah*?" Shumai leaned across the table. The cold steel pressed against his elbows. "I'm supposed to be scared, is it?"

"Of what? Me looking at my phone?"

"Act like you don't care one."

"I do care."

"*Ah* then?"

"I've been told to wait."

"What for?"

Ng decided to make eye contact. He grinned at the handcuffed gangster in the surgical gown. "A tsunami."

"A sue what?"

Ng opened the folder. "Lee Hong Weng. Twenty-nine years old. Changi Prison. Twice already. Short sentences. Unlicensed moneylending and vice. A loan shark and a pimp."

"Fake news *lah*."

Distant, loud voices drifted into the interrogation room. Shumai focused on the heavy, bolted door. There were competing, overlapping noises on the other side. Shumai couldn't quite pin them down. Moving chairs. Moving bodies. Moving closer.

"What's that?"

Ng didn't look up. "The tsunami."

The door flew open. Chaos entered.

A *blur* in a hoodie was around the table and in Shumai's face. A hand found the tattooed neck. The other yanked back his hair.

"You're already dead. It's done. Either in here or out there, you're already dead."

Low's eyes blazed. He was alive to the possibilities of another man's death.

"Do you fucking hear me? I've told who I need to tell. It's done."

Low felt the tentative hands of a wary, junior officer on his shoulders. He recoiled at the thought of a possible counter-attack, a betrayal from one of his own. The inspector used his right hand to push Ng in the chest, hard enough to bruise nothing but the other man's ego. "Fuck off, Xavier."

Ng retreated to his seat, trapped in the eternal Singaporean dilemma. He followed orders, but the orders were wrong. He deferred to a superior voice, but the voice was absolute and unhinged. In doing right, professionally, he was doing wrong, morally. He was closing one eye to an obvious injustice. He was a classically trained Singaporean.

Low's left hand remained a vice. He felt the hair coming away from the follicles. He pulled out a clump. Shumai watched his own hair rain down his face. He yelped in anguish. Instinctively, he raised his hands. Handcuffed. Impotent.

The inspector would not stop. "Do you wanna live?"

Low was even louder now. Raging. Screaming. His bloodshot eyes promised nothing but further torment.

Shumai lashed out in his chair, mustering a final effort to

147

earn a reprieve. But none was coming. Low didn't believe in second chances.

In his experience, they didn't exist.

Ng thought about intervening. He thought about his career. He thought about the built-to-order apartment that he had balloted for in Boon Keng. He could end a guilty man's suffering or prolong his boss' mental breakdown.

"Inspector Low, there are cameras. They'll be watching. Deputy Chua said . . ."

"Fuck Deputy Chua and fuck the cameras."

Low raised his right hand slowly. He needed his intentions to be clear. He wiggled his forefinger in front of Shumai's nose. "Last chance."

Low pressed the finger against Shumai's right eyeball. The gangster wailed like a traumatised child. He grabbed the inspector's wrist. The resistance was weak. Pointless.

Low had a target. He pressed harder.

"You feel that bulging sensation? Your eyeball is gonna explode like a century egg unless you answer my question. Do you wanna live?"

Shumai felt the pressure building inside his head, but refused to answer.

"Do you wanna fucking live?" Low raged.

"Inspector Low, you can't do this."

"Shut up, Xavier," Low snapped. He felt his fingernail scratch the cornea. "I won't ask again, Shumai. Do you wanna live?"

Low increased the pressure. Shumai heard his own eyeball squelch against his skull. The dizziness was overwhelming. He was slowly going blind. "OK *lah*, stop. Bastard. Fucking stop."

Low pressed harder. "No, you gotta earn it. Why you come to my flat?"

"To whack you *lah*."

"But I wasn't home."

"Whack her *lah*. Anyone. To piss you off."

"Why?" Low rotated his finger around the eyeball.

"Ah, fuck. Ah Meng. Ah Meng *lah*," Shumai screeched. "You're killing his business. Too many raids. He's fed up already."

Low stepped away. Shumai covered his weeping eyeball. Ng decided against intervening, on behalf of either man.

Low wiped his finger on Shumai's surgical gown. "Ah Meng? You went after Ramila for an idiot like Ah Meng?"

"Who's Ramila?"

Shumai swiftly regretted his decision to feign ignorance, particularly after the inspector slammed his face against the steel table. "Ah the Indian one *ah*," he said, rubbing his swollen, bloody forehead.

"Yeah, the Indian one. She's a police officer, a British police officer some more."

"Oh shit."

"Yeah. Oh shit."

"I thought she was a hooker."

Shumai decided to stop talking after his forehead met the steel table for a second time.

Low pulled out a chair. "You know why I like women beaters, Ng?"

The younger detective shook his head.

"They're cry-babies. They're easy." Low sat beside Shumai. "Not like last time. No. In the Tiger days, there was respect for women. Pimp them, OK *lah*, but never beat them. Not allowed. Not with Tiger. He killed women. Yes. But only if he had a good reason. He never beat them. Unless he had a good reason. Those *ah peks* were old school, man. And I know them, the ones who are left, inside Changi."

"Yah, so?"

Low leaned into Shumai's ear. "And I saw what you did to that girl at the KTV. Janice, right? You remember Janice? She protected you. But you get no protection from me."

"No need."

"Ah, cos you're a gangster, right? You beat Janice. You beat Ramila. You beat them all, right? But only women. In Changi Prison, cannot. In Changi, got men only. And they like to beat men who like beating women. And I have already given them your name."

Shumai shrivelled in his seat. The puffed-up gangster was disappearing. The tubby kid from Yishun was back, hiding in the playground, clinging to his lunch money.

"But I told you about Ah Meng already," he whimpered.

"And you went to see Ramila already." Low stood up and pushed his chair under the steel table. "Give my love to my Changi *kakis*. I know they'll give it to you."

Chapter 29

The sex workers operated within the shadow of the Prime Minister's residence. Hidden deep inside the lush, Istana grounds, Sri Temasek was a two-storey detached house, built by the British Empire, owned by Singaporeans and maintained by cheap foreigners. Sri Temasek was an authentic Singapore home.

Across the road, illegal masseuses masturbated their wealthiest clients.

Low loved the irony. At the nearby Plaza Singapura, international housewives paid exorbitant prices for imported breakfast tea. In Sophia Road, their husbands paid for imported sex.

Even the name appealed to the inspector's sense of humour. Lady Sophia was the second wife of Sir Stamford Raffles, the founder of modern Singapore. Her husband once screwed Asians. Now expats did the same in the street bearing her name.

Low was a regular visitor to Sophia Road. Since the pandemic, the public's appetite for illicit sex had swiftly returned.

Inside the Peace Centre, the rickety lift was slow, noisy and stank of nicotine. The wood panelling was rotting from the bottom up. Low stepped out at the eighth floor, the lucky floor, and marvelled at the ostentatious tackiness. The Dynasty Spa might have represented Singapore. With artificial grass covering the wall, the façade gave the appearance of eco-friendliness, but the greenery was manufactured and fake. The polished-glass entrance led to a long, gloomy corridor with doors leading into KTV rooms. Gleaming on the outside, grubby on the inside, the faint hope of prosperity hid an underlying seediness. The business operated round the clock for its most prestigious clients. Just like Singapore. And the booming Chinese radio station drowned out all other noise.

No one needed to hear what was going on inside the Dynasty Spa.

The interior was intentionally gloomy. The lighting was low enough to protect the identities of customers and the physical decay of weary sex workers. They sat on cheap, brown sofas, beneath framed prints of China's hinterland, the fading image of a distant, manufactured utopia. As Low entered, three women adjusted their push-up bras. One fixed her skirt and stood up quickly. Her youth betrayed her. She was too enthusiastic. The other two offered the inspector a wry smile. They conserved their energy for one of the six private rooms behind the counter. It was still early.

"You want massage?"

The young woman's heavy make-up failed to hide her sudden apprehension. She had entertained worse customers than the weird Chinese guy in dirty jeans and crumpled hoodie. He wasn't bad looking either. But his eyes terrified her.

"Where's Ah Meng?"

She took a step backwards. "Who?"

"Ah Meng. Your boss. The *towkay*. Fat bastard. Go and get him." Low waved his credentials in her face. "Now."

"No need. No need."

Ah Meng shuffled through a curtain. The curtain hid the six private rooms and the Singapore that locals had little interest in acknowledging. Ah Meng struggled to get around the counter. His stomach spilled over his shorts. His weight was a source of real pride. He grew up stick-thin and dirt poor in a Sembawang kampong. Now he displayed his abundance around his waist.

"I'm here, *lah*. What now, *Inspector*?"

The inflection change was enough. The women spoke little English, but recognised the sudden, abrupt tone. They vanished through the curtain. The police intrusion had already ruined their evening. They would need to entertain more clients now to satisfy Ah Meng.

"Eh, you shut down Selegie Road already. Now you gonna shut down my spa, is it? This one not KTV, OK? This one spa only. I got valid licence. I know the Massage Establishment Act. It says I can ..."

Low stole Ah Meng's voice. He tightened his grip around the fat man's throat. "Why you send him to my house?"

Ah Meng's veins danced around his balding head. Jack Daniels had already taken care of his red cheeks. Low was adding a shade of purple. "One KTV raid and you try and kill me is it?"

"I didn't."

"You sent Shumai."

"The pimp? Why?"

Low registered the bewilderment. Fear was easy. Fear was immediate. Fear was low-hanging fruit. When they were scared, they fought back or they soiled themselves.

They lashed out or pissed on the floor, fight or flight. Ah Meng was doing neither. His darting eyes sought clarity. He wasn't stalling. He was confused.

Low released his grip. "*Your* pimp. Shumai."

Ah Meng stumbled into the counter, coughing loudly. "What did he do?"

"He came to my apartment. To whack me. But he whack my friend instead."

"Eh, you got girlfriend *ah*?"

"Fuck you. The bastard said you sent him."

"Wait ah, wait *ah*." Ah Meng leaned against the counter and inhaled sharply. "Cannot breathe, *basket*." He downed a glass of scotch. "My throat cannot, bloody hell." He took a deep breath and clutched his ribs. "Must lose weight. OK. OK. Can breathe now."

"Then talk now."

Ah Meng clumsily reached for a counter stool. His excess skin flopped over the sides of the small, leather seat. "OK, he say I send him to you for wha'?"

"For closing down the KTV. At Selegie Road."

Ah Meng shook his head, disdainfully. "Eh, come on *ah*. You serious or what? How many times you shut me down. Lost count already. So what? I come to your place and I kill you, is it? Are you mad or what? Yah *lah*, we act *blur* outside. Got no sex inside. Got no party inside. Got no hard liquor inside. Got no singing. Got nothing except *makan*, right or not? All bullshit. Never mind. Once in a while, you whack me. I pay the fine. That's it. Otherwise, what? They go Jalan Sultan. They go Bencoolen Street. Right? So, never mind." Ah Meng covered half his face. "Close one eye. Or cannot survive. Right or not?"

"No, I close your place. He comes after me."

"Please *lah*. You embarrass him. Arrest him. Arrest

him with his cuckoo bird some more. You slap him in front of the girls. He's young. Stupid. So he whack you *lah*."

Low wasn't convinced. "Too neat. I attack him. He attacks me. Simple revenge, is it? Don't treat me like a fucking idiot."

Ah Meng gestured towards the empty brown sofas. The fake leather was cracked in places. The seams were coming away. "You see any customers? You see my girls just now? Three girls. That's all I got here. Every time, I *kena* whack, I lose some more. They leave. That's it. Cannot get any more."

"Come on *ah*, you're one of the only growth industries left in Singapore. During the pandemic, you were operating 24/7."

"Yah, *lah*, but cannot replace."

"Why do you need to replace?"

"*Basket*. They keep leaving. Had so many last time."

"They go to another shophouse?"

"Balls to you. They disappear."

Low looked around the spa. Its appearance was unusual. They were always shabby, but this one was pitiful. The waiting area smelled of musty carpet rugs and last night's sex. The fish tank in the corner was empty. Algae had turned the glass green. Prostitution was recession-proof, but Ah Meng's spa was decaying from within.

"So you cannot get new girls is it?"

"Cannot even get old girls anymore."

Low found the photos on his phone. Twelve faces. All female. None smiling. Grace Chen had even scowled for the officer at the Essex police station. Low had always admired her feistiness.

"Hey, look at this. You recognise these girls?"

Ah Meng took his reading glasses from the counter. He scrolled through the list. "Who are they?"

"You don't need to know. You want me to believe you, then help me first. They work for you last time?"

Low noticed Ah Meng's hesitation over Grace Chen's face. "She looks a bit familiar," Ah Meng muttered. "See her at the KTV last time. Maybe. But never work for me."

The spa owner continued scrolling. "Ah that one I know."

He stopped at a younger woman. Filipino. Long hair. Scared. "Yah, that one I see before."

"Where?"

"My church?"

Low took back the phone. "Bullshit. You go to church?"

"Hey, I found God in prison."

"Yeah? Which one?"

Ah Meng grinned. "The one that got me parole."

Chapter 30

The beeping stabbed Low through the heart. The machine was supposedly keeping her stable, but the unstable one was sitting beside her hospital bed.

He was the reason for the beeping.

Low leaned across the sheets and delicately flicked the hair across her forehead. The fringe covered the swelling. He didn't need to see that now. He was fully aware of the damage. Her damage. His fault.

The staff at Tan Tock Seng Hospital had kindly offered a private room. It was not a private hospital, but the patient was a prominent employee of London's Metropolitan Police Force.

The Minister had made a call.

Low knew that the Minister wasn't entirely happy with the arrangement, but Singapore's obsession with calm exteriors prevailed. That obsession ensured the presence of a uniformed officer outside the hospital room, which amused Low.

Ramila Mistry didn't need anyone's protection. And she didn't need to be here either.

Her superior officer had advised against it. So had her husband. But she had made the trip anyway. Loyalty had compelled her to come, but it was a misplaced loyalty, based on a misunderstanding of past events.

She still thought she owed Low for saving her son. But she owed him nothing.

He softly held her right hand. Not her wedding ring hand. Low knew his place.

He had already asked to call her husband, to make amends, to do something constructive, but she had no time for irrational sentimentality. There was no need to worry helpless loved ones. She wasn't dying.

Low released his grip on her right hand. He struggled to look at her, let alone touch her. The guilt was overwhelming, hammering away at whatever was left of his conscience with every beep of that infernal machine.

The beeping felt accusatory, screeching at the inspector in an otherwise silent hospital room. Low covered his ears, but the noise still penetrated, condemning him. Shaming him. He already knew what he was. He didn't need to be told, repeatedly, rhythmically, eighty times a minute, her heart literally talking to him, over and over again, reminding him of broken relationships. Broken lives.

He tried to think about London. Recent history. Ancient history. Old times. Better times. Or different times with the same woman. Her designations had changed, but her personality had never wavered. Criminology student. Smart arse. Detective inspector. Smart arse. Singapore visitor. Smart arse. He loved that. She hadn't really changed. Nor had he. Good for her. Bad for him. Maybe. He wasn't sure. The contradictions were too many to count, too many to ignore, just like the damn beeping.

Naturally, Low couldn't wallow in his nostalgia. Modern Singapore didn't allow it. Instead, the remorseless city tapped at the window, breaking the spell. The incessant drilling filtered through the thick glass. His home had no time for romanticism or patience for anything that wasn't working. Anything old was knocked down and replaced.

"What's all the noise?"

Her faint voice paralysed him. He was momentarily ashamed of his incoherence. He hadn't wanted her to wake up. He didn't have the words ready.

"It's, er, drilling, outside," he said, looking to the window, away from her. "The national anthem of Singapore."

"Next to a bloody hospital," Mistry whispered, touching the tender wound on her forehead.

"It's Novena. Prime real estate."

"Where's that?"

"Er, what would you know around here? There's Newton over there." Low pointed through the window. "Or there's Balestier next door."

"Oh yeah. I remember Balestier."

Low's skull pounded. The self-flagellating was on its way. Balestier made the best *bak kut teh*. Balestier made the best gangsters. And Balestier made the best gangster out of Stanley Low.

Mistry had once witnessed the transformation.

"Yeah. Sorry." Low sat back in his chair.

"What for?"

"I don't know. Shall we start with everything and go from there?"

"What?"

"I am. All right? I'm sorry for going back to England. I'm sorry for bringing you back here. And I'm sorry that *this* happened." Low gestured towards Mistry's injuries.

"I'm not exactly over the moon about it."

"No, don't do that. Don't do your flippancy thing, like you don't give a shit. I did this. Not you. I put you in here.

Makes me want to smash that water jug and eat the fucking glass."

Mistry glared at the Singaporean inspector. "Are you finished?"

"Yeah."

"Good. 'Cos I need to piss."

Low forced a smile. "You're doing it again. The forced levity."

"Or I could just need a piss. Don't make everything about you."

"I'm not. You're lying in a bloody hospital bed."

"I'm a big girl, Stanley. I chose to come here."

"Because you think you owe me."

Mistry heaved her upper body up onto the pillows. "You saved my son's life. You don't know what that means."

"Of course I do."

"Nah, you haven't got a clue. You're not a parent. And that's fine. Just stop second guessing me. I wanted to catch the bastards who put those women in the lorry. I still do. That all right with you?"

The drilling outside no longer bothered Low. Even the beeping seemed softer. Mistry's outburst had redirected his focus. He grinned at her. "The insect repellent was a nice touch."

"Lucky I couldn't reach your kitchen knives. I would've cut his balls off."

"That could still happen in Changi."

"Good. What was the mask about?"

"Guy Fawkes? Can buy them cheap online. Most of them don't know what it is."

"They don't know the history?"

"Don't know the idea. We don't do revolution here."

"Oh yeah, no protests, right?"

160

"Not unless we run out of toilet roll at the supermarket."

"Toilet! I need to go," Mistry said, rolling back the sheets.

Low peered through the window. He picked out the faint outline of a bore piling machine burrowing its way through a construction site, smashing through an old development to build a new one, a pointless endeavour.

The inspector empathised. Singaporean machines were conditioned to keep going, to destroy and rebuild, over and over again.

Mistry started to sit up. "Bloody shoulder," she said, wincing.

Low hurried over and adjusted the pillows. "Is it that bad?"

"Only when I move."

"What about your face?"

"Only hurts when I smile."

"Wah, lucky *ah*. With your situation, no need to smile."

"Sod off." But she appreciated the humour. She was glad Low was with her.

"Bastard could've killed ya."

"It's a torn rotator cuff and a bad headache. I'll live."

Low plumped the pillows. "You still want to help?"

Mistry touched her tender shoulder. "What do you think?"

"Ok then. Get off that bloody beeping machine. Get better. And then I'll take you to church."

He approved of the new location. An industrial unit attracted less attention and Loyang Crescent was both quieter and closer to the airport. Risks needed to be minimised now. Containing them was easy. Controlling the others was the problem.

They lacked discipline. Focus.

He preferred to use ex-convicts because they usually promised gratitude and diligence. They were grateful for the work. They were wary of returning to Changi.

If nothing else, he recognised the efficiency of Singapore's prison's service. Recidivism was comparatively low. They really didn't want to go back.

But the new location was oppressive. The lack of windows kept out prying eyes, but kept in the odours of desperate women.

He had insisted on a bucket, at least.

The industrial unit lacked a toilet. And he didn't want them venturing outside.

He had even drawn up a simple roster to respect their privacy and personal hygiene. They used. They cleaned. They rotated. The domestic chores kept them active. It was important to him that the women felt valued.

But he couldn't stop their crying. One or two were to be expected. But the weeping was contagious. Tender, private moments became impromptu therapy sessions. He wanted to give them space to process. But the walls of the industrial unit were thin.

The room was also too small. Just three metres by three metres, the temporary living quarters was barely enough room for the dozen women, let alone their luggage.

Every woman was allowed one small suitcase. He had insisted on equitable travel arrangements for all.

But Dewi could not be pacified. She was not quite the youngest, but certainly the noisiest. The problem child.

He decided to join her on the concrete floor, sitting cross-legged to maintain eye contact. He refused to look down on these people.

"Shush now, Dewi." His voice was soothing and calm.

He wiped her cheeks. He pushed her long, black hair behind her ears. She was one of the prettier ones. She was going to be fine. He needed to remind her of that.

"It's going to be OK. A new life is coming."

"I scared." She would not lift her head. She would not look at those eyes.

He nodded in sympathy and rubbed the inside of her thigh. The skirts from the Hope Centre Family Store in Changi had been a wise move.

"I understand. But it's the right decision."

"I scared of him."

She pointed at the mop and bucket propped against a wall. He tutted disapprovingly. "Yes, our tattooed friend with a love of spiders."

He rested a hand just above her knee, for reassurance. "He's gone now."

"What?"

The slumped shoulders suddenly straightened around him. Now, they were all looking at him. They were hanging on his every word.

"Yes, he's gone. Personality clash."

He raised a hand to her face. Her body stiffened in anticipation. She closed her eyes and thought of her boy, back in Jakarta. She was prepared to make the sacrifice. Any sacrifice. But his caress was gentle. His fingers brushed across her cheeks.

"But we don't need him anymore. It's almost over. You're free."

He realised he was getting flustered. Distracted. He was annoyed by the lack of professionalism. He stood up quickly, eager to make a swift exit.

Dewi did not open her eyes until she heard the door lock behind him.

A kind soul took her hand in the darkness.

Together, the women formed a circle and prayed that he wouldn't come back.

Chapter 31

Father Fernandes gazed upon his flock. Sunday services tested his faith. Some came on buses, grateful for the day off and a rare, welcoming sanctuary. The others came in BMWs. The contrast concerned him.

His church had changed. The house of worship felt increasingly like a status symbol, a private members club. They still worshipped, but for different things. They prayed for pay rises and the best secondary schools.

And while they networked, their domestic helpers chased after their children, playing hide and seek among the prestige vehicles in the busy car park.

But Father Fernandes still had a captive audience. If they wanted a path to the Promised Land or a shortcut to affluence, they still had to listen. He held the keys.

Father Fernandes never lost sight of his privileged position.

"It's wonderful to see so many of you on this hot and humid Sunday morning," he said, raising his arms to the congregation. "It's standing room only. It feels like an old Malaysia Cup match. But I won't ask you to perform the Kallang Roar."

His audience tittered politely at the apparent joke.

Most didn't get the local football reference. But he held those keys.

"And I'm sorry to those forced to stand," he added.

The restless souls standing at the back appreciated the acknowledgment, if not the predicament. A well-dressed couple glared at the young women occupying the pews near the pulpit, the best seats in the house.

Maids.

Maids hadn't contributed to Father Fernandes' fund-raisers.

Maids hadn't distributed *hong baos* to those poor people in rental flats.

Maids hadn't earned a seat on one of Father Fernandes' pews.

But the young women ignored the scorn and enjoyed the irony. On Sunday mornings, as long as they arrived early enough, they got to sit down. And the late-arriving Sirs and Madams were forced to stand at the back. For a couple of hours, the church offered the illusion of equality.

"But let's talk about the wider community," Father Fernandes continued, leaning on his stand, warming to his theme. "I had a meeting with my friends at the Inter-Religious Organisation of Singapore this week and it was a reminder of how blessed we all are, sitting and standing here today.

"According to any number of surveys, our religion has the highest number of people living in private property, the highest number of folks with a university degree and, if our busy car park is any indication, the highest number of *atas* cars too."

The laughter came exclusively from the front frows. The well-dressed couple were now relieved to be wedged in at the back of the church. They were less conspicuous and closer to their Lexus.

"Many of us live privileged lives," Father Fernandes said, sensing the discomfort, but not shying away from it. "And wealth, in itself, is not a sin, especially if it comes from hard work and used appropriately and distributed fairly. But the pursuit of wealth should never be championed for its own sake."

The well-dressed couple were delighted to be stationed near the exit now. They didn't appreciate the subtle rebuke and would leave immediately after the service. Besides, their Lexus wasn't parked in a shady space.

Mistry hovered outside the church's porch and remembered why she struggled with Singapore's humidity. The sweat trickled down the inside of her nose bandage. She growled and dug her fingernails deep into the plaster.

The scratching only added to the discomfort, as the exposed soft tissue of her nailbed rubbed against the sticky material.

Low enjoyed the pantomime. "You OK or not?"

"Piss off."

"Itch you cannot scratch, is it?"

"Yeah, now I've got two."

"Ah, I see what you did there. Your itchy nose and me."

"You try scratching your nose without a fingernail."

"I would probably use one of my other nine fingernails."

"Bollocks. I forgot, didn't I?"

"Mind your language outside a church, inspector. Where's your sense of religion?"

"I'm a Gujarati," Mistry said, tearing at her nose. "Our religion is the corner shop."

Low thought about saying something stupid, but the early morning sun caught the battered side of Mistry's face. The shock silenced him. The bandage across her nose covered most of the swelling, but the bruising had spread to her cheek and forehead.

"Yeah, all right. I look like shit. But don't keep staring at me, eh." Mistry retreated into the porch. "That bloody sun of yours."

"You're gonna blame me for the sun?"

"Yeah, the sun, the humidity, the dust, the traffic and that bloody taxi driver who kept asking me where I was from."

Mistry gave up on her tingling nose and peered through a crack in the door. "It's like Wembley in there. Churches are dying in England. What's his secret?"

"The unsaid promise of money, privilege and influence."

"Oh, leave off. You haven't got some Singaporean illuminati going."

"No need. It's out in the open. Raffles Institution runs the country. Anglo-Chinese School owns the country. They teach that on the school curriculum, you know."

"Yeah, well, he's getting a standing ovation so they must be wrapping up."

Father Fernandes watched the last of the luxury cars leave the premises. He waved at the domestic helpers, waiting at the bus stop, clutching their picnics in plastic bags.

The priest took a moment to absorb the noise and smells from the hawker centre next door. The closest stall served Hainanese chicken rice. When the cook prepared the rice, frying the grains in chicken fat and then adding them to the chicken broth, the fragrance drifted across the church.

Father Fernandes' doors were always open, as a matter of principle. But he also adored the smell of freshly-cooked chicken rice.

His stomach rumbled. His service had gone on a little later than usual.

"Hello. You must be Father Fernandes."

The priest didn't know what to make of the incongruous pair loitering around the church porch. He hadn't noticed them earlier.

She was a tall, slim Indian. Her confident poise seemed out of place, considering she appeared to have a smashed face.

He was Chinese, but that was about all he had in common with the world around him. His jeans were covered in stains, but not in the trendy way favoured by teenagers. Even his white T-shirt was full of greasy finger marks. Somehow, the bruised Indian looked more put-together than the restless Chinese guy beside her.

"Yes, can I help you?"

"I'm Detective Inspector Stanley Low. I work with CID. Specialised Crime Division." Low flashed his ID. "And this is Ramila Mistry. She's with the Metropolitan Police in London. She's just an observer. Could we ask you a couple of questions?"

"Oh right. I see." Father Fernandes touched his own nose. "Are you OK?"

"Yeah, fine." Mistry appreciated the concern. "You should see the other bloke."

"That's actually true."

Father Fernandes smiled nervously. "I see. Have you taken your lunch? I'm just heading next door. The chicken rice is very good. Would you like to join me?"

"It's OK. *Makan* already. Look, I don't want to waste your time. Could you have a look at these photos?"

Low had laminated the twelve headshots on a piece of A4. The truck girls didn't deserve anyone's grubby fingers defiling their faces. And Grace Chen certainly didn't. "We were told that some of these girls visit your church. Do you recognise any of them?"

"Yes, I do."

"Which ones?"

"Most of them, actually." Father Fernandes counted several faces. "At least seven or eight, I would say. But this one, *aiyoh*."

The priest's finger stopped on one particular face.

"That's Grace Chen," Mistry said.

"I know," Father Fernandes sighed. "I had to organise the poor woman's funeral."

Chapter 32

The hawker centre was teasing Father Fernandes. He could still smell his favourite dish. The garlic. The ginger. The thick broth of the chicken stock and the coriander leaves all somehow reached the church car park.

He could see them, too, on the other side of the fence, huddled around plastic tables, eating and slurping. Hainanese chicken rice made him proud to be Singaporean.

But Father Fernandes was in a minority. He preferred his chicken roasted, rather than boiled, crispy instead of tender. He even ordered breast meat, a culinary faux pas among friends. Tourists ordered breast meat. Not locals. It was safe, bland and tasteless. Singaporeans ordered legs and wings, gnawing on the fat, bone and gristle.

But Father Fernandes took considerable pride in going his own way. He always made the same joke at the hawker centre. He called himself a free thinker, fully aware of the irony. Singaporeans were religious. Or they were free thinkers. They could never be both in such a literal, binary society.

The priest turned his back on the hawker centre. He was losing his appetite.

"Yah, she used to come to this church," he said, tapping

Grace Chen's headshot. "A lovely lady, a little older than her friends. I think they looked up to her, especially the foreign girls. I mean, she obviously wasn't, you know."

"A maid?"

"I think 'domestic helper' is the preferred term now, Inspector Low."

"Still look like maids to me."

"Sorry, Father Fernandes, you were saying?"

Father Fernandes smiled at Mistry. She had such warm eyes. Hopefully, her injuries would heal quickly.

"Yes, right, I wouldn't say she was a regular. Her Sunday service attendance was erratic, not like the other ladies."

"Like you said, she wasn't a maid. She had a nocturnal job," Low said.

"Oh, I didn't know about her job."

"Oh, I think you did."

"Carry on, Father Fernandes," Mistry said quickly.

"Yes, well, as I was saying, she seemed like a maternal figure to the others, especially the Filipinas. They'd always gather around her, like she was their queen bee." Father Fernandes' face brightened. "She was a kind woman. Always had time for the other girls. And then she just disappeared. Didn't see her anymore. And then a few Sundays ago, a couple of the younger ones came to me and told me the terrible news."

"That she had died?" Low asked.

"Yes. Overseas apparently."

"Who told you?"

"Er, one of the younger ones."

"What's her name?"

"Er, not sure. Dewi maybe. I don't know her surname."

Mistry scribbled down the name. "And you organised the funeral?"

"Yes, well, the memorial service at least."

"Because there was no body," Mistry clarified.

"That's right. But the girls wanted to remember her in some way. So we held a small prayer service for her here. Quiet. Dignified. I encouraged her friends to share stories. They were reluctant at first. But a couple did, which was sweet."

"Yeah, I bet it was," Low said. "She's not dead."

Father Fernandes looked into the Singaporean inspector's eyes, seeking clues, but finding nothing. The eyes were cold. He turned to Mistry for support, for anything that might explain Low's strange utterance. She offered only a rueful nod.

"I don't understand," Father Fernandes said. "We held a prayer service. Her friends said goodbye."

"But there was no body to cremate, right? That's because she's alive and currently giving shit to British policemen for sexually harassing her."

"She's in Britain?"

"In England," Mistry nodded. "A place called Essex. But she's fine."

"But why would they? I mean, why would they?" Father Fernandes rubbed his forehead. Suddenly, he was aware of the encroaching midday sun. The single Angsana tree beside his car park no longer provided enough shelter. His cassock was damp and heavy.

"Don't know. Probably to stop people asking questions about her disappearance. You said she was popular right? The ringleader. Then, she's gone. Cannot be right? Had to explain her disappearance. So there's no more questions."

"It's so strange."

Low noticed the confusion, the fidgeting, the weight-shifting. Instinctive reactions. Father Fernandes was taking stock, making internal adjustments to outdated, former truths. Grace Chen was not dead. The women were not telling the truth. The sun was baking the car park. The heat was rising through the softening tarmac and Father Fernandes' profession necessitated the wrong clothes for the unrelenting climate.

But there was something else. Father Fernandes wasn't asking enough questions.

"Why are you so quiet?"

Father Fernandes didn't understand. "I'm sorry?"

"We just told you that you held a fake memorial service for a dead church regular who isn't dead and all you can say is, 'it's so strange'. She's one of your flock. She was kind and considerate. She rallied the troops for you, brought in the younger ones, filled your benches. Then you find out she's dead. Then you go ahead with a memorial service without doing any checks first, with any family, without any officials. Is that even allowed, Ramila?"

Mistry shrugged her shoulders.

"Of course it's not allowed. We need a permit to have a barbeque in Singapore. Definitely cannot barbeque a person in Singapore. Not without a permit. But you don't even have a person to barbeque. You got nothing except some maids, sorry, domestic helpers, telling you they've got a dead friend. Asking you. Can do a memorial service or not? And, you just say, 'sure, no problem. Bring the girls and we'll tell some fun stories about the dead woman with no body, no death cert, no proof, nothing'."

"We're a church," Father Fernandes said, eager to interrupt the rambling detective. "We try to provide solace and comfort when people need it. We don't demand lots of form filling. We just provide an empathetic service for those in need."

Low gestured towards the hawker centre. "*Wha'*, the

174

chicken rice smells damn good, making me hungry." His head whipped back to Father Fernandes. "Even if that's all true, why you never ask any questions just now? Why you never ask us anything about such a crazy story? You just say, 'it's so strange'."

"Well, it is, Inspector. At least allow me a moment to gather my thoughts."

"He's protecting her."

The men turned to Mistry. She found their quizzical expressions amusing. "He's protecting her. It's his job, right? He's protecting her. I'm guessing you worked out what they all had in common."

"Their love of God?"

Mistry wiped the spittle from her hand. "Sorry. Didn't mean to laugh. Yeah, it could be their love of God. Or maybe it was their moonlighting. What else would a Singaporean sex worker have in common with young Filipino and Burmese maids?"

Low leaned in. "Domestic helpers. He prefers 'domestic helpers'."

"Does he? Sorry. I'll try again. What do you think attracted a number of young women to an older Singaporean sex worker at your church every Sunday morning? Grace wasn't looking for God. She was recruiting."

"And you knew didn't you? You knew what Grace did, what they all did," Low added.

"They were domestic helpers," Father Fernandes reiterated, loosening his collar.

"Yeah, they were domestic helpers earning $500 a month and then Grace comes along and tells them they could earn just as much in one weekend."

"I have never passed judgement on anyone who walks through those doors. I offer support and guidance."

175

Low saw the connection. "That's it. They come to you. In private. They tell you things they cannot tell anyone else. Their employers. Their pimps. Their customers. But they can tell you. Like you said, you offer support. Safety. They can tell you anything. They come to you for advice about personal problems."

Low only needed to glance at Mistry for confirmation. Their history was shared. Their most painful memories were shared. His behaviour. Her decision. Their break-up.

Mistry nodded in agreement. "Grace got pregnant," she said.

"And she had only one choice. In her world. And it's the one choice she cannot make, in your world," Low said.

"She asked you about an abortion," Mistry said.

"I cannot break the seal of confession. It's privileged information."

"Yeah, privileged for who?" Low leaned into Father Fernandes' face. "I can get warrants. I can do stuff, just because I can, because I like it, but mostly because I like Grace. I'm actually standing here because of Grace. Can you believe that? Doesn't matter if you don't. It's the truth. And she came to you for help. And you saw the conflict, the fear, the whatever, and you did what? Tell me. What did you do?"

"I have a moral duty to protect the sanctity of life."

"And I have a moral duty to protect Grace Chen. And these mega monstrosities have a history, don't they? Want me to check the books? The fund allocation?"

"Our financial dealings are always . . ."

"I'll find something." Low eyeballed Father Fernandes. "What did you do? Don't make me ask again."

Father Fernandes exhaled loudly. "I reminded her of the sanctity of life. That's all."

"And what happened?"

"She ran out of the church. Crying. And that was the last time that I saw her. And then I heard the shocking news from her friends that she had passed away. And I'm tested. That's the test of my faith. And now I discover from you that she's still alive and that they all lied to me. My flock. And again, my faith is tested. But it has only strengthened my resolve." Father Fernandes pointed back at the church. "Those doors will always be open. To Grace Chen. To the domestic helpers. To you and Miss Mistry. To anyone who seeks support."

"Unless it involves an abortion," Mistry said.

Low unclenched his fists. "Where do they go?"

"Who?"

"The girls. The abortions. They tell you. Where do they go?"

"Where they always go," the priest muttered. "Back to the original sin. Geylang."

Father Fernandes turned towards the hawker centre, but it made no difference. He could no longer smell the chicken rice.

Chapter 33

The rat disturbed Stella's momentum. Geylang's crumbling alleys were overrun with rodents. They were getting bigger, too. Bolder. This one even stopped to watch.

"Fuck off," she hissed, stomping her stiletto into the concrete.

The rat obliged, eventually. Stella returned to her night job. His groaning was a little over the top, but at least he drowned out the squeaking from nearby dustbins.

The bright side of Geylang's roads belonged to families gorging on beef kway teow and duck rice. The dark side was reserved for rat-infested bins and blow jobs. Stella respected the divide in her adopted home. In Singapore, everyone knew their place.

And she accepted hers. On her knees. One foreigner servicing another.

Of course, he had thought about haggling. The migrant workers usually did.

Stella actually empathised. They were all saving for families back home. They needed to cut corners wherever they could.

He fiddled with his wallet, seemingly searching for

hidden cash. He stuttered. He looked around, considering his options.

Of course, he didn't have any, not in Singapore. As foreigners, neither of them had any tangible rights. But one of them had a pimp. And a migrant worker could not return to his construction site with broken bones.

Of course he was going to pay. "Next week?"

"Can," Stella said, pocketing the cash.

He zipped up and disappeared into the only *lorongs* with insufficient lighting. Geylang's darkness served its purpose. Singaporeans saw only what they needed to see.

Stella took a swig from the Listerine bottle. The night had started well. She gargled hard before directing a mouthful towards the loitering vermin.

"Eh, cannot *tekan* our wildlife."

Stella wiped her mouth. "Who's that?"

"Vice squad."

The sudden light left her momentarily blinded. She covered her eyes. "Eh, I'm not working, OK?"

The light went off. Footsteps approached. She blinked hard to make sense of the two blurry images. One brown and bashed up, the other rodent-like, moving quickly through the alley.

"Yeah, you spend your off days behind Geylang shophouses, spitting mouthwash at rats," Low said. "*Relak lah*, Stella, Not here for you."

"Ah, it's you. But I'm still not working, OK?"

"Never," Low said, winking at the slim Chinese woman. Stella was older than he remembered.

She straightened her mini-skirt. "Who this *ah*?"

"This is my good friend, Ramila Mistry."

"She look like shit. Need a good pimp." Stella grinned as she gargled again.

179

"Yeah, I probably do," Mistry agreed, stepping back as a mouthful of Listerine splattered against the pavement.

Mistry felt like shit, too. The paracetamol mostly took care of the swelling around her nose. But the dull headache above her eyes remained and she could barely move her shoulder.

The location hardly brightened her mood. Mistry knew all about Geylang. Low had once taken her there, three decades ago. He had tried to impress her, intimidate her even, convince her that Singapore was a wild island, too. Just like England.

But Singapore wasn't anything like England. Nobody called her a 'Paki' in Singapore. The multiracial city-state was far too polite for such abuse. Singaporeans kept their best ethnic slurs behind closed doors.

Mistry knew that, then and now. Nothing had really changed. Far too many men surrounded sex workers in the alleyways, examining submissive female bodies like exhibits at a Victorian freakshow. Geylang hadn't evolved. Singapore was a shiny island propped up by exploited, foreign labour in the 1990s. It still was.

So Geylang didn't shock Mistry. It bored her. The red-light district was a cliché. She was eager to move on. "Can we meet your pimp?"

Stella looked away. "Don't have."

"Come on *ah*, Stella," Low said, extending every vowel, stretching out the Singlish. He loved returning to his old stomping grounds. "Your pimp, *lah*. Timmy Chin. My *kaki* last time."

"Don't know."

Low stepped into the solitary light, hanging precariously from a tree branch. He expected to see the thick foundation, understood it even. It was Stella's protection. Her war paint. But there was never enough makeup to cover the eyes.

"Eh, don't do this, Stella. You see me so many times around here. You know what I do. Don't make me ask for your work visa or your employer's name. Don't make me stop you working, OK?"

Low tapped his watch. "Still early. Still got a lot of customers. Don't waste time."

Stella did the sums. It was the end of the month. Pay day. Horny men and cheap Anchor beer kept each other company beside the *longkangs*. Sunrise was many hours away. And she had her children to think about.

"Go straight. Pass the dustbin. Number 28. Got shrine outside."

"Thanks Stella," Low said, smiling kindly. "*Makan* first, OK?"

Mistry noticed the $50 note change hands. The exchange pleased her.

Red Chinese lanterns swayed outside the shophouse. Above the window frame, a pair of golden pineapples glowed through the darkness. A pink, Chinese lattice screen covered most of the shophouse's façade.

There was only one entrance, via a small concrete yard that offered a degree of privacy from the bustling Geylang street. But a deckchair blocked the entrance.

An emaciated runt with tattooed legs rose from the deckchair to meet them at the gate. He had too many teeth missing.

"Eh, who are you?"

"The Avengers," Low said. "I'm Shang-Chi and this is the Brown Widow. Let us in."

"Cannot."

"Who say?"

"Me."

"*Wah*, so tough *ah*. *Win liao lor.*"

The scrawny gatekeeper made an effort to stand tall in his flip flops, blocking their path to the decrepit shophouse. But he was shorter than both detectives.

"Go. Now."

Low grinned at Mistry. "*Wha*, that time damn scary. Are you scared? I'm scared." The inspector scratched his chin stubble. "Look, it's late. I'm the Singapore police and I haven't had any supper. So let us in. Or I'll kick you in the balls and then you'll let us in. Which one do you want?"

The answer came with a wayward fist. The punch was telegraphed. Slow. Obvious. The deckchair dozing and the makings of a premature potbelly reduced the younger man's odds. Low caught the fist. His foot then delivered on his earlier threat. His opponent stumbled into a potted plant. Low stomped on the man's fragile ego, for added emphasis.

"Don't get up," the inspector insisted. "We'll find our own way in."

The detectives stepped over the groaning gatekeeper. They moved quickly through the front yard. The garish red light coming through the lattice panels of the shop-house captured the silhouettes inside. Panicky bodies were running out of the living room.

Low banged on the door. "Open up."

He couldn't stand still. His right foot tapped a steady rhythm against the chipped tile. His fist hammered the door a second time.

"Come on *ah*, open the door."

Standing back a little, Mistry studied her jittery companion. The quieter, empathetic guy in the alleyway, pressing money into Stella's hand and holding on, just a beat too long to check on her wellbeing, had stayed in the alleyway.

"You're enjoying this, aren't you?"

"Of course. "Low pummelled the door a third time. "Come on *ah*, Timmy. Open the door. *Basket.*"

A lock turned on the other side. The door to the brothel slowly opened.

Three schoolgirls greeted Low.

"Hello," said the giggly one with pigtails. "Special service for you?"

Chapter 34

The red light gave them a surreal glow. They had cherubic faces and matching uniforms. White blouses for the sacred. Short, crimped skirts for the profane. Bright lips. Pink cheeks. Identical smiles for identikit sex workers.

Their exposed knees knocked together on the leather sofa. Lucky cats kept them company on either side. They were golden cats, plastic and fake. But the figurines' beckoning paws offered good fortune to prospective customers. In the corner of the humid living room, an altar burned joss sticks for the dead.

The brothel made no such accommodations for the living.

The girls waved at the unshaven Chinese man. They adjusted cleavage. Crossed legs. Blew kisses. Tired routines for a tired custom. They wanted to jump the queue. *Chope* their place. Get ahead of the girl beside them. Every day was a race.

But the Indian woman confused the novices. Customers usually came alone. But the Singaporean had brought his partner. She was pretty. And threesomes paid more.

But she was also a warning. Her nose was bandaged. Her forehead was an unsightly, pulpy yellow. The sex workers recognised the physical effects of a punch in the face.

They had pimps.

A creaking fan on a rickety spine blew the hair out of their eyes, but not the incriminating sweat. They were nervous. They looked like what they were pretending to be. Children.

"You want special service? Both can."

The request came from the youngest girl on the sofa. Her brashness failed to hide her vulnerability. She spoke loudly. Deliberately. Low respected the discipline.

"Very good," he said. "Nice, loud voice, so he can hear in the kitchen. No, we don't want a special service. We want the one you're shouting at. We want your pimp."

Slow, shuffling footsteps announced his arrival. Timmy Chin filled the doorway. He gripped a cigarette between sausage-shaped fingers. "What girl you want?" He brushed the ash from his singlet and stepped into the reddish haze.

Chin dropped the cigarette "Fuck *lah*, Ah Lian."

"Not anymore." The inspector waved his credentials in the air. "This is who I am now."

The girls ended their performance. Flirting gave way to fleeing. They knocked over one of the lucky cats on their way out.

"Please *lah*, Inspector. Got licence. Everything respectful now. You see?"

Chin pirouetted around the living room like a property agent, highlighting the furnishings. A red spotlight sat on a mahjong table. Empty Tiger beer cans were piled beside an empty sofa. A dried condom stuck to the skirting board.

"Yeah, it's the Shangri-La. You should do staycations." Low shoved a laminated A4 sheet of the truck girls into Chin's chest. "Who are they?"

"Don't know. Never see before."

Low took back the laminated A4 and placed it on the

mahjong table, beside the red spotlight. The women's faces glowed.

"Last time, you help me, Timmy. Called you Shitty Timmy, remember? Did all the shitty jobs for me."

"Yah, yah, last time."

"So why you waste my time now?" Low picked up a lucky cat. "Very nice."

The ceramic calico shattered against the wall above the sofa.

"Next time, it'll be your head."

"Ah fuck, *lah*, Stanley."

"No, no," Low wagged a finger in Chin face. "It's Inspector Low today. And Inspector Low can close your business."

Chin dropped to his hands and knees, picking up the splintered remains of his lucky cat. "Close for what? I got visas. Got vaccines. Got everything. You *tekan* me for what? My business screwed already."

"Rubbish. Your business recession-proof."

"Where got pandemic-proof? Where got tourists? Where got migrant workers?"

Mistry's foot swept away a golden paw. "You're complaining because Covid killed the sex trade?"

"Exactly. Fed up, I tell you."

Mistry turned to Low. "Honestly, your country."

Low shrugged. "Sunny island in the sea." He grabbed Chin by his armpit hairs. "Right. You. Up." He yanked Chin to his feet. "You need to see the photos again?"

"I don't know."

The two men were standing nose to nose.

"You don't know if you know the girls or you don't know if you need to see the photos again?"

"Don't know."

186

Low gestured towards the remaining lucky cat. "Inspector Mistry, smash that one."

"Please *lah*. I got to clean up already."

"It's OK. We'll smash the cat. Then arrest you for disturbing the peace."

"OK, wait." Chin shook himself free and picked up the laminated A4. "I'll take a look."

"Thank you, Timmy," Low said. "Eh, your girls can make me a *teh-c* or not?"

"No."

"Eh, why they all dress like schoolgirls?"

"The customers." Chin scanned the headshots. "They like it."

"Fucking hell," Mistry whispered.

Chin glowered at the naïve woman, "Eh, at least my girls are not real girls, OK. My one all correct age. If they dress up, never mind. Customers like it."

"Your customers are paedophiles?"

"*Wah*, she ask a lot of questions *ah*. No, my customers like Japanese cartoon. The anime one. Like to fuck schoolgirls. But pretend only."

"Oh, that's all right then," Mistry said. "Can we shut him down?"

"Just pretend only," Low said. "But if I say it's not pretend, you go to prison, Timmy. Who do you know in the photos?"

"Some only. This one ask me for work." Chin pointed at a young, Indonesian face. "That one also." He tapped the face of a beaming Filipina.

"You were their pimp?" Mistry spat out the words.

"Eh, where you get this one *ah*? Her accent very *cheem* one." Chin peered at Mistry like a museum curio. "You from where *ah*?"

187

"London. Is it relevant?"

"In London, you got pimp? In Singapore, it's different. This not illegal." Chin waved his hands around the living room. "This is legal, OK? In Singapore, I protect the girls. So they don't get abused."

He pointed at Mistry's nose. "Like you."

Mistry stepped towards the smirking pimp. Low stood between them. "Enough *lah*, Timmy. Did they work for you or not?"

"No chance. They were maids. Never employ maids. Very troublesome. No one in Geylang will accept maids. They'll lose licence."

"He's right." Low pointed at the photo of his old friend. "What about Grace?"

"Ah, everybody know Grace. Gave her some work, last time. Very fierce. That one don't need me."

"When did you last see her?"

"When she was pregnant. I told her to see the fat man." "Who?"

"Your friend, *wha'*, Ah Meng. You shut down his place, right? Selegie Road. Thanks *ah*. Reduce my competition."

Low was no longer paying attention. He only saw the last lucky cat beside the sofa. Paw waving. Beckoning him.

"Why did you send her there?" Low could barely concentrate. The lucky cat was still waving at him. Drawing him in.

"For the abortion, *wha'*. Ah Meng got a *kelong* doctor. Worse than *chee ko pek*, I tell you. Likes the school uniforms. Comes here sometimes. So Ah Meng took some nice photos. The doctor with the girls. School uniform some more. And now the doctor must do Ah Meng's abortions. Quite good, actually. I send my girls. Very clean one."

"Lying bastard."

"Eh, it's the truth, OK?"

"Not you. Him." Low pointed at the bandage across Mistry's nose. "That wasn't random. They weren't coming for me. They were coming for you. It's all connected. He says he doesn't really know Grace. Bastard gave her an abortion. Gets them when they're vulnerable. They come to him for help and he passes them on to a snakehead. Singapore to London, or wherever. I'm a fucking idiot."

He jabbed a finger at Mistry's swollen face. "That got in the way. The guilt. I couldn't see straight."

"Oh, I'm so sorry my beating messed with your deductive skills," Mistry said.

Low ignored the jibe. He shut out everything. Mistry's sarcasm. Chin's confusion. The chattering women dressed as paedophile-bait in the kitchen, the punters hovering outside, drawn to the red light. The mahjong table. The beer cans. The shrivelled condom. The goading cat. He followed nothing but the mania.

"*Ah longs* don't *tekan* policemen. They splash paint on the apartment. Throw eggs. Make threats. Run away. They're cowards. And scrawny pimps don't pick fights with policemen just because they lose face. It was never Shumai. It was Ah Meng."

Chapter 35

Mistry hesitated before following Low into the Dynasty Spa. He had a gun. She didn't. She had no idea how the next scene might play out.

Everything seemed incongruous, even the location. The spa was nestled inside the rundown Peace Centre, a short walk from Dhoby Ghaut MRT station, the gateway to Orchard Road. But Singapore's premier shopping district was rather like Mistry's memories of the place. Fading.

Still, the traditional products survived. Beside the money changers and the Singapore Pools outlet, the massage parlours still had hand jobs to sell.

Outside the Dynasty Spa, a list of services promised a relaxing, soothing experience. The fake grass on the wall offered the illusion of healthy living and wellness. As Mistry stepped inside, she smelled last night's sex.

She closed the door quietly, catching a bell above the frame. Low lowered his Glock. "Quiet," he hissed.

Mistry raised a hand to apologise. Privately, she was amused at the latest example of Singapore's baffling incongruity. A 21st Century Asian metropolis still had shop bells from a 1970s British sitcom. The detectives made their way through the waiting area with the leather sofa and the algae-coated fish tank. Low had expected the place to be empty so early in the morning. Ah Meng's line of work made him a nocturnal creature of habit and his employees were still sleeping off last night's special services.

The inspector crouched behind the counter and instructed Mistry to do the same. Sophia Road was busy in the mornings and Low didn't have a warrant. Technically, he was breaking and entering.

Technically, he didn't care.

The Singaporean fumbled through some papers behind the counter. Old receipts. Schedule planners. Lottery tickets. Nothing important. Ah Meng was a modern Singaporean in one sense. He believed in paperless transactions.

Low jabbed the muzzle of his Glock towards a brown, plywood door. "The office."

He felt Mistry's hands on his shoulders, using him for support and nothing more, but the surge in adrenaline irritated him nonetheless.

He couldn't be distracted again.

The office door was already ajar. Low nudged it open. Carnage greeted him. A filing cabinet had been tipped over. A framed print of pandas eating bamboo had been ripped from the wall. The safe behind had its door hanging off. The safe was empty.

Behind a ransacked desk, Ah Meng sat perfectly still.

His throat had been cut.

His eyes were still open.

Ah Meng stared at the silent detectives as the flies began to feast.

Dewi clung to the teddy bear. She did not want to leave. She had heard them outside. Unlocking doors. Lifting shutters. Making jokes.

191

She did not want to leave the dank, humid industrial unit. In the industrial unit, she was still alive.

She watched the other women grab their precious belongings. A few also had teddy bears. They were also parents. Others held photographs. They were doing this for their parents. Whatever the motives, the behaviour was identical now. They clutched their cherished possessions and looked down.

He was in the room.

Making eye contact was unthinkable now, not with him.

So Dewi focused on the teddy bear, squeezing him close to her chest. The teddy bear was roughly the same size, at least when she left her village outside Jakarta. But it wasn't really about the size. It was the smell.

The teddy bear still smelled of her boy.

That's why she never washed him. The women were always being told to stay clean. Wash their hands. Sanitise their hands. He was more worried about travel regulations than their personal hygiene. But Dewi always remembered to dry her hands thoroughly. She didn't want to contaminate the teddy bear in any way.

Some things in her life were going to remain pure, no matter what.

But the teddy bear made her cry. And her tears usually attracted his attention.

She heard the footsteps. She prayed. She hoped that it wasn't her turn.

But he stopped.

She hated his polished shoes. She hated them because the shoe polish was overwhelming. She could no longer smell the teddy bear. She lost the sense of her son.

He crossed his legs, as usual, but folded his arms this time. He always mimicked the women's actions, as if they shared a secret, non-verbal communication.

But she wanted to share nothing with him. Not a second. Every moment with him was one taken from her son. She hoped he would be quick.

"Ah, Dewi."

He rubbed her chin with his sanitised thumb.

"Beautiful Dewi. How can I help you?"

Mistry had investigated many murder scenes. She had served her apprenticeship in East London. Knife crime was routine. She had seen many slit throats. But she had never encountered such a foul stench. She covered her nose.

"No air con," Low muttered, reading her mind. He holstered his gun. "This is what they smell like in Singapore, especially in a tiny room like this, no ventilation."

Low peered into what was left of Ah Meng's congealed throat. "No cold weather to preserve the bodies for a bit."

"The flies don't help," Mistry said, swatting one aside.

"Wait for the maggots. Even better. Low took out his phone and dialled. "Eh Xavier, it's Low. Get pathology and a team down to Ah Meng's place. Sophia Road. Yeah … Yeah, he's dead. Yah, *lah*, Ah Meng, who else? Hurry up *lah*. Before the neighbours complain about the smell."

"So naïve that one," Low said, pocketing his phone.

He stepped around the body, careful not to make contact.

"What are you doing? You can't disturb the scene."

Low straddled a splatter of blood. "Clues."

"Wait for forensics."

"I won't touch anything. And what are they gonna find? This room is perfect. No cameras. No windows. No witnesses. Ah Meng did that deliberately to keep us out. Now it's deliberately killed him. Assuming the guy wore gloves, he's not getting caught in here. Outside CCTV maybe, but not in here."

Low edged his way around the desk. "I'm just hoping he didn't find it."

"What?"

"What I came here for." Low crouched in front of a mini-fridge. He opened the door and peered inside. "Because I'm the only one who knows it's here."

"Oh, leave off, Stanley, they don't hide drugs in fridges anymore."

"Not looking for drugs."

Low pulled out a six-pack of Tiger beer. He tore off the card cover. He judged the weight of each can before settling on the fourth. "Ah, this one." He shook it in the air. The can rattled. Low smiled. "Old *ah long* trick. Cut open the top of the can. Remove the beer and then re-attach the lid. On its own, doesn't work, too obvious. But in a six-pack, it might, if you've got a *blur* policeman during a raid."

Low removed the top of the beer can. "You see?"

"How did you know about that?"

"Tiger taught me last time. Easy way for bookies' runners to hide phones. Betting slips. Whatever." Low pulled a phone from the beer can. "Ta-dah. It's magic. I knew Ah Meng had it. I saw one at the other place, Selegie Road. But I told Ah Meng I wouldn't disturb as long as he played nice for me."

Low looked up at the dead man. "But you stopped playing nice, didn't ya?"

Chapter 36

Detective Sergeant Xavier Ng spun the cellophane bag on the table. His career had taken a turn for the ironic. A few weeks ago, he was raiding Ah Meng's KTV lounge. Now he was fiddling with the dead man's phone.

The rookie cleared his throat. He had rehearsed the speech. A polished delivery might fast-track his promotion, but he hadn't anticipated such a diverse audience.

As expected, Low slouched across two seats. Hands in pockets. Hoodie up. Ng's senior officer loathed the air-conditioning. The Cantonment Complex was always too cold.

But the British woman was both a surprising and distracting addition. Ramila Mistry had remarkable eyes and a mangled face.

Ng was beginning to wish he had prepared cue cards.

When Deputy Director Anthony Chua took a seat at the back, Ng castigated himself about the cue cards. Basic error. He looked like a novice.

So he decided to ignore the expectant faces and focus on the dead one, lying on a mortuary slab, on the projector screen behind him. He owed Ah Meng that, at least.

"OK, thank you all for coming," Ng said, coughing hard in search of a voice.

"All right, Xavier, it's a debrief, not a wedding speech," Low sneered.

"Low." The warning came from the deputy director.

Low yawned theatrically. Ng picked up the phone. He needed a prop to concentrate. "Right, good news first. I've worked with the Tech guys to open the phone that Low brought in. No chat apps like WhatsApp. No text messages. Most of his calls were made to Shumai's phone, especially in the last few days."

Mistry sat up. "When?"

Ng nodded apologetically. "Yeah. Just before your attack."

"Bastard."

"Well, he's got a throat wider than the Causeway now."

"Low." The voice from the back was firmer this time. "Carry on, detective."

"Thank you, sir. Like I said, we're working with Tech to trace the calls. Apart from Shumai, most were made to unregistered numbers. We're checking with the telco companies, but so far they're not matching the numbers with the right names."

"Why?" The men in the room all heard the abrupt tone.

"Why what, Miss Mistry?"

"Why can't you trace the calls to the phone owners? You're Singapore. You're a tech hub. You can't trace a few calls in a murder victim's phone?"

"It's not quite so simple," Chua said.

"I need to show my passport, my proof of vaccine, my blood group and my star sign to get into Singapore, but your tech can't crack a few phone numbers? Are they all drug dealers using burners?"

Ng appeared lost. "Burners?"

"Disposable phones," Low said wearily. The naivety

in the room was tiresome. "No they're not drug dealers, Ramila. They're maids. KTV hostesses. Sex workers."

"And that means what?"

"Foreign workers sell and swap SIM cards all the time, especially if they're leaving. They mix and match. Old phones. SIM cards. Extra minutes. Whatever."

"That's right. We worked that out," Ng said, eager to reassert himself. "So we focused on phone numbers that had been discontinued, rather than sold on."

Low nodded approvingly. "That's actually pretty good, Xavier. Cancel old phones. Cancel old lives. Go work for Ah Meng. Or go overseas. No need the old numbers."

"Exactly. These three numbers gave us a breakthrough."

Ng clicked his laptop. Three female faces filled the projector screen. The youngest woman was smiling and hopeful. The other two were older. Unsmiling. Cynical. Mistry recognised them.

"Those two were on the lorry," she cried. "In England."

Ng took a brief pause. He needed to be sure that the deputy director had registered his breakthrough in the case.

"Yes, that's right," Ng said, extending the dramatic pause with a sip of water. "The one on the left is Achara. She's Thai. Slipped into Singapore before the pandemic on a work permit. Worked on a Thai food stall at first. Ended up in a KTV lounge. Cancelled her phone one week before she was found in the back of the truck in England. Same with the other one. Her name's Linh. Vietnamese. Worked in a nail salon in Far East Plaza. Don't know how long. We called the nail salon. But act *blur* one. Said she just disappeared one day. No message. Nothing. Also cancelled her phone, one week before."

Low leaned forward. "On the same day as the other one?"

"Correct."

"So it was orchestrated. Controlled. Part of the requirements. We'll take care of you, but you must disappear from Singapore. No warning. Just go. But why so *kan cheong*?"

"English would be nice."

"Why so panicky? Why so nervous? Why so scared?" Low was on his feet now, making his way to the projector screen. "They're running this operation. Then we get involved. And pop. Steve Robertson gone. Come back to Singapore. Stumbling around. We know nothing, right? And they *tekan* Ramila. And then Ah Meng, for what? We know he's involved, so what? We keep everything quiet in Singapore. Politics. Gangsters. All the same. No fuss. And now, just anyhow whack. Why?"

Low stood in front of the projector. His face blurred, merging with the three on the screen behind him. "These women disappear all the time. Nobody cares. They're maids. Hostesses. They're nothing. Foreign workers. Invisible. Why panic?"

"We're getting closer," Mistry said.

"You made the connection with Ah Meng," Ng added. "He was involved in the trafficking. He could name names. Give us the money men. The snakeheads."

Low stared into the large, brown eyes of the unknown young woman. "No, it's too much. We don't kill people so quickly in Singapore. Not like that. Too desperate. It's something else."

Low gently tapped the projector screen, running his finger along the unknown woman's nose. The third face. "Who's this?"

"Ah, yes, we think that's . . ." Ng frantically searched his notes on the table. "Yes, there was a number in Ah Meng's phone. A Singtel number. Only cancelled recently. And this number was registered to a Dewi. Just Dewi. Indonesian.

Works here as a domestic helper. That's her work permit photo. We're getting employer and agency details."

Low looked into the young woman's eyes. "You're still here," he whispered, turning to the other officers in the meeting room. "She's still here. And she's next."

Ng looked over at his restless boss. "What?"

"That's why they're rushing. Risk and reward. Why take such huge risks killing Ah Meng? Because the reward is worth it. They can't stop the supply chain. Too much demand. And she's part of the next delivery."

Dewi winced as he clasped her hands in his. At least she could no longer see him. The new darkness was a sudden friend to all of them.

"I know you didn't want to move again, but this will be the last time," he said. "I promise."

Dewi chose not to respond. Her words were usually misinterpreted as encouragement.

He patted her head. She loathed the head patting, found it patronising. She was not a child. She had a child. And that was all that mattered.

"I'm sorry about the lack of light, too. But we are nearly there now. A new life. A new life for all of you."

The girls in the back of the truck ignored his gaiety. In any case, they had been instructed not to speak. Unwanted attention, at such a late stage, might jeopardise everything. The truck was only temporary. It was also cheap and mobile.

No one knew where they were now. Nor did the women. He said it was better that way.

Besides, they had learned not to talk back. When they had moved from the industrial unit to the truck, one of the older women had complained.

He removed her bucket privileges. She had nowhere to pee until she recognised the error of her ways.

"Hey, what was that song you were singing earlier?"

Dewi shrugged.

"Oh, it was lovely. Something about being in my heart."

She shrugged a second time.

"Oh you must remember." He delicately placed his hands on her shoulders. She would not shrug a third time.

"What was the name of the song?"

"'You'll Be in My Heart,'" she sniffed.

"That's it. Such a nice song. Sing it for me."

Dewi turned away and wiped her eyes.

"You can teach me the words," he whispered, caressing her shoulders. "Sing it for me, Dewi."

And while the other women quietly wept in the back of the truck, Dewi sang *You'll Be in My Heart*. It was her little boy's favourite song.

Chapter 37

In the corner of the living room, the maid ironed their clothes in silence. She picked a shirt from a pile on the floor beside her. She pressed it. Folded it. Stacked it on a chair beside her. And started again.

Everyone else in the immaculate HDB flat ignored her. She was present. But she did not exist.

Mistry couldn't drag her gaze from the Indonesian waif standing in front of brown window grilles, hoping for an evening breeze that would not come. The unplugged fan seemed to taunt the young woman.

The promise of a cool breeze was just a generous owner away.

Instead the maid continued, running the iron along the shirt, careful not to drip sweat onto Sir's business attire.

Mistry took note of the yellow perspiration rings on the maid's vest. No one else did.

"Is she OK?"

Poh Cheng Hong and his wife, Angela, did not understand the peculiar question from the foreign woman. They turned to Inspector Low. He would understand. He was Singaporean. Local. He would decipher his partner's strange query.

"My colleague's just asking about your domestic helper," he said, removing the red lid from the plastic container and helping himself to another pineapple tart.

"Damn *shiok*," he said, pointing to a mouthful of crumbling pastry.

"She's temporary," Angela Poh said gruffly.

The HR executive had rushed home from work for the police visit and still found time to put out the expensive pineapple tarts. She didn't like the Indian's tone.

"No, I meant she looks very hot."

Mistry looked up at the ceiling fan, then across at the air-conditioning unit built into the false ceiling above the TV and then finally at the stand-up fan in the corner. None were switched on.

"Yah, if we use the fan, cannot hear the TV," Angela Poh remarked.

"Also, too much noise disturb our boy sleeping," Poh Cheng Hong added. "He's tired after tuition class."

Mistry saw the photographs displayed as part of the Poh family's feature wall. "Is your son a toddler?"

"Ah, those photos quite old already," Angela Poh pointed at her boy's images. "He's two already. Just does one Shichida class, for brain enrichment."

Mistry sat forward. "For what?"

"Brain enrichment," Low interjected, wiping his mouth. "Very crumbly, *ah*? But damn tasty. You got a nice place."

Angela Poh found her husband's hand. They beamed with pride. Their four-room, built-to-order flat had been five years in the planning, making and designing. They had balloted for a Punggol apartment with a sea view and checked their floor and unit numbers with a feng sui master. They had interviewed four different interior designers, before opting for the post-industrial look of heavy greys, high ceilings and matching racing bikes hanging on the walls.

"Yah, only just finished."

Low reached for his Chinese tea. "First HDB flat?"

"Yah," Angela Poh said.

"First home together?"

"Of course. We moved in *after* we got married," Poh Cheng Hong said, rather indignantly. The couple attended mass at Father Fernandes' church every Sunday.

"When did you get the keys?"

"One month already," Angela Poh said.

"That's nice." Low sipped his tea. "First home and second maid already."

Low always went for the tea if a cup was available. In fact, he usually asked for one at home visits. He had the routine down cold. Lift the cup. Cover the face. Prod them. Observe the reaction.

They rarely saw his reaction. The cup was a distraction. But he never missed theirs, over the top of the steaming tea. Every wide eye and heel tap. Every open mouth and sideways glance. Every flicker was a giveaway.

Angela Poh eased her grip. She didn't entirely let go of her husband's hand. But it was too obvious to miss. "Yah, first one never settle," she said. "When they're too young, it's like that. This one better."

She pointed at the only person still standing in the stifling living room.

"That's good. Can be tough to get a good helper," Low said. "Me and my wife had so many problems already. We've had at least five. Maybe six."

Mistry felt the whiplash. Her neck spun around to examine the features of her lying partner. Low offered only an empathetic smile. "Actually, I think seven."

The inspector had a captive audience. Angela Poh was clearly engrossed. "Really, *ah*? How did you find the right one?"

"Older, better, more experienced. Plus their kids grown up already," Low said. "Otherwise, they're always thinking about *their* kids, instead of looking after *my* kids, you know? Of course, we're sympathetic, right?"

"Of course," Angela Poh agreed.

"But still paid to do a job, right? Not spend all day on Facetime, talking to their kids. No, older helpers are definitely better."

"What did I say?" Angela Poh flicked her husband's arm. "I told you, right? Older, better. But you said get a younger one."

"Young one fitter, work faster," Poh Cheng Hong said. He looked across at the other man for moral support. The Indian's scowl was beginning to annoy him.

"Definitely," Low said. "The ball is round, right? Anything can happen. My old boss said to me, you gotta treat maids like pets. Break them in first."

Low anticipated the horror in their faces, as expected. Their curiosity took a moment to catch up. "Yeah, I know. Sounds terrible. But honestly, after so many maids and agency fees, my boss was right. You set the rules. Set the boundaries. From the first day, I tell you, and then you'll be set."

Angela Poh nodded along. "Yeah, yeah." She peered over at the maid, cringing as the maid clumsily dropped a hanger.

The maid grimaced as the hanger clattered against the marble tiles. Her employers rolled their eyes. The maid crouched behind the ironing board and retrieved the hanger. Low waited for the maid to resume her ironing duties before continuing.

"You see? Got to break them in early. Train them. First day. Over and over again."

"I feel like I'm in Battersea Dogs Home here," Mistry said, loud enough for Low to hear, but no one else.

"So what happened with Dewi?"

Low's sudden, cheery tone and the mention of that woman's name caught the Pohs off-guard. "I don't understand," Poh Cheng Hong said.

"Was she too slow?"

"No, like you said, too young, too homesick," Poh Cheng Hong added. "Kept complaining about missing family, kept crying about her son back in Indonesia. We tried to support her, even let her use our phone to call her family on Sundays, when we got back from church. But it didn't help."

"She didn't have her own phone?"

Again, the Pohs were taken aback at the Indian woman's strange question. "No, didn't have enough money," Angela Poh said. "But I let her use mine. On Sundays."

"Got free data on weekends," her husband pointed out.

"Yeah, good enough," Low said, standing up.

He eased away from the Italian sofa. He wandered over to the feature wall. Glass lightboxes surrounded the TV. Each one either had a framed photograph or garish pieces of objets d'art.

The inspector ran his finger along the shelf, moving towards the window grilles and the maid. "Do you keep those windows open?"

"Yeah, all day, must give her some fresh air," Poh Cheng Hong said.

"That's good." Low stopped at the window. Singapore's latest construction site greeted him. "Not much fresh air though, not in a new development. This block is finished.

But those ones are not. Got a car park and a coffee shop being built down there. New concrete boxes. Built to order. But every one of them is the same, right?"

He turned back to the puzzled couple. "Bit of an oxymoron, right? Come live in a built-to-order apartment that looks just like every other apartment in Punggol. And we can't have that, can we? Can't spend all that money. Two parents working full-time. Never see the kid. Just to have an apartment that looks like everyone else, right? So what do we do, eh? Do you know what one of the biggest growth industries is in Singapore, Inspector Mistry?"

She had no idea where he was going with this. Low spun around the room, arms outstretched, performing, channelling.

"Interior design," he shouted. "Remember your old council houses in London, Ramila? Remember how everyone painted over the red bricks as soon as they bought them, to show they weren't council houses anymore? Well, in Singapore, we can't do that. We spend half a million on our council flat, but we can't even decide the outside colour. The *gahmen* paints our little Lego boxes for us. So we spend all our money making our interior different to all our neighbours. Interior design sets us apart from the rest. And this one is perfect. It's like a show flat. It has everything, except this."

He held his forefinger in the air.

"Dust. There is no dust. Anywhere. You are surrounded by construction. Heavy drilling. Concrete and sand everywhere. You've even got the salty sea air to blow all the construction crap into your apartment. And look." He flashed his forefinger in front of the Pohs' startled faces. "Not a speck of dust, with all these open windows on the . . . what is this floor again?"

"Eighth," said Angela Poh.

"Of course. Lucky number for the lucky home. Perfect home for the perfect family. So you want it perfect, no matter what. No dust. No dirt. Nothing. Just shiny floors and piles of freshly ironed clothes. And in the corner, what?"

Low aimed his dust-free finger towards the silent woman behind the ironing board.

"A 24/7 cleaning machine for your improbably clean home. That's what you wanted. That's why you wanted her young. To work her hard. Look at this one. Almost 9pm. She's still ironing in the living room. In silence. So you can watch TV. The last one was the same, right? No day off, right?"

Angela Poh tried to hide her reddening face. "We gave her one Sunday off a month, as stipulated in the contract."

"One day off a month?"

Low waggled a finger at Mistry. "No, it's stipulated in the contract. Don't bring your woke values here, Inspector Mistry. We're giving these girls a better life in Singapore, right, Mr and Mrs Poh?"

Low stood over the couple. "But you didn't, did ya? You didn't even give her the Sunday off, not even one a month."

"We did."

"No, you didn't. In your eagerness to convince me how good you treated her, you only showed me how bad. You said you let her use your phone on Sunday. After church. Back home. Here. Making lunch. No day off."

"We compensated her," Poh Cheng Hong insisted.

"But she asked for more."

"All the time. She was meeting with her friends. Outside. They were telling her how much she could get for working Sunday. Telling her to ask us for money. They spoil market. We treated her well, OK? And still not enough."

"No, you made her work seven days a week to clean your built-to-order mausoleum and she got fed up and left, right?"

"Yeah, she went back to the agency. In Katong. Cannot even get our maid levy back."

"Your maid levy?" Low was in their faces now. Shouting. "She's been picked up by people smugglers and you're worried about a maid levy? She could be dead."

In the corner of the oppressive living room, the maid continued to iron their clothes in silence.

Chapter 38

Katong Shopping Centre looked like a modernist Meccano set. The blue and yellow layers and the concrete port-holes hinted at the last days of rebellion in Singapore. In the early 1970s, even the architects hadn't fully conformed. The fading building was out of touch with its glassy surroundings. But the landlords and tenants were holding on for a collective sale. Singaporeans always came together. For money.

Mistry followed Low down the staircase and into the deserted mall. Empty units sat beside neglected watch repairers and frame makers.

Dying industries for a dying mall.

"Well, this is all a bit 'the land that time forgot'," Mistry said, passing a geomancy centre.

"Eh, first mall in Singapore with air-con, you know."

"That's nice. No income, but high electric bills. How do they survive?"

"Who cares? They're waiting for an en-bloc sale. Sell the entire estate. It's the East Coast. Top postcode."

"Why bother staying open?"

"Rich people still need them, right?" Low nodded towards the young women.

There were six of them, in matching yellow T-shirts,

sitting on stools inside the shop. The glass frontage framed them, like a surreal living tableaux. In the shop window, a seventh woman stood behind an ironing board, pressing a pair of trousers.

Mistry pointed at the spectacle. "What the hell is that?"

"What?"

"She's ironing a pair of trousers in a shop window."

"Yah. Quite good, *ah*? No creases."

"But everybody can see her. Walking past the shop."

"Then they'll know she's good at ironing."

"It's degrading."

"Nah, it's marketing. Put your best items in the shop window, right?"

Mistry took in the neon sign of the business, shining brightly above the ironing lady.

Happy Maids.

"Unbelievable," she muttered.

The detectives greeted the young women on the stools. The women's suitcases were piled in the corner of the shop. An older woman, sitting behind a long counter and playing Farm Heroes on her phone, cleared her throat.

The girls responded to the guttural command, immediately improving their posture. No hunched backs. They pressed their knees together. And they smiled sweetly at the mixed-race couple.

"This is doing my head in," Mistry said, under her breath.

The woman behind the desk heard the accent and put down the phone. She was already running a customer profile. *British. Expat. Woman. Got money. Chinese husband. Definitely got money. Need maid quickly. Fees no issue.*

"Hi, I'm Christine. Can I help?"

Christine Yeoh slid her phone out of view and gave the

mixed-race couple her full attention. Mixed-race couples always needed her full attention. They were difficult to read, especially the foreign ones.

The detectives took a seat at the desk, turning away from the macabre pantomime. Mistry was grateful. The girls' imploring eyes were driving her crazy. "Yes, we're looking for a maid," she said, reaching for her handbag, looking for the headshots.

"Domestic helper." Yeoh delivered the clarification with an insincere smile.

Mistry stopped. "What?"

"Domestic helper," Yeoh said cheerily. "In *Singapore*, we don't say *maid*. Not so nice. We say domestic helper." She grinned at her stable, one of whom was now ironing a tea towel.

"As opposed to where? India? Is that what you mean? I don't know what they call maids—sorry, domestic helpers—in India. I'm from England. We don't have maids. And we don't have them ironing clothes in a shop window."

"Eh, come on *ah*," Low said, turning to Yeoh. "You'll have to forgive her. She's been a bit jet-lagged for about twenty-five years."

Yeoh took comfort in his local accent. He would understand. "Ah, no problem. They like to keep busy, you know. They take turns."

"Who?"

"The domestic helpers. Doing small jobs for me. Otherwise, they get bored."

"Understand." Low took the headshot from Mistry and pushed it across the desk. "Did Dewi get bored?"

Yeoh rocked a little in her leather chair. "Oh you're not looking for a maid, is it?"

"It's domestic helper," Mistry corrected.

"Yeah. We're looking for this one." Low dropped his police ID beside Dewi's tender face. "You can guess why, right?"

Yeoh picked up the photo. "Ah this one *ah*. So troublesome. I put her with a nice, young family in Punggol. Still complain. I tell them to pay her extra for working Sunday. Still complain."

"She's supposed to get a Sunday off every month, right? You represent her interests, not the employer's. You are her agent."

"Cannot control everything inside the home, right? Mus' be give and take."

Mistry leaned across the desk. "And what did you give Dewi?"

"Hey, I give her a lot, OK? I let her sleep on the floor here one time."

"That's very kind of you."

"I drive her back to their apartment, several times I tell you. In Punggol, some more. I meet with the family. And she kept running away."

"Where is she now?

Yeoh threw her hands in the air. "I don't know. The family complained a couple of weeks ago. She left home again. I ask around. I look for her. I go TWC2."

"What's TWC2?"

"A welfare organisation, for migrant workers," Low said. "They help the maids."

"Yeah, something like that," Yeoh sniffed, not impressed.

"And then?"

"Yah, they said she had gone inside. They told her to come back to me. To discuss. But she didn't. Completely disappeared."

Yeoh returned to her desktop computer. They were not customers. No need to pretend anymore.

212

Mistry looked nonplussed. "And that's it?"

Yeoh found the foreigner's smugness annoying. "What else can I do? They run away all the time. They always get found. At a worker's dorm. A shophouse. A charity. They always come back in the end."

Mistry was surprised at Yeoh's confident tone. "How do you know that?"

Yeoh looked away.

"She keeps their passports," Low said.

"Jesus Christ."

"Ah, but I never had Dewi's passport, OK? The family keep it. They look after it for her. And then they tell me, it's gone. That's why it's better to keep it here. At the agency. Safer. Can protect them."

"*Control* them."

Yeoh was out of patience. "You think my business so easy *ah*? You think I want them to be unhappy, is it? Unhappy, they don't work. Unhappy, they cause me problems."

"I'm sure Dewi's disappearance must have caused you a lot of paperwork."

"Eh, Singapore not like England, you know. All women must work here. Must have helpers. Cannot be a kept woman in Singapore."

"I'm not a kept woman, you silly cow." Mistry started to rise. Low gently placed a hand on her shoulder. "Get your hands off me," Mistry barked. "I'm a bloody detective inspector, *love*. I'm not a kept anything."

Mistry tapped her finger against Dewi's photo. "And you've sent this girl God knows where. You know she's part of a trafficking operation, right?"

"Ramila ..."

"No. Be quiet for a change." Mistry returned to the unsettled agency manger. "You know she's gonna end up

213

in the back of a lorry, right? Or repeatedly raped. Or dead in a ditch, all because you lot never saw *12 Years A Slave.*"

"SIT DOWN."

Low's outburst silenced everyone. The girls in the matching yellow T-shirts froze. They did not speak English well enough to know if the ranting, screaming couple still intended to take one of them home.

Slowly, Mistry returned to her seat. Low took a deep breath.

"Now I appreciate that this is an emotional case. For all of us." He stared at Mistry. "But I am the ranking officer here. I am the *only* officer here. And we all need to calm down. We all want to find this young woman. We all want answers. So, Miss Yeoh, what can you tell us that might help us find Dewi?"

"I don't know. I don't speak their languages," Yeoh said. "They would chat outside when they went to the toilet. Some people would come in and talk to them. Normally, I just ignore. But one time, a local Chinese, about my age, disturb my girls. I saw her talking to them, a few weeks ago. I scolded her. She swore at me."

Mistry retrieved a photo of Grace Chen. "Was it her?"

"Yah, yah, how you know *ah*? Was she running an agency?"

"No. But she was trying to recruit them," Low said. "You must tell us if Dewi had somewhere she might go for help."

"I told you *lah*. Same place they all go," Yeoh said. "TWC2. Go tell all their problems. And then we get a fine from Ministry of Manpower. They always talk to TWC2. Don't know why."

Mistry took back the photos. "Maybe it's because they don't make their girls iron clothes in a shop window."

Chapter 39

James Richmond checked the case file. He had another cigarette burn coming in. Hopefully, the burns were minor. He was working the evening shift and the polyclinics were closed. Hospitals were more expensive. The office was low on cash until the next fund raiser.

Richmond opened his wallet. It was empty. Luckily, he hadn't breached his credit card limit. But he was getting close.

He really needed those cigarette burns to be minor.

But he loved his work at Transient Workers Count Too. He had been there since the beginning, one of the founders, in fact. He remembered arguing over the unwieldly name, insisting that it wouldn't matter. Singapore was a land of abbreviations and acronyms. Everyone would refer to the fledgling organisation as TWC2.

And they did.

And Richmond was rather proud of TWC2's achievements. A modest man, he acknowledged the collective sacrifice of every board member, full-timer and volunteer, but he had personally drafted the original proposals for a fixed day off for domestic helpers.

The idea was commonplace now. Its implementation

remained a work in progress, but Richmond was a patient, optimistic man. He always saw the best in people, which was why he hoped the cigarette burns would be minor.

He really didn't fancy the prospect of another horrific injury.

The forceful knock on his door didn't suggest a weakened soul. He put his wallet away, feeling relieved. The cigarette burns were definitely minor.

"Come in," he said.

They were not burns victims. If anything, they resembled the perpetrators. She had a permanent grimace. He looked like a charity appeal. Richmond rose from his chair, instinctively respectful. "Can I help you?"

Low seemed surprised. "You James Richmond *ah*?"

"Yes."

"You don't look like a James Richmond."

The common response was tiresome. Richmond's lineage could be traced back to the Second World War. He was taller than most Singaporeans and had a fairer complexion. And the obsession with skin colour remained.

"Wow, racial profiling already. Cos I'm not an *ang moh*, is it? OK. Well, I am a Singaporean. My family is Eurasian. Hence the surname. And my father is a big 007 fan. Hence the first name. Is that good enough? Do I pass the Singapore test?"

"Ignore him. We're having a bad day," Mistry said, offering her hand. "I'm a British Indian. Get it all the time."

"I can imagine." Richmond adopted a strong Singlish accent. "Where you from *ah*? No, seriously, where you from *ah*?"

"Yep. All the time. There and here, strangely."

"At least you're brown. I'm half brown with a western name. I need to take my passport for every taxi trip."

216

"Ah, but at least you don't get called a *paki* in Singapore."

"I've been called plenty of other things. I mean, look at me. I can be anything, right?"

Low looked on as the other two giggled at their racial profiling anecdotes. "Yeah, it sucks when you're not part of the majority race. Can we move on?"

"Sorry, who are you?"

"I'm Detective Inspector Low. This is Inspector Mistry from London."

"London? Wow."

"Yeah, 007, you wanna do national profiling as well?"

Richmond almost found the surly character amusing. "Are you always so antagonistic when you meet new people?"

"This isn't antagonistic for him," Mistry said. "We're sorry for the intrusion, but we're looking for this domestic helper."

She handed over Dewi's photo. Richmond examined the young woman's features. "They're so young, aren't they? Still children really. I don't think I've met her. What's the problem?"

"She's part of an ongoing investigation. We believe she might have gone missing. Maybe other girls, too. Her agency said she came here."

"It's quite possible." Richmond took a second look at the photo. "I'll check the records. This place is packed at weekends, especially Sundays obviously. One of the volunteers could have taken her details. Why did she come here?"

"Couldn't get a day off," Low said.

"Yeah, that's the most common one. Over work. Or withholding salaries."

"Where would your staff tell her to go?"

"Well, if there were no signs of abuse or mistreatment, we

217

can register a complaint with the Ministry of Manpower, inform her agency, liaise with her employer and then follow up."

"But she didn't get a day off."

"Understand. But we estimate around forty per cent of domestic workers in Singapore do not get a day off. Their wages are low. Their recruitment fees alone can take six months to pay off. They are working in a stranger's home, behind closed doors, poor and powerless. What can they do?"

Richmond picked up the photo. "I admire the girl for coming forward so quickly. Most don't. Too risky."

Mistry was curious. "Why?"

"Their work permit is attached to the job. No job. No permit. No chance of staying in Singapore. They can't really job hop. Very hard to switch employers. Maybe if they have a good agency. Do you know hers?"

"Happy Maids in Katong." Low caught Richmond's rueful sigh. "You know it?"

"Everyone knows it. Are they still putting girls in the window?"

"Yeah, we just come from there. One of them was ironing clothes in the window."

"Been told so many times. Even got in the newspapers. And they're still doing it. Not the best agency that one. A lot of complaints."

"They didn't seem to care that this Dewi might have disappeared," Mistry said. "How could this girl just vanish?"

"I'll show you." Richmond turned to Low. "You're Singaporean. How many helpers do you know by name?"

"Don't know. Hardly any. Unless I arrest them for moonlighting."

"Exactly. We used to have cowboy movies with the man

with no name. Now we've got a million men and women with no name. Migrant workers from all over Asia, coming here, almost a fifth of our population. And what are their names? What do we call them? Maid. Helper. Construction worker. They disappear behind these impersonal terms. They're invisible. It's not surprising that they disappear, Miss Mistry. It's surprising that we ever see them at all. And when we do, it's because they've been abused, starved, neglected." Richmond picked up his file. "Or they've got arms full of cigarette burns."

"Bloody hell."

"Ah well, cigarette burns are commonplace. It's the really sadistic ones I don't get. I once took a young Indonesian helper to Tan Tock Seng hospital. Her boss came home and twisted her nipples until they bled. One of them had to be stitched back on. When we finally got the case to court, the boss blamed the stress of work. She'd had a bad day, come home and tore off her helper's nipple. I'm never surprised when they run off, Miss Mistry. I admire them for hanging around for so long."

Mistry looked to Low for something, a cutting remark, a remorseless jab, anything to temper the mood. "Sunny island in the sea," he whispered.

"They must have protection," Mistry said.

"They have the Employment of Foreign Manpower Act, sure, but how many are going to be in a position to utilise it? Their employers must comply with the work permit regulatory conditions, which lays out what helpers can and cannot do, but who's going to know behind closed doors? Who's going to complain? More importantly, when can they complain? Realistically, helpers can only access our outreach support if they get a Sunday off. And many employers are still reluctant."

"They don't wanna *spoil the market*," Mistry said.

Richmond leaned against his desk and breathed hard. He truly believed his work made a difference, but fresh cases kept coming. "Sorry, guys. I hate to sound so cynical. Long day and all that. After this, I've got to speak to this girl with cigarette burns. She's younger than my daughter. I want to help you if I can."

He took another look at Dewi's photo. "We might have her details. But I don't know what they'll give you. What are you looking for?"

"Friends, contacts, anyone who might have visited TWC2 with her. Anyone who might be able to make a connection between her and these girls." Mistry handed over the laminated photos of the twelve trafficking victims. "These girls were found in a lorry near London."

"In England?"

"Yeah. Luckily, they were found alive."

"Well, I know at least two of these girls. Maybe even three or four," Richmond said. "They came here a few times."

The detectives huddled around Richmond's desk. He was pointing at younger women. Different nationalities. Same haunted faces. Mistry took out her notepad. "Are you sure?"

"Yeah, she was Filipino, I think. She was probably Indonesian," Richmond said. His finger underlined the images. "And these two were from Myanmar. That one I'm not sure, but I'd have to check. But you could just ask her anyway."

"Ask who?"

"That agent you just met," Richmond said, matter-of-factly. "These girls all came from the Happy Maid Agency. You knew that, right?"

Low tried to temper the dizziness. The dots were racing across a distant horizon line, gathering momentum. He could only try to keep up. Follow the patterns.

"Why did they come?" Low struggled to keep up with his own words. "To TWC2. To see you. Why did they come? What was their complaint?"

"Abuse."

"It's always abuse. What kind of abuse? Not Sundays, right? Not long hours, right?"

Richmond shook his head. "No, physical abuse. They were beaten."

Low punched the desk hard. The photos danced in the air. Female faces. Smiling. Tumbling. Low watched them fall. His fault. Always his fault.

"The hanger. The fucking hanger," he shouted.

Throughout the office, the empathetic, dedicated volunteers of TWC2 tried to concentrate on their case work as a scruffy detective ran past their desks, raging against his incompetence.

Chapter 40

Low left his car in Northshore Crescent. He expected a ticket. Street parking was not allowed around the housing estates. Unsightly vehicles belonged in concrete labyrinths beside Punggol's latest utilitarian blocks. Cars were treated like any other problem in the self-proclaimed 'city in nature'. They were hidden. The façade was all important.

The inspector hurried through the manicured greenery. Shady rain trees and bougainvillea bushes offered shelter and colour all the way to the lift lobby. The sea air provided a cool breeze. Off-shore industries brought the dust. Everything came with a compromise in Singapore.

Low hit the lift button. Eighth floor. Lucky floor. Not for Dewi. Not for the poor girl ironing in the corner. He felt the raised dots on the lift button. Braille signs. On the surface, a considerate gesture. Singapore was a considerate country, on the surface.

He ran along the corridor, passing the neighbours' horticultural acts of defiance. Too many potted plants balanced precariously on too many rusty shelves. Decorative flora today. Killer litter tomorrow. It was tokenistic anarchy for the greater good, as long as the neighbours closed one eye, to overhanging plants and maids being battered.

The façade was all important.

Low hammered on the grille. A sleepy Poh Cheng Hong opened the door. He was wearing a white singlet and boxer shorts, rubbing his head, trying to make sense of the unannounced intrusion. "What is it?"

"Unlock the grille."

Low had no warrant. Poh Cheng Hong wouldn't ask for one.

The inspector barged past the confused flat owner and found Angela Poh lying on the Italian sofa, watching a Korean drama. In the corner, the maid was ironing a school uniform.

"Fuck *lah*, does she ever stop ironing?"

Low went for the ironing board, raising both hands. Instinctively, the maid recoiled, dropping the iron and covering her face. Angela Poh sat up on the Italian sofa and straightened her nightie. Poh Cheng Hong ran into his own living room, feeling helpless, enfeebled.

Low leaned over the ironing board and reached for a pile on the chair behind. "This is when I should've known. When she dropped this."

He held up a clothes hanger. "She dropped this and jumped. OK, that one understandable. We all jump. But she didn't just jump, did she? She practically leapt out of the window. And look at her now? Hiding behind the ironing board like it's Fort Siloso. Why? Just because I raised my hands. You know I'm a police officer, right?" Low's voice became softer for the maid. She nodded.

"And yet, you still jumped back. Instinctively. Out of habit. Out of necessity." Low turned back to the Pohs, now together on their Italian sofa. "Because of you."

"Now look." Poh started to get up.

"Sit down or I'll knock you down."

Poh decided not to get up.

"You beat her. Don't you?"

The Pohs left the question hanging in the air, as if hoping it might dissipate.

"I don't need you to answer now." Low took out his phone. "I'll bring down a female officer and my new *kakis* from TWC2 and they can investigate this ... I'm sorry, what is your name?"

For the first time in hours, Low remembered how to smile. "Tell me your name."

"Indah." She continued to fold clothes on the chair.

"Indah. Nice name." Low allowed the smile to linger. He wanted to feel its warmth. "I like that. Indah."

He returned to the Pohs. The scowl was back. "So you beat, Indah? You know it's a crime, right? I'll charge you under the Employment of Foreign Manpower Act. You remember the other woman with me? The British one? She's with TWC2 right now, putting a file together."

Low's fingers hovered in front of Poh Cheng Hong's face, stopping between the cowed man's eyes. "On you. Do you know about the Employment of Foreign Manpower Act?"

"A bit."

"Yeah, a bit vague, right? Deliberately, I think. Covers a multitude of sins. But still got prison, you know. You think you can do prison time, Cheng Hong? In that vest? You know what the *ah bengs* will do to you, right? I got a friend inside Changi, you know, got a big tattoo of a spider's web, right here." Low touched the left side of his neck. "Right on the jugular. He likes beating women, too. You two will have so much to talk about."

"I didn't bloody touch them, OK?"

Low had anticipated the husband's aggression. Their relationship dynamic was almost too obvious. "Yeah, I knew that already. Your wife dominated the conversation last time. Your wife earns more money than you. HR manager. Quite stressful, but pays well, right? You are what?"

"I work in IT."

"Yeah, something boring. Less money. She dominates you. Do you like Korean dramas, Cheng Hong?"

"What?"

"Do you like Korean dramas?"

"Not really."

"No, and you probably don't like her laying across this new sofa either. But she dominates both. The sofa. The TV. Everything. She brought in the interior designer. And she brought in the maids. Like Indah, here, ironing herself to sleep. And before that. Dewi."

Poh Cheng Hong raised a hand. "Eh, just wait *ah?*"

"Hey, I get it, just by looking at you both. I get it. She's an eight. An eight at least. And you're more like, what, a five? Got a pot belly already. Dyeing your hair already. I get it. You've overachieved marrying this one. Good for you, man. So, you ignore some of her other shit. The crappy Korean dramas. The sofa. The maid beating. Nobody's perfect, right?"

"Inspector, I really think . . ."

Low cut off Poh Cheng Hong with a dismissive wave of the hand. "Don't care what you think. I already know. Everyone in this room already knows because the only one who hasn't spoken yet is the one with the most to lose, right or not?"

Even Indah had stopped pretending to fold clothes. She hadn't expected the night to take such a positive turn.

"I didn't do anything, right, Indah?"

Angela Poh locked eyes on her employee, confirming her desperation. Her whiny plea sought validation from the only person in the room with no voice.

225

"No, no, that ship sailed already," Low said. "It's gone. No point using her name now. Like I said, my colleague, Miss Mistry, is on her way with some people from TWC2. And some uniformed officers. Females. Tough buggers. We use them for the maid beaters. They will interview you. There will be a court case. And you will go to prison. That's it."

Angela Poh's eyes filled with tears. Low found the pitiful scene hypnotic. He allowed her realisation to take hold, to really fester, before continuing.

"All you can do, Mrs Poh, is make things easier for yourself, by giving me as much information as you can about your last helper, Dewi."

Angela Poh wiped her cheeks. "Do I need a lawyer? Can get a lawyer, right?"

"For what? This is Singapore, not one of your Korean dramas. And in Singapore, maid beaters not so popular anymore. Not like last time. Now got TWC2, HOME, all these social workers, bleeding hearts, all helping these women. And they'll make you famous, Mrs Poh. Our Government loves scapegoats, right or not. They use people like you to set an example. Your little boy will point at his iPad and say, 'eh, that's Mummy. Why she got her head down, Daddy? Why she got handcuffs, Daddy? Why Mummy not coming home, Daddy?' And Daddy will say, 'Mummy's in prison, son, because she beats women who do not fold your school uniforms properly.'"

"Eh, it wasn't like that. It was just one time, OK."

"I doubt it, but let's start with Dewi shall we? What happened?"

Angela Poh paused to blow her nose. "A few weeks ago, we came back from church. And I was already quite stressed. Getting work calls on a Sunday, during the church service, on my day off. Was supposed to take *makan* to my mother's place. But when we got home, lunch wasn't ready. And we found her asleep on our son's bed. He's got an allergy, OK? She cannot sleep on his bed. So I dragged her off."

"How?"

Angela Poh hesitated.

"How did you drag Dewi off the bed?"

She bowed her head and gestured towards her scalp. Low peered into her watery eyes. "By her hair? You dragged her by her hair?"

"A little bit only. But she screamed and lost her temper and started punching me."

Low tutted. "These maids, eh? So troublesome. And then?"

"I, er, pulled her over there." Angela Poh pointed towards the ironing board. "And we had a fight."

"And then?"

"She had left the iron on."

Low wearily shook his head. "And then?"

"I told her so many times not to leave the iron on. So dangerous. Especially with our boy running around. And she left the iron on and fell asleep some more. So stupid."

"Yes, they're all so stupid, And then?"

"I was angry and tired."

"And then?"

"My boy could've run into that iron?"

Low sighed. "So you hit her with it?"

"Once only."

"Yah, once only," Poh Cheng Hong echoed.

"Where?"

"In her back. But I stopped when I heard that, you know, that sound."

"That hissing sound of burning flesh?"

"Yah, but it was once only," Poh Cheng Hong reiterated, clutching his weeping wife's hand.

Low used his fingertips to massage his eyebrows. He needed a break from their entitled faces.

"And then she ran away," he finally mumbled through his hands.

"Yah."

"Did you take her to the hospital first?"

"No. We weren't sure if . . ."

"Your insurance would cover," Low interjected, cutting off Poh Cheng Hong. "And you have no idea where she went?"

"Yah. She went back to the agency," Poh Cheng Hong said, comforting his wife.

Low looked over his fingers. "What?"

"She went back to the agency, to complain about us."

"To Happy Maids?"

"Yah. Why?"

Low did not reply. He did not say anything until after he'd finished kicking the walls of the lift and the bougain-villea bushes on his way back to the car.

And then he swore at the parking ticket on his windscreen.

Chapter 41

"**Y**ou pimped them out, didn't you? You sold the abused ones," Low said, pulling himself away from Mistry.

The British copper was aware of the bystanders. The other retailers along the narrow corridors of Katong Shopping Centre were pulling down their shutters. It was late. The regular patrons of a neglected mall had long gone home. Only the tenants remained, along with the weary girls of the Happy Maids Agency, still wearing their yellow T-shirts, still believing in fairy tales.

But Mistry did not seek to silence Low. She wanted them to hear. The naïve girls needed to discover where the road ended.

"You fucking passed them to Ah Meng, didn't ya?"

Christine Yeoh had dropped the keys. She was on her knees, her fingers reaching across the tiles. The agency manager had been locking up for the night, fumbling for the bottom lock, when Low had turned up, screaming in her ear.

She counted before answering. Six. That was the number. That was how many yellow T-shirts crowded around her, waiting for a response. She had hoped to end the day with only five, but the paperwork had been delayed. She still had six mouths to feed, rather than five. Domestic servitude was a costly business. Her clients never appreciated the overheads involved.

"You made me drop my keys." Her response was feeble. Her voice weak.

"Never mind your keys. Get up." Low towered over the woman.

"Must get keys first." Yeoh watched her hands reach out. "I drop them just now."

She was talking to herself, shutting out those around her, withdrawing. She blocked out his filthy tongue, but his scuffed trainers crossed her eyeline. He kicked her keys across the tiles, towards that Indian woman, way beyond Yeoh's reach now.

Mistry bent down and picked them up. "Now we've got your keys."

"Get up," Low growled.

Yeoh nodded to herself, as if answering internal questions. "Yah, OK."

Eye contact was beyond her.

"Girls, go wait for me by the van outside," she said, staring only at the tile that had once occupied her keys.

"No, they stay," Mistry said.

"It's better if they go back and rest."

"They stay." Mistry's tone settled the matter.

"OK, for a little bit only," Yeoh said, desperately trying to save face. "Go wait on that bench over there."

"No. They stay here." Mistry walked towards Yeoh, making the agency manager flinch. "They listen."

"To what?"

"To me telling them who you really are," Low said, pointing at the young women. "You are not their agent. You are their pimp. You pimp out your problems. You send them away."

"Send them away why?" Yeoh was slowly recovering the voice that had given her one of the most profitable maid agencies in the East Coast. "How does that help me? I lose money."

"No, you lose a pain in the arse like Dewi. Always get one like that, right? Always complain. Too lazy. Too home-sick. No matter what you do for them, it's never enough. They do a lousy job, so you must send them back. Lose money on them."

"Yah, lose money, *lor.*"

"No, not anymore." Low produced the laminated head-shots. "You see these girls? Found on a truck in England. Smuggled out of Singapore. You recognise them?"

Yeoh gave the sheet of paper a cursory glance. "No."

"Yeah, you do. You know why? Because they are braver than you give them credit for. You see these ones here?"

Low pointed at three woman on the sheet. "Look at them."

"Yah?"

"You couldn't silence them. You couldn't scare them about recruitment fees. They still went behind your back to TWC2. Did you know that?"

Yeoh said nothing.

"Nah you didn't," Low said. "But these girls told TWC2 all about you. Tell her."

Mistry read from her phone. "We met James Richmond, a co-founder and member of the executive committee at TWC2. He has files on all three of these women. They all reported cases of physical abuse to TWC2, after they first reported the abuse to you."

"Not true."

Mistry glowered at the agency manager. "I wasn't fin-ished. They all visited TWC2 at different times. Two of them didn't even appear to know each other. They came through your agency at different times. But their stories were all the same. You sent them to abusive families. They complained. You did nothing. So they went to TWC2 for help. And then they vanished."

The yellow women in the T-shirts whispered among themselves, sharing fragments to those in the group not yet blessed with the language of their former colonial masters.

Yeoh spotted the horror in their tender faces. They were all the same, still burdened with the idealism of youth.

"It's bullshit," Yeoh said. "These people are lying. You're not even Singaporean. You don't know how it works."

"No, you're right I don't know. I don't know how any of this works." Mistry gestured towards the shuttered shop units. "I don't know how you can survive in a dying shopping centre. So I asked James Richmond. And he told me. It's well known within TWC2. Christine Yeoh doesn't just take on every abused maid—"

"—She takes on every maid abuser," Low finished.

"That's right. According to the staff and volunteers there, it's like an unwritten rule in your industry. If dodgy employers keep losing their maids, they go to Happy Maids. If they get a bad reputation, they go to Happy Maids. After a while, even the maids find out. They talk to each other, in chat groups, and they learn about Happy Maids, too. They avoid this place like the plague."

"Which leaves you with these poor bastards," Low said, smiling kindly at the women in yellow T-shirts. "Straight from the village. Too young to know any better, too clueless to complain if they get whacked with an iron. But one girl will always complain in the end. A girl like Dewi. Girls like these." Low waved the laminated sheet in Yeoh's face. "And they don't stop complaining. To you. To TWC2. And then how? TWC2 puts a case together. TWC2 has social media platforms. No good for Happy Maids. If only they would just go away, right? I mean, they're only maids, right? It's not like anyone's going to miss them."

"No, I don't know. Maybe that older one, last time, the Chinese one."

"Yeah, Grace Chen. That's good, Christine. Smart. You know she's in England already. Her picture is on here with the other girls. You think you can blame this on her, right? Because she's gone already. But I know Grace. And Grace looks after Grace. She might get some sex work for the girls, but she's not a bloody snakehead. Tell me about Ah Meng first."

Yeoh's eyes widened at the mention of the dead gangster's name.

"I know he was involved. And Shumai. He did that to her face." Low pointed to Mistry's bandaged nose. "Nice guy, *ah*. He's in prison now. And Ah Meng is dead. You knew that, right? Ah Meng is dead. This is not just a salary anymore. They're killing people now."

"No *lah*, they're helping people."

"Who's helping people?"

"Ah Meng was actually nice to me, you know. The others were animals, especially that Shumai. But Ah Meng was all right *lah*. They wouldn't kill him. No way."

"They killed him straight after I went to see him. They'll kill you next."

"What?"

"Next shipment too important. Cannot stop now. Who are they?"

The Happy Maids Agency manager looked up at the lightbox sign above the shop. She had chosen the sunny colours and the font. The sign was inviting. Welcoming.

233

"Who are they, Christine?"

Yeoh didn't want to look at her shop anymore, or the insufferable detectives, or the six women she still had to feed.

"Look at the owners of this place," she mumbled.

"I thought you were the owner."

"The real owners."

Chapter 42

Andrew Mogg never grew tired of his treetop view. Every evening, the Seraya trees danced for him. They were reported to be the tallest trees in Singapore and many had been chopped down to build the Seraya Country Club.

Mogg stood on the cantilevered pavilion, the club's architectural jewel, and watched Bukit Timah forest's latest performance. Mother Nature never disappointed.

On an overhanging branch, a long-tailed macaque groomed her baby, picking away at his fur until she was satisfied. Even the monkeys were clean in the sanitised city.

Mogg took a sip of his iced water. The speeches were about to start. The subject was boring, something about maids, but the speakers were exemplary. They befitted their lush surroundings.

Mogg shooed a mosquito from a table setting. The general manager of the Seraya Country Club made a mental note to call Rentokil in the morning. There was no place for mosquitos in such a natural, equatorial setting.

The location, the architecture and especially the clientele made Mogg immensely proud of his heritage. In the late 19th Century, a few good men sought a venue that befitted the halcyon days of empire. The hills of Bukit Timah proved arduous for the local builders and several tigers needed to be shot, but the Seraya Country Club became the pillar of social life between the wars. Indeed, the British missed the place terribly, after leaving the locals to face the Japanese Occupation.

But the Seraya Country Club continued to flourish, serving the elitist needs of the island's masters. Pets and maids were not allowed. Members paid a premium for their peace. The symbol of the tallest tree was picked with good reason. The Seraya blocked out the unwanted. And the hill-top pavilion allowed members to look down on the rest of Singapore. The British always understood the natural order. And, finally, the Singaporeans were recognising it, too.

They mingled together freely on the pavilion, clinking their champagne flutes and oohing at the monkey business. Mogg was genuinely disappointed at the prospect of ending the wildlife spotting. The members' photos always looked terrific on social media. But the first speaker had arrived. He was early, but Mogg hurried to the lectern in any case. The speaker was a billionaire. Only his schedule counted.

"Ladies and gentleman, I'd like to thank you all for coming to this wonderful evening, a charitable evening, where I hope we can all contribute to a deserving cause."

Mogg paused as his guests put down their Dom Perignon to applaud the initiative. "And we know this is just a teaser of our special guest's upcoming Second Chance event. But he's a proud patron of Seraya Country Club and he kindly agreed to say a few words tonight. Let's give a warm welcome to Mr Patrick Lin."

Behind the lectern, the projector screen displayed Lin's side profile. Arms folded. Face turned. The dignified pose of choice for the class of LinkedIn. Lin made a point of hushing the crowd, before speaking.

"Come, please, really, no more clapping. Look, I'm a very busy man."

The raucous laughter befitted a billionaire's status. Lin checked his white shirt for sweat stains. The rainforest air was still and humid. He noticed the monkeys.

"Hey, I think I had a Zoom meeting with those guys today."

More laughter. More clapping. No one wanted to be seen as the first to stop.

"Look, I'll keep this short. I know the chef is putting on a great menu. Later this week, my Second Chance charity will be publishing this."

He held up a small textbook.

"This book is long overdue. This is the first comprehensive guide on the working rights of migrant workers in this country. Whether it's your domestic helper, your construction worker, your office cleaner or your gardener, this will help them to know their rights in Singapore."

The applause was muted this time. Members didn't attend functions at the cantilevered pavilion to think about Bangladeshi gardeners.

"The book is not only written in our four national languages, but also in Tagalog, Thai and Burmese for our South-East Asian friends."

Lin sensed his audience's discomfort. He was not bothered in the least. They needed to hear this. "Look, you know my background. *Ah beng*. Gangster. Studied economics in prison. Learned how to read the stock market and here we are. But this is what you maybe don't know. I used to sweep the streets down there." Lin pointed down the hill. "Bukit Timah. Stevens. All the way down to Newton Circus. Part of my rehabilitation. Community service. You know how people looked at me back then?"

Lin enjoyed a couple of *tai tai*s adjusting their jewellery and looking away from the lectern. "Exactly. They looked at me how we sometimes look at people in this book. And with your help, we're going to put this book in every school, library and community centre in the country. Because our migrant workers don't just need to know their rights. We do, too. So buy as many copies as you can tonight. I've signed them all. Just for you."

The rapturous applause returned. A book with Patrick Lin's signature was worth more on eBay.

Mogg returned to the lectern, clapping Lin to his seat. The general manager needed a quiet word with the billionaire later about renovating the swimming pool.

"Wow, a signed book, we are honoured, Mr Lin."

"You certainly are."

Mogg tried to block out the projector's lights and find the voice. A blurry figure made his way through the small, distinguished crowd.

"We are indeed," Mogg said, slightly confused. "In fact, Mr Lin has been a patron of the Seraya Country Club for many years now and ..."

"The secret owner of the Happy Maids agency."

Low leaned against the back of a chair occupied by a well-dressed expatriate. "Did you know that, Mr Country Club? I didn't know myself until an hour ago. I couldn't believe it. One of his many, many companies, and my God, he has *so* many companies, this shell company, that shell company, Panama this, British Virgin Islands that. Not many British virgins in here, eh? Sorry, shouldn't joke."

Low had already picked them out at the back of the pavilion. Hulking figures. Overdressed. Earpieces. Private security. Billionaires never left home without one. They were on their way, through the tables, nothing but a nod and a wink. Discreet. Effortless. Low didn't have much time.

"And here he is, with a guide to help maids, when he actually sells maids. Help maids. Sell maids. What's the difference, right?

The two security men separated at Low's table. One clockwise. One anti-clockwise. Without speaking. No sound. Minimal distraction. Low respected the training.

"But do you know what he really does with these maids? Shall I tell you?"

They were almost there. The left one went for his inside pocket. The right one already had the handcuffs. Such efficiency. Such coolness. Low almost applauded them.

"Well, Mr Lin uses Happy Maids for the really unhappy Maids."

The right one went for a rugby tackle. Low hit the floor hard. His nose found a guest's Jimmy Choos.

"Call the police," the one with handcuffs whispered to his colleague.

"I am the police," Low replied, through gritted teeth.

"Not tonight," the one with the baton hissed, slyly jabbing Low in the ribs.

The inspector was hoisted to his feet, shocked to find himself confronting the silent partner of the Happy Maids agency. "Oh, hello. I know who you are."

"Everyone knows who I am, Inspector Low. We are both men with a troubled past. I have come to terms with mine. I wish you all the best with yours."

Mogg hurriedly ushered his members towards the popular Stamford Bar, while pondering alternative sources of income for his swimming pool renovations.

Chapter 43

The Minister had asked to meet them at the National Gallery. He rather enjoyed the banana muffins at the Courtyard Café. Besides, the location was ideal. Across the road from Parliament, the heritage attraction was deserted most mornings. The National Gallery didn't make money. Its purpose remained tough to grasp.

The Minister made a point of thanking the waitress for the muffin. She was young. Attractive. She would almost certainly have an Instagram account and he was still one of the most popular cabinet members on social media.

"Still warm," he whispered, patting the top of the cake as if it were a small boy. "Best muffins in Singapore, right on my doorstep. They really deserve greater footfall."

"Stick that on one of your 'buy local' campaigns."

The Minister chuckled as he bit into the muffin, allowing the banana custard to trickle across his tongue. He still enjoyed the company of Detective Inspector Stanley Low. Even now. The officer's intellect belonged in government. His temperament belonged in a padded cell. Keeping him away from both had been an intriguing challenge.

"Not a bad idea," the Minister said—after swallowing

first, of course. An elite education bought impeccable manners, in most cases.

The sunken-eyed ruffian sitting across from him tested that theory.

The seating area of the Courtyard Café was essentially an annexe of the National Gallery, joined to the imposing neo-classical structure by a sloping glass roof. The sun reflected favourably upon one of Singapore's finest colonial structures, but left Low looking like a rotting sampan.

"A wonderful example of British architecture, eh?"

The Minister addressed his question to the only British resident at the table. Mistry feigned interest in the twee surroundings. "Yeah, it's nice."

"Does it remind you of your home?"

Mistry almost choked on her cup of expensive English breakfast tea. "Not really. My parents ran a corner shop in East London. The first time I saw anywhere like this was on a school trip to the National History Museum."

"Ah, Kensington," the Minister said brightly.

"Yes." Mistry was surprised.

"I studied in London. Like you and Inspector Low."

The Minister's wry smile was deliberate. He liked to give the impression that he knew everything about those brought before him, mostly because he did. Everyone had a file in Singapore. Even foreigners.

That's why he'd asked to see all four of them. Low was a cliché, a timebomb forever in search of a new detonator. Mistry was presumably a second-generation Asian immigrant, in awe of quaint western values like neoliberalism and equality. And Deputy Director Anthony Chua was the classic product of the scholarship system. He'd endorse anything official and the Minister didn't need a parrot right now. He needed something vaguely resembling balance.

The Eurasian with the straggly beard and the nervous disposition was the best available at such short notice. The Minister offered him a little encouragement. "Are you OK?"

"Yes, I'm fine, sir."

James Richmond wasn't fine. He wasn't fine when he was summoned from his bed to prepare for a quick chat with the Minister. And he wasn't fine when he discovered why he'd been called. The reason was sneering in the chair beside him.

The Minister lowed his muffin. "So, Inspector, you had an eventful evening, eh?"

"No more than usual. I think I'll get a muffin." Low waved at the waitress and pointed towards the Minister's half-eaten snack.

"Luckily it was a private event. No media."

"There will be an internal investigation, sir. As soon as I get in the office, I will prepare the paperwork."

The Minister waved away the deputy director's obsequious promises. "Patrick Lin does not want to press charges. The Seraya Country Club did not want to register a complaint, for the same reason I like to sit here with a banana muffin after my daily run around the Civic District. You know why?"

"No, sir."

"No fuss, Deputy Director. Everyone minds their business. You want to know the biggest misconception about Singapore, Miss Mistry?"

"OK."

"*Kan cheong*. Everyone thinks we're *kan cheong*, which is nervous or jittery in Cantonese, on edge, permanently stressed. Look around you." The Minister nodded towards the café's windows. "That's the Singapore Parliament building. Right there. I'm sitting in a café having a banana muffin, as I do most days, a member of the Cabinet. Does this scene scream '*kan cheong*' to you? Where are the armed guards? The security restrictions? No, what we cherish here, Miss Mistry, are our calm exteriors."

Low laughed loudly. "*Wah lao eh*, that really is your bloody catchphrase eh?"

"It has allowed a tiny island surrounded by potentially hostile neighbours to navigate a safe passage for almost sixty years. We must keep our eye on the bigger picture."

"And close the other eye on everything else? How money and people flow in and out of this country? How we treat people?"

"*Women*," Mistry muttered.

The Minister was rather disappointed. The British-Indian woman had built an impressive career in a male-dominated environment in an obviously archaic country but she was such a feminist stereotype.

"Why do you think I'm here, Miss Mistry? I'm listening. A brutal murder is always a concern. If you tell me the death is possibly connected to further deaths in the UK, I will not only listen, I will demand an investigation. I oversee the Inter-Agency Taskforce on Trafficking in Persons. We're on the same side here." The Minister focused on the social worker's hands. They had stopped shaking. "Mr Raymond, I admire what you do for migrant workers at TWC2. Tell me what you know."

Raymond fumbled with his file, in search of papers he could not find.

"It's OK, James," the Minister purred, making the most of his public speaking classes. "I just want your view."

Raymond closed the file firmly. "Trafficking is a real issue here. We know that Singapore is used as a transit point.

Sex and labour exploitation are the driving forces. We have a unique situation here. A small country with more than a fifth of its population being foreign, poorly paid and often poorly managed, unsure of their rights and legal protections, which, frankly speaking are not great. Sorry."

"Carry on."

"Right, we have more than a million migrant workers. We know that a percentage top up their income with sex work. That's thousands of unlicensed, unknown sex workers. And we see hundreds of them. Sexually abused. Violently abused. We see them regularly. And then, they just stop coming. They disappear. We follow up. But we just get stuff like, 'oh, they went back' or 'they found another job'."

"That might be true."

"Not for these girls."

Raymond produced the headshots of the girls on the truck. "Three of these girls came to us at TWC2 quite regularly. And then they stopped."

"And they ended up on the back of lorry, in a swamp in England," Mistry said. "All terrified, waiting to be executed, it seems. But the lorry driver was killed instead. It seems the killer was then disturbed."

"One of them is Singaporean," Low added, pointing at Grace Chen's photo. "I know her. From last time."

The Minister raised an eyebrow. "From your other life."

"Yeah, we helped each other's lives back then, eh, Minister?"

The Minister rolled his fork over a piece of muffin. "What are you planning for her?"

"I'm arranging to bring Grace back, once I think it's safe to do so."

"Safe? If she's a Singaporean citizen, I think she'll be fine, Inspector."

244

"What? Like him?"

Low dropped a photo beside the Minister's muffin. A close-up of Ah Meng's slit throat. "That one not his IC photo. But he did have a pink IC. He was local. Does he look safe in Singapore?"

The Minister eyeballed his deputy director, waiting for an explanation.

Chua shifted uneasily in his seat. He didn't have enough savings in his CPF account to retire. He still needed to please. "Yah, this was Zhi Hao, nicknamed Ah Meng, because he was fat, like the orangutan last time," Chua said. "Convicted for loan sharking before. Then ran KTV lounges, some spas. Shut down and fined during the pandemic, several times."

"Appalling behaviour. A tragedy. But this is gambling, sex and violence. These things go back to the days of Raffles' cock-fighting," the Minister said. "I'm sure CID is investigating?"

The deputy director nodded vigorously. "Absolutely, sir."

"Then why is Inspector Low harassing a prominent Singaporean businessman?"

Low turned to Richmond. "Tell him."

Richmond held up the photographs again. "Er, well, these girls were from the Happy Maids agency in Katong. In fact, many of our complaints come from Happy Maids."

"Then report your findings and the Ministry of Manpower will investigate and take action if necessary."

"The agency is partially owned by a company called Phoenix Holdings. Patrick Lin is an investor," Low said.

"Honestly, I'd be surprised if he wasn't."

"Oh for . . . Seriously? Cos he's a *towkay* right? Investments everywhere, right? Like he has stock in a Genting casino in Essex?"

"Every major Chinese investor in South-East Asia probably has an interest in a casino, Inspector. You of all people should know that."

"Same casino where he met this guy? Show him, Ramila."

Mistry placed Steve Robertson's crucifixion beside the Minister's teapot. "According to sources, Mr Lin had helped Mr Robertson find a regular supply of illegal labour, which Mr Robertson then transported across the UK, using his freight company."

"Illegal labour from the Happy Maids agency," Low said. "Whenever they get an abused one, an angry one, they sell them to any country that's got a labour shortage, which right now is every bloody country."

The Minister stirred his tea. "Maybe we could lower the volume a little, Inspector?"

"Please *lah*. This is an art gallery, not a shopping mall. There's no one here."

The Minister continued to stir, careful not to touch the sides of the cup. He was disciplined. Controlled. He liked the tea to cool first. Cold tea reminded him of his army days. He had risen through the ranks quickly and still cherished the core values.

He spoke slowly. "So, to summarise, a wealthy trading investor is using his tenuous links to a maid agency, one of literally hundreds of businesses that he has a stake in, to send maids who complain to England, via a trucking company, owned by a man he met at a casino?"

"Check with the MP in England. He introduced them," Low added.

"An MP in England? Sure. I'll get right on it." The Minister faced the social worker. "Do you have any information on this?"

"No, sir."

"Any of the women ever mention anything about potential human trafficking?"

"No, sir."

The Minister returned to the detectives. "Is there any evidence to support this allegation, this connection, in the UK?"

"Not yet," Mistry said. "But my boss in England, DCI Wickes, he's staying in contact with the case, following up with the local murder squad in Essex."

"Well, that's good. What about in Singapore?"

"We know that these girls came from the Happy Maids Agency," Low said. "We know that they ended up on a plane to the UK. And the agency manager herself said that he was involved."

"How? Did she mention him by name?"

"No, she just said the owners of the business were involved. That's all she knew."

"Along with trying to save herself." The Minister wiped his mouth with a napkin. "OK, Deputy Director, please continue the murder investigation. Mr Richmond, if you can put together a full report on this errant agency, I will see that it gets dealt with immediately. Also, in the longer term, perhaps we might consider a detailed research paper on human trafficking. Put some meat on the bones. Frankly, what you've told me so far, I could get from Google."

Richmond was crestfallen. "No, don't get disheartened," the Minister added. "You're on the side of the angels. Keep going."

The Minister gazed at Mistry. Sustained eye contact conveyed empathy. He added a rueful shake of the head for emphasis. "And I'm so sorry about what happened to you, Miss Mistry. I'm told the Singapore Police Force are taking care of the medical bills?" The Minister paused for Chua's assurance. "Good. The least we can do. And the Deputy Director will write up a favourable report, I'm sure, for your superior officer back in London. Cooperative relationships are so important."

"And what about me?"

Low's question was rhetorical, but the Minister indulged him anyway.

"Go back to vice. Clearly, these illicit establishments are still not getting the message. And you're doing a great job there. A great job. You should cherish your career. Both of you."

The threat was barely implied, but it was enough to impress Low. The Minister used the only weapon at his disposal to stop Low.

Her. Nothing else would stop Low. Except her.

"Yep, Ramila does have a career worth cherishing," Low muttered, already edging away from the table.

"Anyway, thanks for your time," the Minister said. "I must finish this muffin."

The others left without being asked.

The Minister waited for the waitress to clear his plate while picking up his phone. He needed to hurry. The first tourists were arriving.

"Morning, yes, I'm just finishing up here, coming over now." The Minister spoke quietly, while signalling for the bill. "Yeah, they're gone. He's out. She's going home. Yah, Chua can handle. No problem."

The waitress was heading back with a bill on a saucer. The Minister raised a finger. He wasn't done on the phone yet. The waitress froze. He was a minister.

"Yah, should be OK now ... Don't know ... That one

ah? You never know, right? Didn't go to our school, did he? ... Of course, I heard the rumours. They're like that sometimes. The new ones. A bit overzealous ... So how?"

The Minister laughed. "Yah, we want more billionaires, right?"

The Minster finished the call, but held his phone in the air. There was still time for a selfie with the pretty waitress.

Chapter 44

The palms swayed in the moonlight. Mistry found them strangely robotic. A manufactured line of trees, running from one end of the East Coast to the other. Same size. Same height. Equidistant. Hundreds of them. Maybe thousands. A long, unnatural nature display, from Marina Bay to Changi Airport, showcasing a country's intent. Even the palm trees did as they were told in Singapore.

"This place never changes," she said, staring through the window.

Xavier Ng grinned at his British passenger through his rear-view mirror. "East Coast Park? Yah. Lee Kuan Yew knew it would be a tourist's first impression of Singapore, straight from the airport. "Not bad, right? Part of our 'city in nature' concept."

"Yeah, our city in nature, built on reclaimed land,' Low grumbled. "Foreign workers clean it. Expats use it. And the most popular place is Burger King."

He had no interest in looking to his right. He focused on the construction site for the new MRT train line on his left. That was the authentic Singapore, cutting through finite spaces and building for the future. Besides, his past was sitting on his right.

"You took me to the East Coast once," Mistry muttered. "That funny place with the water slides. What was it called?"

"Can't remember."

"Yes you can."

"Big Splash."

"Yeah. That was it. First time I went down the water slide, I nearly threw up. The pool at the bottom was full of salt water."

"It was built by the sea. We're practical."

Mistry picked out a couple walking their dog through East Coast Park. The Singapore Strait shimmered behind them, a picture postcard shot. "You took me to that hawker centre after, on the beach. First time I had satay, with the peanut sauce. Delicious." Her voice trailed off.

"Yeah, you dropped one on your T-shirt."

"So you do remember."

"You looked like you'd shit on your own shirt. Hard to forget."

Mistry found his hand on the back seat. "Are you gonna be all right?"

"I'll survive."

Low was surprised at his instinctive response. He felt gratitude. For her. She was going home to a better life. He was pleased.

The Changi Airport Control Tower appeared in Ng's windscreen. "Almost there," the rookie detective said, keen to break the tension.

Ng's earpiece flashed. He pushed the phone on his dashboard. "Yes, sir. Dropping her off now. Yes, sir. The check-in counter. I'll let you know after. OK, bye."

Ng found her face in his rear-view mirror. "Sorry."

"They really want me to go, eh?"

"You're a loose end," Low said.

"So are you."

"Yeah, but I'm Singaporean. The bastards are stuck with me."

Ng wisely decided to wait in the car. He was under orders to escort the British detective to the check-in counter. But he was working hard on his emotional intelligence. Low was still his boss. And his boss was clearly damaged. The least Ng could do was give the unusual pair a few minutes on the kerbside.

Low wheeled a trolley over to Ng's car. He lifted her suitcase. "You travelled light."

"No winter clothes." Mistry breathed in the humid air. "I'll miss the weather."

"And nothing else." Low bundled her suitcase onto the trolley.

Across the road, a glassy, steely dome dominated the landscape. The Jewel housed one of the largest airport retail complexes in the world. Families hurried into the air-conditioned behemoth. "I'll miss the shopping," Mistry said.

"Piss off."

The detectives laughed together. She always had an endearing laugh. "Do you think he's watching us?

"Little Xavier? Of course. Someone is always watching us. They'll expect a full report. I'm surprised he's not handcuffed you all the way to the plane."

"Bit disloyal."

"Not really. Just a junior officer with a new mortgage."

Low gestured towards a long line of identical cars, idling outside the terminal. "What else is he gonna do? Drive a taxi? Singaporeans don't get many options."

Mistry shook her head. "There were twelve women in that lorry. There'll be another one soon. With Dewi."

"Yeah."

"They won't stop."

"I'll shut down the maid agency."

"And then what?"

"And then I'll go back to raiding KTV lounges."

"You know it's a cover up."

"Cover up? Here? We're a blissful, law-abiding utopia." Low leaned forward and gently touched her bruised cheek. The swelling had almost gone. "Go back to your family. Go see your little boy."

"I'm still gonna chase the murders on my end. I'll get Wickes on board."

"I know."

"And I'll send Grace home."

"Yeah, I promised her."

"She'll be fine."

Mistry tapped Ng's passenger window. The young detective waved back and turned away. He was talking on the phone.

In the window's reflection, Mistry caught a glimpse, over her shoulder, of the guy that had once taken her to the East Coast Park for satay. But he'd been stripped back. Hollowed out.

She hugged him. "Don't give 'em an excuse, Stanley."

"What?"

"They're waiting for you to fuck things up. Don't be, you know, *you*."

Chapter 45

The great and the greedy gathered at the grand ballroom of the Ritz-Carlton. Singapore's finest were dressed up to toast their superior DNA. Black ties and fluffy gowns gathered in the photo booths, a dress rehearsal for the fashion awards later. The winners usually made the glossy pages of the next edition.

Elite Magazine's 25th Anniversary Ball was both a celebration and a chance to raise funds for Patrick Lin's Second Chance foundation. He was a billionaire. *Elite Magazine* was essential reading for landed property owners. Two birds. One party. Win-win.

There were no losers at *Elite Magazine*'s 25th Anniversary Ball, except those topping up glasses before retreating to the darkened crevices of the grand ballroom.

And a detective inspector making his way through security.

Low's ID was enough to see him past the trio of doormen. His credentials revealed only his profession, not his psychiatric report. He offered no threat. On paper.

His heart rate indicated otherwise. He couldn't control his breathing. Or the shaking. A couple of vodkas on the way in had barely registered. He couldn't control the internal images, flashing past, like a PowerPoint presentation of a life less orderly. *Ang mohs* nailed to pallets. *Ah longs* sliced open. Loved ones saying goodbye. Always saying goodbye. They never stayed. He never really wanted them to stay. For their protection. For their safety. From him.

He couldn't control himself.

Only the mania sustained him, directed him, past the crowds, the odious masses of endless consumption. They ignored him. He did not dress like them. He held no value to them, no networking potential, no purpose.

They air kissed around him, posing for selfies with equally important people and perused the menus. Seven courses. Asian fusion. Organic produce and handcrafted chocolates. Whisky bars and cigar lounges. Photo walls and gaming rooms. Property magnates and tech entrepreneurs, old money and new, all tastes were accommodated as they raised funds for ex-convicts.

The guests thought it was *so* important to give back to society.

Low grabbed a glass of Champagne Pierre Paillard from a passing waiter. Downed it. Dumped the glass. Grabbed another. The silver trays were refuelling stations on his way to the finish line.

The grand ballroom stage.

The final destination for the evening, for the case, for his career. He wasn't sure. It didn't matter. They were minor details. Trivial concerns. The prize was the end of the show. His performance. He was going out on his terms.

He flew over the stage steps. The mania made him soar, sharpened his vision. He saw everything. The stunned host on stage, with the wholesome persona and the husband in the closet, and the event planner off stage, screaming into her headset. And he saw the faces in the crowd.

The glorious, stupefied faces. Cowering behind Remy Cointreau bottles. Clutching pearls. Stealing glances. Not at Low, obviously. He was not a person of financial interest.

All eyes were on the guest of honour, sitting at table one, flanked by useful acolytes.

Patrick Lin expected to be the centre of attention. He paid a high price for it.

So he did nothing. He watched and waited for the man on stage.

Low grabbed the microphone from the host. "Eh, you don't mind, *ah*? Your comedy not bad one."

The inspector raised the glass in his other hand. "Hello everyone, here we all are, gathered for such a prestigious occasion. Making the sequel. Crazy Rich Arseholes." Low embraced the sharp intake of breath. He craved it. The mutual hatred satiated the mania. "*Relak lah*, just joking," He peered beneath the spotlight, examining the audience. "Let's see who we've got here tonight."

Silence filled the cavernous grand ballroom, allowing Low to hear the footsteps at the entrance. On the move. The three doormen with broad shoulders and no necks were on their way.

Low picked out a perspiring face. "Ah, I remember you from last time. Head of one of the media companies, right? Yeah, you remember me, from the CPIB bust. Found you in the private lounge, Russian hooker on each knee, right or not?"

They gasped, fumbling for air like guppies smothered in Gucci.

"What? He likes the blonde ones. Did your wife give you a second chance? If not, we can help you with this charity tonight." Low moved across the stage. "Ah table three. The *towkay* table. Your wife still battering maids or not? No more already? You gave her a second chance? Fantastic."

Low clapped his microphone and champagne glass together. "That's why we're here, ladies and gentlemen, giving people from all walks of life a second chance, except our host on stage. He's a brilliant comedian. Good actor. But gay. Gays don't get much chance in Singapore. But at least not illegal anymore, eh? Let's see a show of hands for all the gay CEOs in the room? See? No one coming out tonight, *ah*?"

Low caught the doormen in his peripheral vision. He moved quickly, looking down at another horrified table. "Ah, look there's my good friend, Father Fernandes. Never misses a charitable event and the free *makan*, right? Always willing to give everyone a second chance. Except young women who make a mistake. For them, cannot right? Speaking of young women, who brought their maids here tonight?"

They coughed in the audience. They sipped their champagne. They prayed for security to run faster and put the irritant down.

"Nah, no maids here tonight? You know why? 'Cos he put them on trucks. Your generous benefactor." Low directed his microphone towards Lin. "Former convict. Famous billionaire and secret people smuggler. Hey, Patrick, *ah*. Are you still gonna smuggle the next lot? Still got time *ah*? I'll drink to that."

Low emptied his glass and threw it over his shoulder. "His case was going to be my second chance. You know that? Second chance with the love of my life. No, not in that way. I didn't want to shag her." He spotted a *tai tai* at table five, clutching her necklace, horrified. "It's OK, dear. I'm not a pervert, not like your husband. Saw him at Orchard

257

Towers last time. Do you know Orchard Towers, madam? It's known as the four floors of whores in Singapore. You know it, right? Yeah. I think your husband had a season ticket there. Anyway, I didn't want to sleep with her. No, I just wanted to make things right with her. That's all. Settle the case and settle things with her. But I fucked it."

Low sighed as the doormen closed in. "I always fuck things up."

The three men, in matching black suits, leapt onto the stage. But they hesitated, seeking guidance from table one. They needed an executive order.

Sitting beside Lin, the Minister gave a slight nod.

Low could only marvel at Singapore's bureaucratic efficiency. He clenched his teeth. Loose jaws were easier to break. "OK, let's get this over with."

A flying microphone caught the first one in the forehead. A follow-up head butt sent the disoriented slab of muscle tumbling into the Basque burnt cheesecakes on table seven. A kick winded the second doorman. But the third surprised Low with a rabbit punch from behind, jarring his skull, stealing his balance. The second restored a little pride with a sly dig in the solar plexus.

Low's early advantage was gone. The two doormen had the numbers. Singaporeans expected the majority to prevail. Opponents were supposed to succumb, especially at the grand ballroom of the Ritz-Carlton, where the clientele had no patience for childish acts of rebellion. The doormen soon restored the status quo by cracking a couple of Low's ribs. They needed to satisfy an instinctive, violent urge to save face. Their employers were watching.

Low dropped to his knees. He was done.

The doormen handcuffed him roughly, reasserting their authority in front of the people that mattered. Table one.

The inspector leered at the assembled dignitaries. "Hope I ruined your evening. You've fucking ruined mine."

The car park wasn't ideal, but it was the only secluded space within the vicinity. Nonetheless, he checked the vehicles around him, just in case.

He decided to send the message. He was determined to see this one through. The risks were always there. Nothing new. But the reward was everything.

Still, he used a different SIM card. It was simpler. Cleaner.

He typed slowly. He really wasn't fond of texting.

He kept the message brief.

"Send them first. Make a decision after."

Chapter 46

Low was struck by the familiarity. Holding cells always looked the same. Singapore. Malaysia. Even the UK. He had visited them all, as an inspector, an undercover detective, a fake gangster and a foreign observer. The décor rarely deviated from the stock sets of old movies. Small. Square. Grey. In Singapore and Malaysia, there was either a hole in the floor or a bucket in the corner. In England, there was usually a proper toilet. But then, the *ang mohs* always did things upside down. They treated their villains like pets and their politicians like dogs.

In Singapore, the lines were clearly drawn. The bad guys got a plastic bucket.

Low stood over the bucket and deliberately missed. The cell already stank of piss.

He pressed one hand against the concrete wall, careful not to touch the dried excrement, and loudly sang "One People, One Nation, One Singapore".

He often worked his way through the country's National Day jukebox in police holding cells and interrogation rooms. He found the juxtaposition amusing. And the confined space offered outstanding acoustics.

"Very patriotic."

Of course, Low recognised the voice. He had expected to hear it sooner. "Yeah, Jeremy Monteiro got nothing on me." The inspector didn't turn round. He was still going.

"You should sing at the next National Day Parade."

"Nah, I'm a 'singing in the shower' guy."

"You and I must have very different showers."

Low shook himself, zipped up and turned round. "OK, we've done the shit banter. What happens now?"

The Minister stood in the doorway, making a snap judgement not to step inside. It wasn't the holding cell or the lingering odour of bodily fluids. He was a legitimately proud supporter of the Second Chance project. His education was elitist and privileged, naturally, but his school's religious heart had always been in the right place. He was taught to acknowledge the wealth, but give something back. Time. Wisdom. Money. Whatever. All donations were welcome.

So he visited prisons, hospices and old folks homes. He gave out *hong baos* and care packages and not just to fill compliant news pages either. He believed in the mission.

He had sacrificed weekends to clean rental flats far worse than Low's holding cell. So it wasn't the room or the smell.

It was the inspector.

The Minister didn't want to go anywhere near such a toxic personality.

His inability to analyse Low actually alarmed him. He could explain a complex budget to a low-income family in his constituency. But he could not explain Low.

"That, as always, depends on you," the Minister said. "What do you think should happen now?"

Low wiped his hands on his jeans. "I think your billionaire *kaki* should be dragged in here and covered in that bucket of piss."

261

"What about you?"

"I'll be the one throwing the piss."

The Minister tutted. "I don't need to be here, Inspector. I shouldn't be here."

"Then why are you?"

"I'm supposed to break you."

"Cannot. Already broken."

Low gingerly lowered himself to the cold concrete, pushing hard against his ribs. He leaned back against the wall and exhaled.

The Minister pointed at the inspector's chest. "Does that hurt?"

"Only when I breathe or take a shit." Low looked around the holding cell. "Luckily, I've only needed to do one in here."

The minister noticed Low wince as he shifted his posture. "Have you seen a doctor?"

"No treatment for cracked ribs. Just rest."

"Can you rest?"

"Not since secondary school."

"Same." The Minister realised they were both grinning.

"Are you expecting a hug or something? This isn't a Chinese drama."

"No, I'm expecting, I don't know, penitence maybe?"

"Wah, so *cheem* your English. Talk like *ang moh* some more."

"I'm supposed to fire you, Inspector. You understand that, right? If I follow procedure, I tell the deputy director to find a bit of backbone and fire you."

"Chua couldn't find his backside with both hands. If you wanna fire me, then you fire me. Justify that huge salary of yours."

Low allowed the inevitable silence to pass. "Cannot

right? Too much history. Too many cases. And they all messed with the message. Didn't show our sunny side. Low crime doesn't mean no crime, right? I'm literally the clue in your slogan. The face of ugly Singapore. You need me. But you cannot talk about me. You use that handsome officer in uniform, right? Got his cardboard cut-out in every shopping centre. The acceptable face of Singapore. I'm the other one. The invisible one. Like the maids. I clean up your mess. And you pretend you cannot see me."

"So why am I here?"

Low twisted his torso slightly. The adjustment made no difference. He needed paracetamol, but would never ask. The pain was warranted. His fingertips pushed the intercostal muscles into the splintered bone. The stabbing sensation energised him.

"You're here to make sure I'm not a vindictive data dump. I know where the bodies are buried and all that. But don't worry. I'll use that bucket for my leaks."

"Why?"

"Because it's the right thing to do. Just because I work on the shitty side of the street, doesn't mean I don't appreciate that the other side still exists."

The Minister wasn't convinced. "So why the big ballroom scene?"

"I had to let that fucker know."

"Will that be enough?"

"Does it matter? You need to uphold your calm exterior, right?"

The Minister's chuckle echoed through the holding cell. Low's unfiltered analysis was still missing from the spoon-fed education system. The man had everything required to advise the fourth generation of political leadership. Except sanity.

"I'll ask Chua to reassign you delicately. Nothing too strenuous. This evening's guests value their privacy. There'll be no media coverage. No phones. You're lucky."

"Do I look lucky? I'm sitting next to a bucket of my own piss."

"You'll be released after this." The Minister pointed at Low. "But, Inspector, please, leave it alone now. We've had a mutually beneficial relationship over the years. We solved problems. For each other. But it has to end now. I can't help you anymore."

"You don't have to. She will."

The Minister felt the warm air on his neck. He turned to find the bruised face of Detective Inspector Ramila Mistry smiling at him.

"Oh look," Low said, rising to his feet. "It's the ghost of girlfriends past."

Chapter 47

The Minister could not comprehend this alien situation. He had been blindsided. He was catching up with events, instead of shaping them. Ordinarily, he set the agenda. He signed off on the press releases and they reappeared in the mainstream media at a time of his choosing. The Minister was not a newsmaker. Such quaint descriptions belonged in naïve, western publications obsessed with impractical freedoms.

The Minister was a news controller.

But he didn't own the narrative now. The British interloper was supposed to be on a plane, not reuniting with Singapore's lost cause in a filthy holding cell.

"Well, well, Miss Mistry. I was under the impression that you were heading back to your actual job in London," the Minister said.

"I forgot to pick up my duty free."

The Minister did not understand her response, tone or physical appearance. He was accustomed to deference. Unlike England's crumbling social order, Singapore retained a rigid class structure. There were those with money and power. And those without. And everyone behaved accordingly.

She wasn't doing that. She was being tediously flippant and noncompliant, like a political science undergrad discovering Marx for the first time. The Minister expected it on panel discussions with idealistic students. He enjoyed the batting practice.

But Mistry was a grown woman. And yet she stood tall before him. Indifferent to his status.

"It's very late," the Minister said. "And my wife will be waiting for me."

"Which one?"

The minister turned to his fellow Singaporean. "*Et tu*, Inspector?"

"Etta who? Sorry, Minister, didn't go to your *hao lian* school. My Latin not so powerful one."

"Yes, yes, your *ah beng* routine. Made you a hero with young policemen everywhere, but please do not insult my intelligence any further."

Low was suddenly aware of his body odour. He reeked. The vodka and champagne seeped through his pores, mixing with the dried blood. And the pain kept him in check, reminding him what he was.

And what she wasn't.

Ironically, Mistry had never looked more beautiful. Standing in the doorway of a cell that still held Low—and his bucket of warm piss—she towered over the grubby testosterone. But the bruises, though barely visible now, still remained.

That was enough.

Low gestured towards her facial injuries. "That's why she's here. Right there. That. You showed her no face."

"I'm sorry?"

"All of you. No face. When I was in England two years ago, I also ended up in hospital, right? But that one was my fault. Fair enough. But this wasn't her fault. This was a piece of shit. Broke into my apartment. And nearly killed her. Why? To protect some snakehead. OK. Part of the job. But all you could think about, you and your task forces, was saving *your* face. Hers gets smashed and your first reaction is to save yours. Typical *gahmen*. Typical Singapore. And then you kick her out. She's nearly strangled trying to help my case, a Singapore case, and you kick her out. And you use your *cheem* Latin on me? Balls to you. There's only one traitor in this room."

The mania propelled Low across the cell. He peered into the Minister's eyes. "There are many things wrong with me. Up here." Low prodded his own forehead. "Everyone in this room knows what they are. I am the fucking gargoyle that keeps on giving. But she stuck by me." Low jabbed a finger at Mistry. "She's loyal and so am I. I'm also a vindictive bastard, but still loyal. What are you?"

"Loyal to the people of Singapore."

Low laughed in the Minister's face. "So you send home an injured woman to protect the Singaporean people, is it? How fragile are we?"

"It wasn't personal."

"Yes, it was. When your people made my people follow her. When you put Xavier on her tail, when you made that Mini-Me detective spy on my friend, then you made it personal. So we made it personal. We took our case back."

Finally, the Minister understood. He understood everything. He even chuckled at the ingenuity. "You set us all up. Both of you."

"We had to let people know that we were out of the picture," Low said. "So business could resume."

"They would've been nervous to continue if we were still around," Mistry said.

"Yeah, so thanks for kicking her out and throwing me in here to shit in a bucket. It worked like a dream."

Mistry frowned at the bucket in the corner.

"No, of course I haven't," Low said. "I've only pissed in it."

The Minister rubbed his face. He appeared to growl into his palms. "Ah, you didn't come to the ballroom to let him know, like some Shakespearian farce. The whole thing was a bloody distraction."

"Yeah, had to be a bit *wayang*, so Mistry could sneak around on my behalf."

"You could be a minister."

"Learned from you. Calm exteriors, right?"

"That was you being calm?"

"Didn't kill anyone, did I?"

Reluctantly, the Minister addressed the mendacious foreigner. "So, I guess, Miss Mistry, this is where you tell us that you've made some sort of breakthrough?"

"Yes, sir."

"And do you actually have any proof of people trafficking this time?"

"Yes, sir. We've arrested the trafficker."

As Xavier Ng hit the record button, he realised that he was jittery. Hopefully, his boss wouldn't notice. Chua was busy pouring water into three plastic cups.

Ng held the cup to his mouth. He sipped slowly. The rookie detective flushed easily, especially after a couple of Tigers, and wasn't sure if he was flushing now. He was certainly nervous. The sudden, dizzying events at Changi Airport had turned Low's fantastical hunch into a legitimate case.

A wild goose chase had produced a human trafficker,

presumably caught in the act. Hopefully. In theory, the eye-witness accounts were still circumstantial. The interrogation would make all the difference. Ng's first major interrogation.

The room was deliberately cold. Standard tactic. Singaporeans couldn't *tahan* the cold. Other countries starved their suspects. Singapore tortured theirs with air-conditioning.

But the temperature didn't help Ng either. He couldn't feel his fingers.

The unexpected drop of blood hardly improved his nerves. Ng and Chua watched it form a tiny, red puddle on the steel table. Fortunately, the blood missed the cups and the deputy director's paperwork. The veteran civil servant prepared his files with fastidious care.

"Clean it up." Chua pushed a box of tissues towards Ng, reminding everyone present of their respective ranks in the interrogation process.

Ng went to work on the blood stain. Chua grabbed a handful of tissues and offered them across the table. They were rejected.

"OK, fine. I'll just leave them here." Chua dropped the tissues. "Shall we start then?"

"No comment."

Chua nodded to his colleague. He wanted the rookie to take the lead.

Ng cleared his throat. "OK, right. Right. OK. Can you confirm that you are Christine Yeoh?"

"No comment."

"Are you the manager of the Happy Maids Agency in Katong Shopping Centre?"

"No comment."

"Er, Miss Yeoh, the bleeding is getting quite bad."

"Yah. Bastard tried to kill me."

Chapter 48

Low's sudden presence in the interrogation room was an indictment of Chua's failure. The deputy director had made no progress. The stubborn woman had offered nothing.

Ng had played nice. Chua had resorted to stereotype. Good cop. Insane cop.

But Christine Yeoh had forced a change in personnel. Ng was out. Low was in, against Chua's better judgement.

And still, Yeoh was unmoved. She dabbed her bloody forehead and parroted the same line. "No comment."

She flicked back her hair, emphasising the gash above her left eye. She wanted the wound to remain the centre of their attention, especially for that inspector.

"That's a bad cut," Low said.

"No comment."

"But you know who did it?"

"Bitch."

"You mean Miss Ramila Mistry?" The inspector pointed at the large mirror on the wall. "You know she's on the other side, right? Watching. That's a two-way mirror. And she's watching you. Does that bother you?"

Yeoh faced the mirror. Her reflection saddened her. It

wasn't the blood. She had been a KTV hostess for years. She had suffered worse. It was the lines. The wrinkles. The eyebags. Her current line of work was withering her.

She grinned at herself. Then she pointed at herself. Then she pulled back her head.

They watched her splattered saliva dribble down the mirror.

"Bitch."

"Yes, you like that word," Chua said, tapping his file on the table. "Would you like to explain what happened with Miss Mistry? I'd like to know, too."

The deputy director glared at his deceitful colleague. He'd deal with Low later. Once he'd used him.

"Ah, that part is easy, Deputy Director. I used my old friend, Shitty Timmy, to follow this one, right or not, Christine?"

"No comment."

"Yah, no comment. Very good. You watch those Netflix crime shows, is it? Maybe you watch those instead of watching Timmy. But Timmy owes me. I do stuff for him. Once in a while, he does something for me. Owe money. Pay money. *Ah longs* never forget, right. You know why I call him Shitty Timmy, Christine? Does all my shitty jobs for me, like following people for me. Do you know why I use him? He's a pimp and pimps are the best. They live in the *longkangs*. The alleys. The shadows. They work in the dark. Like Batman. No need Gotham. We got Geylang. And Timmy is always hiding in Geylang. Cannot be seen. And you never saw him. All the way from Katong to the airport, right or not?"

"No comment."

"Don't need you to comment. Got Shitty Timmy."

Low opened the file. "You like this? It's like a photo

album. Got you leaving Katong. Got you driving into this industrial estate. Then standing outside a big truck. And then, *wah*, look at this Christine. This is the big one. This video. Should put on TikTok. Watch this." Low reached across the table for the laptop. He turned the screen towards Yeoh. He slowly found the button. A grainy image filled the screen. "Bit blurred at first. Shitty Timmy very excited one. Then he focused. And look at that."

Yeoh watched two, large Chinese men open the shutters.

She watched the men pull young, frail women down from the truck.

She watched the women wipe their eyes. Holding hands. Seeking support.

She watched the timid woman cling to a scrawny teddy bear.

Dewi.

And she watched another woman roughly push Dewi towards a black mini-van with tinted windows.

Herself.

She was watching herself take part in a trafficking operation.

She was watching herself grab Dewi by the arm. *That* arm. The arm that had been held up to the light in the Happy Maids Agency to reveal the purple swelling. The battered arm that had convinced Dewi that she could not go back. No matter what.

"Do you see, Christine? We know that's Dewi. We know she came to you. For help. And you did this instead. You sent me chasing red herrings at TWC2 while you rushed them out of the country. But you screwed up and here's why."

Low slid a folder across the desk. The TWC2 logo was stamped on the cover. "You didn't count on good guys like Mr Richmond, keeping files, remembering faces, checking on their wellbeing, all the things that you don't bother with. Every beaten maid is a real headache for you, right? Lose money, right? They get sick, lose money. Catch Covid. Lose money. Get abused. Lose money. What to do? Heck care *lah*. But James Richmond cares. His office cared enough to keep a detailed record of every one of your abused victims. It's all in here, weeks, months and years of sustained abuse." Low held the file in the air. "And your flimsy house of cards . . ." Low slapped the file against the table. "Fucked."

"No comment."

"Yah, yah, yah, no comment. But why *ah*? Is it because of her?" Low pointed at the mirror. "Did it piss you off what she did? A foreigner some more!"

Yeoh turned to the mirror. "Bitch."

"Yah, we get it already. Bitch. No comment. Bitch. No comment. Don't want to tell us anything except how much you hate the bitch behind the mirror. I get it. She hit you. Caught you some more."

Low faced his frowning boss. "Timmy followed them to the airport. This one drove the girls in the mini-van. And you know what? She even made them get out, one by one, separate, go to check-in counters separately. Don't mix in front of the CCTV cameras. Fantastic. But she was paranoid now. Looking everywhere. Rushing. Checking if she's being followed. Time running out. So I tell Timmy to back off. You know why?"

Low raised a finger slowly towards the mirror. Now he grinned at his own reflection. "Hell hath no fury like a woman punched in the face by a pimp. I had her at the airport. Waiting. We knew the girls were coming. Just didn't know when. So Mistry waited. For hours. She's patient. Tenacious. Never gives up that one. And then, she saw you. Loitering around the check-in counter, checking your phone. We were right. But we were late. Their plane had already taken off. British Airways, direct to London. But Mistry tried to detain you anyway, didn't she? And you resisted arrest. And the rest is, well, a woman being punched in the face by a female inspector."

"Bitch."

"Absolutely. What a bitch," Low stood up and leaned across the table. "What an Indian bitch. Looking down her nose at your agency. She doesn't understand our culture, right or not? She doesn't understand how it works in Singapore. You're just providing a service for overworked families. And then she whacks you in the face at the airport. For what? You're just doing your job. Following orders. I get it. Even if she doesn't. But it's over now Christine. You're going to prison. Too much evidence already. And when we check your phone, we'll have even more. So why stay quiet now? You're not hurting that bitch behind the mirror. We've already caught you. You're just hurting yourself. From this point on, Christine, you can only hurt yourself more or help yourself, just a little bit. Who made you put those girls on the plane?"

"No comment."

"We know about Dewi. Who are the other girls?"

"No comment."

"What's going to happen to the girls?"

"No comment."

"You are not the brains here. Clearly. Why are you protecting him, Christine?"

"No comment."

"Say his name, Christine."

"No comment."

274

"Say his bloody name."

"No comment."

"*Wah lan eh*, can you say anything other than no comment?"

Now it was Yeoh's turn to slowly raise her index finger towards the mirror. "Bitch."

On the other side of the mirror, Mistry and Ng watched Low floundering, a rare experience for both parties.

"He's getting pissed off. That usually helps," Ng said.

"No, something's missing. Did tech get back about the phone?"

"On the way." Ng pretended to check his phone for updates. "Sorry about the Changi thing, checking up on you. I feel like shit."

"I know."

"I told them you had checked in and went through departure. I knew you hadn't."

"I know."

"How?"

Mistry gestured towards the screaming inspector on the other side of the mirror, stomping towards the door. "He said you wouldn't grass me up."

"Grass?"

"Tell tales. Tell your bosses."

"How did he know?"

"He said you're not an arsehole."

"Really?"

"He knows how to spot arseholes. He lives with one."

Ng's polite chuckle eased the tension. For a second or two. And then Low arrived.

"I don't get it," he shouted, slamming the door behind him. "I don't get her motive. Stonewallers are fine. I like stonewallers. Gives me something to work on, to break down. But she's not stonewalling. She's gone. Checked out. Left the building."

Mistry recognised the traits. Low was talking too fast. Avoiding eye contact. Shifting his weight. Walking the line between revelation and self-loathing.

"She's scared," Ng said.

"Of course she's scared. She's going to prison. She'll talk to help herself."

"She'll be killed, like the others," Mistry said.

"Then she'll be killed. Talk or no talk. She's dead anyway. Might as well seek some protection, right? Give her better odds of not getting her throat cut."

Ng's phone buzzed. He took the call. "Hello . . . It's Tech. They've traced her SIM card records. Singtel. Quite easy actually. She should've thrown away the SIM card first."

"She was busy being punched in the face by this one," Low said, nodding at Mistry. "Put it on speaker."

Low spoke into the phone quickly. "Hey, this is Inspector Low, any texts, WhatsApp messages?"

"Yeah, hundreds." The voice on the line was muffled. "You want me to read all?"

"No need, the last one or two. No wait. Stop." Low did the calculations. "What have you got after 8pm tonight? Close to 9pm."

"OK, hang on."

Ng felt rather lost. "Why those times?"

"Went to the ballroom after 8pm. See if they took the bait."

The voice on the phone returned. "Yeah, only one. It's a text message from a blocked number. We'll check that. But it says, 'send them first. Make a decision after.'"

Low didn't hear the rest of the conversation between

Tech and Ng. He was already heading for the door. "She's not scared. She's stalling."

"Why?" Ng wondered.

"To see what we know about the girls," Mistry said, chasing after Low. "To see if they need to be killed."

Chapter 49

Răzvan Lupo sipped his coffee and thought of home. Industrial Essex reminded him of Bucharest. Everything was daubed in grey. The sky. The drizzle. The docks. A world of metal and rust stretched from one end of his windscreen to the other.

But a river ran through the lot. And Lupo loved to stare at the Thames.

As a kid, he had foraged for scraps on the banks of the Danube, looking for anything of value, not realising the priceless commodity was flowing past him daily, leading into the Black Sea and a different life in Western Europe.

Romania had taught him the value of Europe's waterways. The swampy banks on either side produced nothing. Just scraps. Money only flowed through the rivers. Essex had confirmed it. A grey place for the natives. A golden opportunity for those passing through.

Lupo clutched the polystyrene cup with both hands. The foreign spring weather still deceived him. Warm evenings. Frozen mornings. He had considered switching on the heaters, but the lorry's engine was far too noisy and conspicuous for the time of day.

Besides, he had his coffee. And the foggy view. Essex by the Thames, just before dawn, took him back to Romania. The nostalgia would keep him warm for a bit and provide a handy distraction.

Their singing was driving him crazy.

In the back of the lorry, Dewi waited patiently for her turn. She was in no hurry. The singing was comforting. The singing blocked out the silence. And the silence bothered them more than the darkness.

Darkness was familiar and consistent. Their eyes and minds soon adjusted. But the silence was uncertain. They didn't know what was coming next.

But they knew how to sing. From church. From work. They knew how to escape, to fantasise.

That's why the other girls mostly picked ballads. Love songs. In their own languages. The words were alien to others, but understood by all, huddled together in a lorry filled with false hopes. A yearning to be discovered, to be seen, to be swept up and carried away in their homelands.

They wanted a reason to believe.

But Dewi already had one. He was waiting for her, back in Indonesia, with their old *Tarzan* DVD.

"Homework first," Dewi muttered to herself in the back of the lorry, in Bahasa.

That was the instruction left with her parents. Homework first. Then he could watch their special movie and reminisce and dream and wait for her return.

The muted applause brought her back to the darkness. They had been ordered not to make too much noise.

"Dewi." The voice was soft and kind. "Go."

Dewi held her teddy bear and sang their song. One more

279

time. The last time like this. The next time, she would see him on screen. Chubby face. Bright, brown eyes. Giggling. Always giggling.

And they would sing their song together.

You'll be in My Heart.

Their singing was starting to grate. Lupo was hungry. There was a McDonalds drive-through along the A13 and he always had an egg muffin after dropping off a load. It was a tradition. He had never been able to afford McDonalds in Romania.

He checked his watch. The Essex boys were late. No surprise. He preferred the Chinese. They were punctual. Rude, but punctual. The Essex boys turned up late and shared their life stories. Lupo had no interest in small talk.

He was not a patient man.

But he was a cautious one. He had picked them up at different places around the M25, using only country lanes and laybys. He had parked the lorry beside the Rainham Marshes, away from prying eyes and CCTV cameras. He had followed every instruction.

But he was still collecting the first load since that Chinaman had fucked up. Lupo was under no illusions. He was the guinea pig, the test case, the expendable one. Nothing could go wrong.

And something clearly had. Sunrise was on its way. Exchanges never happened in daylight. Lupo checked his watch a second time and cursed the death of a Chinese driver. Essex boys were just not as reliable.

Lupo watched his phone dance along the dashboard. He read the message.

"It's off."

Lupo swore in Romanian as he found the gun beneath his seat.

He had been really looking forward to an egg muffin.

Lupo jumped down from the driver's cab. He inhaled sharply, taking in the competing smells of low tide and a nearby landfill site: the sublime and the shitty. His stomach grumbled, forcing him to check the time again. He was starving.

Lupo slapped the side of the lorry twice. That was their prearranged signal to gather all belongings. Time to go.

They were going nowhere, but Lupo saw a strategic advantage anyway. His hand signal would bring them together at the door. Less chance of scattering. The work should be cleaner. Faster.

Lupo felt a little better as he examined the gun. If he finished up quickly afterwards, he might still make breakfast.

Every woman jumped. They had been briefed on the signal. They knew a double slap on the side of the lorry was coming at some point. But they hadn't known when.

Dewi was the first on her feet. Her excitement was palpable. She grabbed a nearby arm. "My song."

"Yah."

"He bang on my song."

Dewi shouldered her rucksack. She wanted to hold nothing but her boy's teddy bear. He was definitely with his mother now, guiding her along. He had given her a sign. A definite sign.

The song. *Their* song. She was going out into a new world on their song.

You'll Be in My Heart.

He was practically talking to her.

281

The women crowded around Dewi at the back of the lorry. They waited by the double doors. They heard the muffled footsteps. A clanking lock. Turning.

Dewi smiled as the other girls applied lipstick and foundation to cold, weary faces. They needed to impress the new men waiting for them. She didn't.

She was already taken. She had her boy.

Dewi pressed her face against the teddy bear. She could still smell him. Even now.

As the door slowly opened, the lorry's container was suddenly filled with laughter.

The women could not stop laughing. And hugging. And crying.

But early dawn confused them. Jet-lagged brains tried to decipher the sudden, alarming images, as if ticking off items in a grim tableaux.

There was a grey, foggy swamp.

There was a grey sky.

There was a grey man.

And there was a gun.

The women stopped laughing. The grey man was their driver.

He was on his knees. The swamp had swallowed most of his legs.

The gun rested against the back of his head.

Behind him, a taller man stood upright. His hand was steady, his finger frozen on the trigger.

"Good morning, ladies," he said. "I'm Detective Chief Inspector Wickes of the Metropolitan Police. Who fancies a nice cup of tea?"

Chapter 50

Yeoh only had eyes for the Indian bitch. The interrogation room was full of police officers now, but Yeoh focused on the foreigner. Deputy Director Chua stood at the back of the chilly room, clutching a file to his chest. The younger local, Ng, hovered by the door. And Low sat on the other side of the table, alongside Mistry.

But none of the men concerned Yeoh. She ran a maid agency. Before that, she was a KTV hostess. Men were her business. She provided a service for them. And women often hated her for it. Her products undermined the matriarchy. Whether she was selling maids or herself, her existence made other women feel inadequate. She offered something that others could not provide. She sold answers to questions that no one wanted to ask. So she recognised the disgust in Mistry's eyes.

Yeoh would not give the sneering detective any kind of satisfaction.

"You keep staring at me," Mistry said.

"Bitch."

Still hovering in a gloomy corner, the deputy director cleared his throat. "Mrs Yeoh, I've allowed Miss Mistry to join us as a courtesy. Please extend her the same courtesy."

"Bitch."

Mistry leaned across the table. "It's OK. You're still angry, Christine. I get that. But I had to try and detain you until Inspector Low contacted the airport police. Does your head still hurt?"

Yeoh considered spitting again. But she was already handcuffed. She didn't want to be gagged, too.

"No comment."

"Does my presence make you feel uncomfortable?"

"No comment."

"What is it like? Trafficking abused women?"

"Bitch."

"Mrs Yeoh, I will not tell you again," Chua said. "As Miss Mistry has been involved in this case from the beginning, I agreed to her request to ask questions. Just a few questions." The deputy director paused long enough to expose his true feelings on the matter. "You will answer them or this interview will be suspended."

His eyes found the only interloper. Mistry took the hint. She was a foreigner in a Singaporean interrogation room. She wasn't earning her privileged position. She tried again. "What were you doing at the airport?"

"No comment."

"Why did you see me and run?"

"No comment."

"Do you have a problem with all women or just maids?"

"Bitch."

The hatred was palpable and undiluted. Low was impressed at Yeoh's honesty. There was no effort to conceal or pretend, just an unvarnished disgust for the other woman. Yeoh did not care. Yeoh did not flinch. Instead, she rested her palms on the table. The handcuffs clinked against the hard surface. She sat upright, barely moving.

Her posture was close to perfect, the instincts of a former hostess.

"*Wah*, not bad," Low said finally, as if admiring an artwork. "I asked the deputy director to let Mistry sit in here, opposite you, just to irritate you. At first, he said, 'no'. She's a foreigner. And this is private Singapore business. But I knew she would definitely annoy you, look down at you, and you'd hate it. And you do. Look."

Low pointed at the handcuffs. "If you didn't have them, I'm sure you'd try to strangle her, like your friend Shumai. But you won't take the bait, eh? You won't break."

The Happy Maids agency manager turned to the repulsive inspector. His smug grin reminded her of a past life, of long nights, sore feet and too many men. They had usually sneered as they made their selections, perusing the offerings on the kerbside.

So she had smiled. She was trained. Programmed. Her smile was sexy and submissive. Every man's wet dream. But she didn't need to smile for anyone now.

"No comment."

And she sneered, just like the rest of them.

"Yeah, very good. Got attitude some more." Low tapped the file. "Just like last time, eh? Surprised our paths never crossed. You with the KTV hostesses. Me with Tiger. On the streets. Doing the same thing. Working with scum. In some ways, nothing changed, right? We're still working undercover, right? You close one eye with the maids. I close one eye with everything. Typical Singaporeans, right? Protect our rice bowl. But they died, Christine."

Low took in the responses of the women in the room. He was impressed. Mistry looked straight ahead. Yeoh flinched, but only slightly.

"Yeah, they're dead. All twelve of them. Mistry's people

found them in London. In an abandoned truck. Shot. No survivors. No witnesses. So you're saved, right?"

"No comment."

"Yeah, that's what Mistry's colleagues got in London. No comment. Because they're all dead. Twelve dead girls. Twelve 'no comments'. But we did get this."

Low pulled out a Polaroid photo of a blood-stained teddy bear beside a handwritten note. "You recognise that teddy bear?"

Yeoh turned away.

"Of course you do," Low continued. "That's Dewi's teddy bear. You remember Dewi, right? She's only got one name. Like Madonna. Like Beyonce. Like dead. But you remember her when she was alive, right? Came to you when she was being abused. Wanted to escape from her nightmare. So you put her on a truck. Not your problem anymore. Heck care *lah*. And now's she dead. Definitely not your problem anymore, right? But she did this for us."

Low took out a second photograph, a close-up shot of the handwritten note, and waved it in Yeoh's face.

"Can you see what it says, Christine? It's scrawled and messy and on a torn scrap. She was writing in the dark. In the back of that truck. Can you read it, Christine?"

Yeoh sneered at the photograph. She sneered at Low and Mistry and the other officers in the oppressive interrogation room. She had nothing else to offer.

"I'll help you Christine. It says, 'Miss Yeoh do this. Maid woman.' That's what she called you. *Maid Woman*. Sounds like a superhero from hell. And we know what your super power is. Making abused women disappear. But Dewi had the real super power. She came back from the dead. A brave woman resurrected. Because you killed twelve women. And one of them came back to point the finger." Low held up the photograph again. "Miss Yeoh do this. Maid woman. Miss Yeoh will hang for this. Miss Yeoh is a dead woman."

"I did not kill them."

Low visualised the line bobbling on the surface of the water, a gentle tugging, the ripples increasing. The fishing imagery pleased him. He recalled simpler times with his father, Bedok jetty at dusk, waiting for a bite that rarely came.

But Yeoh had taken a nibble. Her first proper sentence.

"You took them to the airport. Mistry saw you. You received a text, giving you the order. *Send them first. Make a decision after.* Of course, you deleted it. But our geeks in Tech found it. Found the text to your phone. Send them first. Make a decision after. And we made the decision for you. Mistry made it for you, slapping you in the face at the airport. And suddenly, you didn't have twelve cash cows on a plane anymore. You had twelve live witnesses in a truck. No point anymore. Too much risk. Cut your losses. Kill them all. But she made the connection for us. A real woman. Dewi."

Low held up the photograph for a third time. "A dead woman gave us what we needed. And now, instead of being charged with just human trafficking, we can also charge you with criminal conspiracy to commit murder."

Yeoh found her sneer again. "Then I talk for what?"

"For him."

Mistry pushed a photograph across the table. The teenager was handsome. Beaming. New blazer. Neat tie. Modern student. Traditional background.

"It's funny how school photos look the same all over the world," Mistry said. "My little boy's photo is just like this. Head and shoulders shot with a cheesy backdrop. Same angle, same lighting. I heard that your boy, Noah, wants to go to the UK to study engineering. And he's got a good chance. Goes to a really good school. Now."

"*His* school," Low interjected.

"Earned a scholarship for an overseas internship."

"*His* scholarship," Low added.

"Got everything he needs for a bright future."

"Except a mother. She'll be in prison."

Yeoh grinned at her son's toothy grin. The braces had been worth every cent. She had made every sacrifice. One more wasn't going to matter now.

"What do you want?"

"I want his name, Christine. In a signed statement. I want names, dates, places and transactions. I want his fingerprints over every one of them."

"Cannot."

"You help us or you'll never see your son graduate."

"Cannot. He doesn't get involved."

"He got involved with you."

"No, not him, his company maybe. His people. They helped me last time. So hard to survive. So much competition. Everyone else got cheaper product now. From Indonesia. From Myanmar."

"*People*. Everyone else got cheaper people, Christine. Women. Domestic helpers. Maids. Sitting in shop windows. On display. Ironing clothes. Modern marketing for modern slavery." Low saw the line. Wriggling. Sinking.

"And you hate it right? Everyone looks down on you, now and then. At least last time, it made sense, right? You were a prostitute. They were customers. They needed you, craved you, so they hated you. Because they hated themselves. And now, the same. You're the boss and they still hate you. Cos you're the pimp now. You're selling young women now. Exploiting poor people. And what do you get in return? Complaints. Problems. This one lazy. That one lazy. This one runs away. That one pregnant. It's never-ending. If only they would all just go away. The bad ones. Disappear. And he makes that happen for you. He makes your problems vanish."

Only the photograph deserved Yeoh's attention now. Her finger traced his smile. He was such a handsome boy. So intelligent. So pure. She would do right by her son.

"He's got nice eyes," Mistry said.

"Yeah."

"Do you wanna see them again, Christine?" Low shouted. "Do you want to see your son again, regularly? We charge you with murder. No chance. You co-operate. We downgrade. You might get out to see your grandchildren."

"He looks so happy in this photo."

"Yeah, like the maids in your shop window. Where is he, Christine?"

"You think I can get a reduced sentence?"

"You definitely won't if you don't help. And I'll make sure all your prison privileges are withdrawn. And I'll cancel your son's scholarship. If he's lucky, the kid can mop floors at a coffee shop."

"Why would you do that?"

"'Cos I'm a bastard. Where is he?"

"Where he should be," Yeoh whispered.

Chapter 51

Patrick Lin lit a candle for the dead. This was a test. He knew that. His faith was absolute, unshakeable. But his moral compass was complicated. He was human, vulnerable, fragile and weak. They all were. That was the point, the contradiction to overcome. What made him waver then, made him weep now.

Lin closed his eyes, but still saw them. They had the brightest of eyes, the dreams of the naïve. They were him, all those years ago, looking for the light.

The candle flickered. Lin was no longer alone. The heavy door kept out the non-believers and kept in the cool air. Everything functioned in Singapore. Everything had a purpose, even the church door.

The footsteps were light. Dainty. Female.

They were also slow and tentative.

A domestic helper.

Lin opened his eyes and looked upon his salvation. Contrary to popular stereotype, He didn't move in mysterious ways. For those who believed, He moved in rather literal ways. The path was clear, the signs obvious to all, except those who wilfully looked the other way.

The footsteps stopped, just over his right shoulder. The

pew creaked. She was sitting down. Lin heard plastic bags being lowered, rustling against the natural stone tiles. She was definitely a domestic helper.

Once again, Lin questioned his worthiness. Why was he being afforded so many opportunities to atone, to make amends for poor choices earlier in his life? Why was he being blessed, time and again, with a chance to shine?

Lin had nothing to give in return beyond his tears, the only physical manifestation of immeasurable gratitude that he could muster. He expressed his thanks with a nod, praying that his deep appreciation would register. He wiped his face and checked his appearance. An overhanging shirt flap was unsightly. Lin tucked it deep into his black trousers, remembering he had loosened his belt during confession.

Once the shirt flap was fixed, Lin felt ready. Polished shoes. Pressed trousers. Parted hair. He took pride in his appearance. First impressions mattered. Especially now.

He turned around.

She was even younger than he'd expected. He sighed. His fellow Singaporeans continued to disappoint him. Their maids were getting younger and poorer. As working and educational conditions improved in the region, fewer women were turning to domestic work as a source of income.

Singaporeans were no longer picking from the barrel, but plucking them straight from the tree, not yet ready, not yet ripe.

And they bruised easily.

She was barely an adult. And yet, the purple marks and scarring on her left arm were unmistakable.

Lin struggled to contain his excitement. He had to pause until the blurriness cleared. He could not stop crying. He was so fortunate, so blessed, to have such a clear path.

He inhaled sharply. His deep appreciation was over-whelming. Finally, he left the altar and made his way along the carpeted nave. The carpet was red. A lucky colour, promising prosperity and abundance. The symbolism was overpowering. Lin was almost too eager to breathe.

The church was empty, just for him. Lin had left his driver outside and Father Fernandes was back in the par-sonage, preparing for Sunday's service.

They were home alone.

And Lin felt home. He loved his church. He had paid for the restoration of the stained-glass windows, but the building pleased him more, the hybrid architecture, a bit of everything, the best of everything. The neoclassical façade came from the *ang mohs*. The cooler, rattan-backed pews came from the indigenous peoples of the region. The church stood as a resilient example of shared sacrifice for a common goal.

Outside, the wide verandas provided shade from the tropical sunshine and privacy for Lin. He would not be disturbed.

When he reached her pew, he noticed the shudder. She flinched. She tensed. She really needed his help.

Lin squeezed between the pews. The church had broad-ened his mind. The personal trainer had taken care of his body. He felt the rattan against his lower back, a familiar comforting sensation.

"Ah, that's better. Needed to sit down. It's hot in here, eh?"

Lin savoured her silence. Her apprehension. Her fear made his work more important.

He pointed towards the stained-glass windows. "You see those windows? I paid for those windows."

Now, Lin had her attention. He had mentioned money.

She had none. The power structure was clearly defined and understood.

He waited as she took in the elegance and beauty of his contribution to the church's heritage.

"You see all those figures, standing together in the window? That's known as the Romano-Byzantine style. It's like a mixture of Roman and Medieval art. It combines the best of different cultures to show the best of humanity."

The young woman appeared confused.

"It shows people doing good work," Lin added. "I'm very proud of my windows. Do you like them?"

"Yah. Very nice."

Lin allowed the words to wash over him, to cleanse and absolve him. She was responding, making a personal connection. He had never felt more righteous. "Yeah, I like them. I like this church. Is this your local church?"

She shook her head. "No. First time."

"Ah, where is your church?"

"Don't have."

"Why?"

"I'm new."

"You just moved to Singapore, is it?"

She nodded.

"Ah, I understand. Where are you from?"

She fiddled with her shopping bags. "Myanmar," she whispered.

"Myanmar? I often do business in Myanmar."

The young woman decided to make eye contact, joining the dots. The Chinese stranger had paid for the church windows. The Chinese stranger had business in Myanmar. The Chinese stranger deserved eye contact.

"You have pretty eyes."

The young woman did not recoil or look away. The

man had church windows and business in Myanmar. He had possibilities.

"Very pretty eyes," Lin emphasised. "Like a child. Let me see them."

Lin reached out and gently pinched her chin between his thumb and forefinger. She did not resist. He delicately tilted her head towards the light streaking through his stained-glass windows. She did not resist. He pressed his other hand into her thigh, silently pinning her to the pew. She did not resist.

"Do you know Father Fernandes? This is his church. And he says that we reveal our souls in here. We expose ourselves. We can see through each other."

His nose brushed against hers. "And I can see you. I can see your pain."

Lin's hands moved towards her left arm. His fingertips brushed against the fresh scars. "And I can make it go away. I can make all of this go away. Would you like me to do that?"

She did not answer. She did not know the right answer.

"It's OK. I have friends who want to help. Do you need help?"

Finally, she nodded. They usually did in the end.

Lin sat back and exhaled. "Good. Good."

He pulled out a small bottle of hand sanitiser from his hand and cleansed his hands. "What's your name?"

The young woman peered up at the stained-glass window. "Janice," she muttered.

"Janice? Nice name," Lin said, adjusting his waistband.

"Well, today it's Janice. Tomorrow, it'll be whatever she needs it to be, right?"

Lin felt a calloused hand on his shoulder. But he didn't turn round.

He knew the voice.

The church's long and high ceiling provided excellent acoustics, allowing Low's laughter to drift towards the pulpit.

Chapter 52

The Minister was not amused. He was missing his nightly rounds of visiting poor people in rental flights, handing out *hong baos* and goodie bags.

Across the polished table, Low scratched his stubble. The bureaucrats were wasting time. *His* time.

The inspector's mania was finite. He understood that, even if no one else did, not even his shrink. He needed to go in now, to attack, to eviscerate. He craved destruction to avoid addressing his own. Interrogations stalled the self-doubt.

But Deputy Director Chua had boxes to tick and bonuses to protect. Sitting at the head of the table, he adjusted the tie, the only man in the room wearing the sartorial relic, the only one unsure of his social status, the most eager to please.

Mistry had also been allowed to join them at the emergency meeting at the Police Cantonment Complex, as an observer. She was a woman and a foreigner. An irrelevance. She had no voice. But then, none of the others did either, except the one in the open-necked white shirt.

"This should not have happened." The Minister's voice was soft. It was not his job to shout. It was the job of Singaporeans to listen.

"Agree. I did not sanction this arrest." Chua's voice was desperate. "And I do not sanction the interrogation of Mr Patrick Lin."

"*Wah lao*, so much you don't sanction *ah*? You Russian, is it?"

"Now look, I am the Deputy Director. You cannot talk to me like that OK?"

"OK, now you sound Singaporean."

The Minister covered his mouth. He realised he was smiling. The career politician had often found Low's antics amusing, like a lab experiment, a Singlish-spouting hamster on a broken wheel.

The Minister cleared his throat. "You should have gone through the proper channels."

"Proper channels for what? He's the guy."

"Oh for heaven's sake." Chua slapped the table. "He's your killer is it? In both countries? Kills two in England and one in Singapore?"

"And runs a trafficking operation, smuggling vulnerable women," Low added.

"*Aiyoh*, this is crazy. You know what I think?" Chua dug an elbow into the table and pointed at Mistry. "*Her.* You're so eager to impress her that you're talking cock. The man's a billionaire, he runs foundations, he's a local legend."

"Balls. He's a Singaporean blind spot. Got money, we look the other way. He wears his wealth like a bulletproof vest."

"That's it. Enough nonsense." Chua pushed back his chair. "I will not let you ruin my department's reputation. The media will make us look like a joke."

"Please *lah*, they'll will print whatever he tells them to print." Low nodded towards the Minister.

"Careful, Inspector. That sounds almost slanderous," the Minister purred.

"Balls *lah*, it sounds like the mainstream media."

The Minister turned towards Mistry. "Colourful, isn't he?"

"He has his moments."

"Is he having one now?"

"I don't understand the question."

"You have followed this case in two different countries, Miss Mistry. You have participated in the apprehension of a prominent and highly successful Singaporean businessman, who denies any and all wrongdoing. And I understand you've had a successful career in London's police force. *So far.* So I suppose my question is, who do you believe? The respected businessman waiting in the interrogation room? Or the unshaven officer who still has chicken curry stains on his T-shirt."

"It's *teh tarik*," Low corrected.

Mistry felt the eyes of cynical men upon her. She found the sensation strangely familiar. In school, it was working-class white boys, so many white boys, telling her what she was. An outsider. A foreigner. A *Paki*. At university, it was middle-class white boys dragging her to parties to show off their liberal credentials. A useful minority among the eternally guilt-ridden. And in the police force, it was male officers dismissing her promotions as political correctness gone mad.

And now, in Singapore, it was conservative men looking to maintain the status quo.

What these men wanted, what they always wanted, was validation.

And it made her laugh, then and now. "You lot are hilarious."

The Minister was intrigued. "How so?"

"You're weak. You're all so weak."

"Now I don't understand."

"You're scared of him." She flicked her head towards Low. "You're a minister and you're scared of *that*."

Mistry encouraged the senior politician to examine Low's state. "Look at him."

The Singaporean inspector was lying back in his chair, picking at the *teh tarik* stains on his T-shirt.

"He can't even eat and drink properly," Mistry continued. "He can barely function. And yet you lot can't function without him. You're all desperate for him to be wrong to preserve your weird, archaic view of the world, that money is always right. Have you not seen our British scandals lately? Rich men can be arseholes. You lot need to catch up."

The Minister leaned forward. "So I can assume you're in Camp Low?'

"There aren't any camps, Minister, but I got the patronising undertone."

"My apologies. It's been a long day for everyone. And you've made it abundantly clear that you trust Inspector Low's judgment."

"With my life." Mistry smiled at her old friend. "With my son's life."

The Minister possessed the emotional intelligence to let the comment pass. He had read about the London case.

Chua was not similarly blessed. "*Yah lah, yah lah.* You trust him. Fantastic. But the evidence is circumstantial. You got three dead bodies in two countries. Lin wasn't anywhere near them. You got the trafficking women, but no direct links to Lin. You got some hazy connections to his companies, but nothing like a motive. OK *lah*, you got testimony, but from unreliable witnesses. Pimps. Hostesses. It's their word against Patrick Lin. Not enough. I'm telling you, if you go in that room and make a mess, it's over."

"He's right," the Minister said. "This one got no safety net."

"*Wah*, your Singlish not bad, *ah*." Low stood up. "Your *gahmen* never give us a safety net. Must be self-sufficient, right?"

Low headed for the door, singing loudly. *"Who wants to be a billionaire? I do."*

"Stanley, wait."

The use of his first name surprised Low. He was not usually on first-name terms with the Minister, not in the presence of others anyway.

"What?"

"Are you sure you want do this?"

Low stopped at the door. "No choice."

"Why?"

"The bruises," Low mumbled. "I'm tired of seeing their bruises."

Chapter 53

"It was the bruises, right?" Low didn't sit down. He didn't concern himself with formalities. He knew that Chua would handle the recording equipment. The deputy director was the fastidious one, the proper Singaporean.

Chua would go by the book. Low would go by the mania.

"It was the bruises, Patrick, right? Can I call you Patrick? I mean, I know that I'm supposed to call you, Mr Lin, technically, because you're helping us with our enquiries and you're a billionaire so I'm supposed to kiss your arse, but I feel like I know you, Patrick. We had the school talk together, then the stage show at the *atas* ballroom, with all your bigshot *kakis*. You remember that one? They had me thrown out, which was awkward. But we did have the church, didn't we, Patrick? We definitely had a moment there, don't you think?"

Patrick Lin ignored the deranged inquisitor and focused on the Indian sidekick beside Low. She was prettier. She was also quiet.

"No, don't look at her, Patrick. She's just an observer. Besides, she's not your type. She's not emotionally fragile or physically abused. Or maybe she's not bruised enough? You only like the really broken ones, right? Like this one."

Low pressed the play button on his phone. He turned up the audio. Two voices filled the boxy interrogation room, one concerned, the other timid:

"Ah, I understand. Where are you from?"

"Myanmar."

"Myanmar? I often do business in Myanmar."

"You have pretty eyes ... Very pretty eyes. Like a child. Let me see them."

Low dropped the phone on the table. He inhaled loudly through his nose, filling his chest, seemingly growing over the table.

"Yeah, I can see why you wanted to see her eyes. So pretty. Like a child. Just like you said. But that wasn't why I picked Janice. It was the bruises. The scars. They turned me off at the KTV lounge where I found her. Being raped. Well, it wasn't really rape, Patrick, cos he was her pimp, so consent is a grey area, right or not?"

Lin never reacted. His arms stayed rigidly folded. He gazed at the ranting inspector. His eyes fixed on Low's sweaty forehead.

Low nodded, as if seeing something in Lin's blank expression. "No, that's wrong, isn't it? You wouldn't know, not anymore. Last time, yes. Last time, you were living a different life, like me. I was Ah Lian. Undercover cop pretending to be a gangster. And you were a maths genius pretending to be a gangster. You knew the hookers then, right? You knew Christine Yeoh last time; before she was trafficking abused maids for you, she was a KTV hostess, too, like Janice. Did she have bruises when you found her? The bruises turn me off, but they turn you on, right?"

302

Lin almost grimaced. He caught himself, but it was a change in expression. Low nodded. "No, they didn't turn you on. But they drew you in anyway. The bruises. You saw Janice's bruises and you went over. And she recorded you." Low picked up his phone. "As a favour to me. For showing her some compassion. Just like you. But I didn't touch her. Not like you. Face, arms, legs, you moved around quite quickly, eh? You know that's molesting right? So we got you for molesting already. And you know what we do to molesters? When it comes to perverts, we follow your book. Old Testament. No chance for molesters. And in a church some more. Your church. You paid for the stylo-milo windows, right? So you can grope women in a nice, private building, is it?"

"No!"

The tiny interrogation room fell silent. Lin's voice was loud and defiant. Low slowly returned to his seat, allowing the tension to fester.

"No, Patrick? No, what?" Low fumbled for a piece of A4 on the table. "I have a written statement from Janice. She says that you grabbed her chin and then rubbed her thigh. Yes, I know, it's a bit 'he said, she said', and your expensive lawyers could probably cry, 'entrapment', but it's not gonna look good. Even your boardroom *kakis* in the media cannot bury this one. Very embarrassing for the charitable billionaire."

"No."

Low and Mistry exchanged glances. "No, what, Patrick? You're beginning to sound like a parrot."

"I will not have this. I will not have you mocking my beliefs."

"No one is mocking your beliefs," Mistry said. "No one has mentioned your beliefs."

"His inferences. I'm fed up with his inferences. I know it's normal in *your* country, Miss Mistry, but in Singapore, we are proud of our religious harmony."

"You're not going to sing are you, Patrick?"

"Yes, Inspector Low. You make fun of me. You mock our faiths, our personal choices. And for someone like me, the mockery is even worse because I made my choices later in life."

Low perused Lin's file. "Yes, you found God in the old Queenstown Prison, which was lucky. Most convicts found pornography."

"Yes, ridicule me. Mock me. It's all you have. But I will not accept this." Lin addressed Chua. "You are leading this investigation, Deputy Director?"

"Yes, I am," Chua said, adjusting his tie.

"I agreed to this because I believe in second chances. I had one. And based upon my own reading, Inspector Low has had plenty. I'm willing to help and support anyone. That's why I'm here. But this constant goading is unacceptable. I agreed to assist you. Remember?"

Chua watched as Lin checked the cuffs on his shirt. He turned to the perspiring, fidgeting colleague beside him. The Deputy Director shook his head.

"No, Mr Lin, you didn't agree to anything. Inspector Low arrested you on suspicion of people trafficking and conspiracy to commit murder. Answer his questions, please. Or I'll have you charged with molestation right now."

Lin sat back in his chair. "OK, Deputy Director. Let's do it your way. And then, later, I'll do it my way."

"*Wah lau*, now he's Frank Sinatra."

"OK, fine, make your jokes. But I will file a legal complaint later, Deputy Director."

Chua pondered the threat. He thought about his CPF

savings and the home renovations that he intended to complete before retirement. He considered his kids' academic aspirations. The youngest one still harboured dreams of an overseas degree.

And he looked at the two men sitting on either sides of the table. Both had the potential to ruin him, professionally and financially.

He faced the billionaire. "If you wish to file a complaint, that's your prerogative, sir. " Chua turned to Low. "Carry on, Inspector."

Low cleared his throat. Compliments confused him. Hatred was easy, but endorsements were complicated. They slowed him down. He needed a diversion. He spotted Mistry's watch.

"8.52," he muttered.

Mistry frowned. "What?"

"Nah, we'll come back to that." Low swivelled in his chair, returning to the impeccably dressed businessman. "You know the girls are not dead, right? We got there just in time."

"What girls?"

"Your girls. Your abused girls, the ones you get Christine Yeoh to smuggle out of your country, through your maid agency."

"I don't know what you're talking about."

"I'm sure you don't. 8.52."

"What?"

"Yeah, you won't know Chief Inspector Wickes. A nice guy, for an *ang moh*. He's also Mistry's boss. And he arrested your driver, some Romanian guy, which really ruined the driver's plans, apparently. He was about to shoot all twelve girls in the back of the truck. 8.52."

"What?" A puzzled Lin looked for guidance from the

305

other officers in the room. They offered nothing. "What truck?"

"Ah, this new truck was freelance. Outsourced. Smart. We outsource everything right? Truck driving, manual labour, domestic servitude, murder, it's all the same to us, we don't do it ourselves. Plus you had that connection to Steve Robertson's truck company. You remember Steve Robertson, right? Apparently he said that you could supply some Chinese drivers for his trucks and then he said something to us and you killed him, right?"

Lin shook his head in disbelief. "What on earth would I possibly gain from killing this man? Especially if one of my companies was supplying him with migrant labour—legally, I might add."

"'Cos he was talking to us. He had gambling debts in your casino, the Genting one in Essex. And you're like me right, deep down, still think like an *ah long*. Owe money, pay money. You can smell it. Can't help yourself."

Lin exhaled in exasperation. "Inspector Low, I came to terms with my past a long time ago. I set up the Second Chance Foundation, among many other charitable initiatives, to acknowledge my past and try to stop others from heading down the same path. I am not the one stuck in the past here."

"No, you're stuck in the present, where smuggled girls were found alive in a truck that your shell company invests in. And they were sent across by a maid agency that you also own, facilitated by traffickers like Christine Yeoh and Ah Meng, people from the old KTV scene. Like you. And when the KTV clowns tried to crawl away and save themselves, by talking to us, you had them killed. The China driver in England. Ah Meng over here. Even the *ang moh* Robertson. You had him crucified, which was a bit heavy handed in the symbolism."

306

Lin sighed. "Inspector Low, before we wrap this up with my lawyer, let me reiterate, again, I have investments in companies across the region, Asia and the UK, where there are presumably hundreds of crimes committed every day. My companies employ thousands of people. I can't be held responsible for their actions."

"Even when it's murder?"

"Oh, Inspector, I wasn't even in England for those crimes you mention. If murders are committed on a Facebook video, is Mark Zuckerberg culpable?"

Low leaned back and applauded. "Wah, that's good, Patrick. Did you memorise that one? The Facebook murder and Zuckerberg? I like that one. That's a good one. Nah, of course Mark Zuckerberg isn't culpable, but he wasn't responsible for 8.52."

"What is 8.52?"

"8.52pm to be precise," Low said. "That was the time that you hanged yourself."

Chapter 54

The other officers were determined to look only at the suspect. Both Mistry and Chua were trained, in their respective countries, to give nothing away during an interrogation. No occasional glances. No raised eyebrows or involuntary responses. Remain professional. A blank canvas.

So Mistry and Chua found Patrick Lin's bewildered face a useful distraction. They could focus on his confusion to hide their own. Like Lin, they had no idea where Low was going.

"Tell me about 8.52," Low said. "Tell us all. For the record. 8.52pm. The timing must be scorched on that born-again soul of yours. Unburden yourself."

"Inspector Low, I'm assuming this is some sort of counter-intuitive interrogation technique, but I fear you may be embarrassing yourself."

Low welcomed Lin's self-assurance. Self-assurance was halfway to complacency. The other half was uncertainty. Low was ready.

"No, not this time, but I did embarrass myself at 8.52. Do you remember? On stage. Your monkeys had me removed from the ballroom. And you sent a message. At 8.52. Incriminating yourself."

Low found a piece of paper from the file. He held it aloft. "Read that text message."

"I haven't got my reading glasses."

"Then squint."

Lin craned his head, narrowing his eyes. "Send them first. Make a decision after." He shrugged his shoulders. "What does that mean?"

"It's the message you sent. 8.52. It popped up on Christine Yeoh's phone. Your maid agency manager and people smuggler. You sent that message. 8.52."

"No, I didn't. I'm sure you'll check my phone records."

"We are," Chua said.

"It doesn't matter. I saw you. As I left the room. Agitated. 8.40. And I saw you get up. 8.41. And I saw you leave the table. 8.52. And my rookie detective, Xavier Ng, watched you after 8.52. He was a waiter. A very convincing waiter. Kept giving me champagne. In fact, he's more convincing as a waiter than as a policeman. But he saw you. Panicking. 8.52. Whispering to your people. The best in Singapore society. They sit on every board, every *atas* alumni association. They pray to the same god and own the same country. And they were shitting themselves at 8.52. I was ruining everything at 8.52. Maybe. You didn't know for sure. So the message goes out as a precaution. Send them first. Make a decision after. They can leave Singapore. See what we know first. Can always kill them later. But I've got you. 8.52. With Xavier Ng. On camera. Same time the message was sent. Same time you panicked. Same time you decided you might have to kill the women in the truck."

"That's absurd."

"When did you actually decide? After 8.52. When did you decide to kill them?"

"You're insane."

309

"Probably. But I've never ordered twelve women to be killed before, not like you. That's real power. That's real influence. A nod in the grand ballroom and they all die. A quick chat in the car park and they all die. But why? That's the bit I don't get. What's the Faustian bargain?"

"My lawyer will destroy you, Inspector Low."

"He'll have to get in line. Why did you try and kill 'em? Because you couldn't fuck 'em?"

Low saw the blood vessels. The widening, traitorous eyes. Lin blinked repeatedly, but he couldn't hide the internal treachery.

Low was on his feet, jabbing a finger between reddening eyes. "Yeah, you can't shag 'em on the righteous path. Kill 'em? No problem. Molest them when no one is looking? No problem. But you can't shag 'em. Definitely cannot shag 'em. And that must dredge up the rage, right? The old rage, from your *ah beng* days. It's still there, right? Like it is for me. You can't kill it. Can't kill the urge, the shameful urge. You can only try and kill them."

"I would never kill those women."

"Not personally, but on your behalf? Sure. That's what I'll leak on social media anyway. That's what I'll tell your *kakis* in *gahmen*. At 8.52, you gave the order to smuggle those women out of Singapore."

"No."

"At 8.52, you gave the order."

"I would never . . ."

"At 8.52, you calculated the risks involved."

"I didn't."

"At 8.52, you told your people to wait first."

"I will not take . . ."

"At 8.52, you realised I was coming for you."

"Inspector . . ."

310

"And you panicked. You wanted them dead. You decided to kill twelve women because you couldn't shag 'em."

"Fuck you, *lah*. I was saving them."

Lin's vitriolic outburst silenced the room and appalled him. But he had to draw a line. He accepted the derision. The cynicism from non-believers. He knew his dedication was hard to swallow. But he would not be deterred.

"I was saving them." Lin lowered his voice. "I didn't mean to swear, but I was saving them. I will not allow you to muddy my mission, Inspector Low, or besmirch its legacy. I was saving every one of those women."

"By killing them? What does that mean? You can't make an omelette without murdering twelve women?"

Lin took a deep breath. "You really don't see it, do you?"

"Please. Enlighten me."

The billionaire looked to the Englishwoman for moral support. "Inspector Mistry, what do you know about Gladstone?"

"Never heard of him," Mistry said.

"Does he play in the English Premier League?"

"No, Inspector Low. He was a British prime minister. William Ewart Gladstone. In the late 1880s. I'm surprised you aren't aware of him, Inspector Mistry. He's one of yours."

"One of mine?" Mistry sniggered. "I think we were still shopkeepers in Gujarat back then. There's not a lot of interest in our imperial rulers."

"No, Gladstone was misunderstood. He was a good man. A true believer. Even as prime minister, he would walk the streets of London as part of his rescue and rehabilitation work, saving British prostitutes. He spent his own money. And was ridiculed. We always are. In fact, there were preposterous rumours that he might be Jack the Ripper, even though Gladstone was old and frail by 1888. He was just a good man, a pious man, mocked, because his devout beliefs were different to others. Just as you are doing to me now."

"No, I don't think you're Jack the Ripper," Low said. "You're far too boring for that. You just smuggle and kill 'em."

"*Save* them. I save them just as I was saved. And yes, to use your facile analogy, I was bruised, too. And He came for me. So I came for them. I gave them a second chance. But the path is hard. So many temptations to fall back into old habits."

"Yeah, they do, don't they? They fall into old habits," Low echoed.

He understood now. He saw them. Every woman. Falling back. Retreating. Taking the familiar path, the easier option.

"They just can't be told," Low said.

"They just need guidance. Patience."

"Yeah, but that's still not enough, is it? These women. They don't know what's good for them. Look at the maids. They get abused. Time and again. Whacked with a clothes hanger and what happens? They go back to the same abusive employer. Cigarette burns? Go back again. And you keep praying for them, over and over. You pray for them at church. And they still won't let you save them. So ungrateful. Hostesses are the same. Get abused by pimps like Shumai. And they keep going back. Got police like me for protection. Charities like you. And they still go back. The abused keep going back to the abusers. How dare they? Women like Janice. And Grace. They go back to the scum. You try to save them, but they just won't bloody listen, will they? They won't follow the path. Like Dewi. How many times was she offered your path? Because it has to be your

312

path, right? That's the real Faustian bargain. Yours is the one true path. Your path brings wealth. Just look at you. And still, they won't listen. These women. They're lost and they won't be found. Or saved. No matter how much money you spend, they just won't follow your path."

"It's frustrating."

"Which part? That they won't do as they're told or won't follow your special path?"

"It's frustrating because once you've seen it, once you *really* know, you just want to share it. You want others to see it. To embrace it."

"Oh for god's sake," Mistry snapped. "History is full of men like you. You're always saving us on our behalf, aren't ya? Always correcting our ways. Where would women be without men like you?"

"You would be where you are right now," Lin said calmly. "Lost."

Low stretched out his left arm, instinctively, blocking Mistry's lunge across the table. He looked down at his shoes. He didn't want the others to see him smiling.

In such a tense moment, he was surprisingly philosophical.

Low knew he'd never again meet anyone quite like Ramila Mistry. But he was grateful for their time together. He also appreciated what she did to men like Lin.

The billionaire was incredulous. Dumbfounded.

"You really are confused, aren't you? By her reaction," Low's voice raced to keep pace with his thinking. "She doesn't get it. You really think you're helping people."

"I am helping people." Lin sounded assertive again.

"I believe you. Because you really believe it. The mission. It's not about money, or casino debts, or trucking companies and bloody supply chains. Heck care *lah*. You're a billionaire, not a *blur* pimp. You're Patrick Lin. The founder of the Second Chance foundation. That's what you do. Give second chances."

"With all my heart," Lin said softly.

"You send them away to save them. You actually believe this shit. But some people just cannot help themselves. They must be forced to help themselves. Grace and Dewi and the others have to be shown the way. You save them from themselves."

"Yes. Yes. I've saved hundreds of them. I took them off the streets. Like Gladstone. And I gave them new lives. Abused maids. Raped hostesses. I saved all of them."

"You exploited vulnerable people for profit," Mistry said.

"What profit?"

Low found himself nodding along. "Yeah, it's not for profit. It's real. It's genuine. You save them. Whatever the cost. It doesn't matter. Some don't make it, but never mind, as long as the majority make it. The Singapore way. There's always a few fuck ups in any society. Like the truck driver and Steve Robertson and Ah Meng."

"I saved hundreds of young women."

"And those guys were collateral damage?"

"I didn't have any part in that. I wasn't even in England for the first two."

"But you were here when Ah Meng was killed. Silenced."

"It's a tragedy. But none of them really understood what we're trying to do here. They still thought it was about money. That's the trouble with people today, especially in Singapore. They see me and they just see the net worth. Do you know people actually Google my net worth? My staff tell me. One of the most popular Google searches in Singapore is 'net worth'. They never Google about Second Chance. They never ask about the real work. The only work that matters to me now."

Low sighed. "And they were putting the work at risk."

"Like you said, Inspector. Some people just do not want to be saved. They turn to craven vices instead, like lust, blackmail or greed. My Second Chance foundation will never succumb to such grubby temptations."

"Even if three men died?"

"Hundreds of women were saved."

"So it's a numbers game?"

"There's no game, Inspector, just the work. His work."

"Nothing else matters to you now, does it? Sincerely."

Lin unbuttoned his cuffs and rolled up his sleeves. The interrogation room was stuffy. "Precisely. They were putting my life's work at risk. My legacy. And once the first one goes, it becomes an exercise in containment."

They didn't speak for a while, listening instead to the faint rattling of an air-conditioning unit. Low noticed that the old machine was leaking.

"You'll go to prison," he said finally.

"That's no sacrifice. I sacrificed myself to Him years ago. Our work will endure."

Chua cleared his throat and pretended to fiddle with the recording device. "I think that's enough for now. Unless there's anything you want to add, Mr Lin?"

"Yes, I would." Lin rested his elbows on the table and clasped his hands together. "Sorry for the bad language earlier, Miss Mistry. What must you think of me?"

Chapter 55

Chua joined the other officers in the adjacent room. The deputy director declined a Tiger beer from one of his subordinates. Chua was never off duty.

But he wasn't tactless. In a quieter corner, Low and Mistry were deep in conversation. Chua decided not to intervene. They were presumably saying their goodbyes. They had a history. Low had demons. Chua had no interest in going there.

Instead, he made his way through the crowd of junior officers, gawking at the large glass screen, like kids on their first zoo visit. Being relatively new in the job and Singaporean, they hadn't been in the presence of such a prominent criminal before.

On the other side of the glass, Patrick Lin sat alone at a table. He was praying.

His arrest and subsequent charge had confused most of the impressible officers in the room. He was rich and supposedly guilty of heinous crimes. That didn't fit the prescribed narrative.

Chua passed them all, nodding politely and accepting the odd congratulatory comment. The praise left the proud man distinctly uncomfortable. The deputy director oversaw the case, but this had not been his case. The mad one in the corner, whispering sweet nothings to a former lover, had dominated from start to finish.

Chua felt like an empty suit, a bureaucratic shell, relying on rogue detectives to solve his problems. He felt a fraud. But he would retain his dignity.

He found Xavier Ng sitting against the far wall, holding a polystyrene cup filled with Tiger. The beer hadn't been touched. The case had aged the rookie detective. Or maybe following Low around the city had taken its toll. Ng looked ravaged.

"I just wanted to say, congratulations," Chua said, looking at the top of Ng's head. The younger man already had grey hair.

"Thank you, sir." Ng stared at his beer.

"Did you watch the interrogation in here?"

"No, sir. Had to do some reports outside."

"Must admit. Low was good. And so were you, from what I heard."

Ng looked up for the first time. "Sir?"

Chua chuckled at the irony. His officers were trained to follow orders and respect authority. To keep up the pretence of both, Ng had to lie now.

"It's OK. I know about the ballroom," Chua said. "I should be an arsehole now, right? You never told me. Went behind my back some more. Undercover as a waiter. Technically, I should be pissed off."

Chua pointed at the glass screen. "But you helped with him, I suppose. Just amend your report, with accurate times and dates. I'll counter sign."

"I don't understand."

The deputy director was less amused now. Singapore's rigid adherence to its clearly defined societal structures

317

maintained the rule of law, but it often came at the expense of intuitive behaviour. "Just take the compliment. Amend the report."

"But I wasn't a waiter, *wha'*. When was I supposed to be a waiter?"

Chua suddenly felt dizzy. But he was going to suppress it, ignore his instincts and give the benefit of the doubt. "With Low. At the ballroom."

"I wasn't with Low. I was at Changi Airport. Watching Mistry. Following your instructions, sir, which I still feel bad about. I apologised, but I'm sure she hates me. You think I should apologise again?"

But Chua wasn't thinking. Or listening. He was running, pushing through the starstruck onlookers gazing at the praying billionaire. Chua caught a glimpse and briefly envied the piety on display. The deputy director needed prayers now.

"You lied." Chua's palm caught Low's shoulder blade. The inspector's reflexes took over, spinning him round, confronting his dramatic interrogator.

"What?"

"The ballroom surveillance. Following Lin. There was no one there, except you. Being a clown on stage. You never sent Ng there. He was doing as he was told. Watching you."

Chua pointed at Mistry. She turned away.

"So it was the pair of you? I'll bloody whack you for this, Low."

The deputy director realised his volume had reached the other officers, momentarily dragging their gaze away from the freakish, live art installation through the glass.

Low shook his head, wearily. He had never felt more alone in his own world. Chua and Ng both shared the same race, culture and passport as Low. But they were aliens to him. They conformed. Without question.

"Ah, Xavier told you the truth," Low said.

The inspector wasn't disappointed. He empathised. Ng had just put down a deposit on a new flat in Boon Keng and Singapore was so small. The rookie had nowhere else to go. And Chua never saw the value of colouring outside the box, to ignore the lines and challenge conventional wisdom.

The deputy director was the conventional wisdom.

Low could only make do with what he had. "And now you're pissed off. I get it."

"Don't patronise me, Low."

"I'm not. I'm really not. You took my side during the interrogation. I'm grateful."

"It was either you or a people smuggler."

"I'm still grateful."

"It was a tough decision."

"I'm sure. But you agree?"

"That you're marginally better than a possible murderer?"

"That he did it."

Chua peered over his shoulder. Through the glass, Singapore's most prominent billionaire was talking aloud in an empty interrogation room.

"Probably."

"And now we've got him."

"With false information. We have no direct connection to the message sent to Christine Yeoh's phone. We have no eyewitness reports of him doing anything at 8.52, apart from him being irritated by your bloody *wayang* acting. We don't even have a formal confession. He won't write down anything."

"Because he didn't do anything. Look at him. He's guilty of nothing. He needed to tell us that. He had to tell us that. He'll confess to nothing except doing His work. He'll go to court and say exactly the same. And the judge will either send him to Buangkok or Changi, but it doesn't matter. He's done."

"The evidence is still circumstantial."

"No, it isn't. Not to him. The work isn't circumstantial. The work is real. His work is finding lost women. Saving them. He'll say that in court, proudly, honestly. He has a cause. A mission. There's nothing circumstantial about his mission. He'd be deeply offended if anyone said as much."

"Even if that's true, he didn't physically kill anyone. The killers are still out there."

Low shrugged. "Hired hands. *Ah longs*. They'll turn up. Wickes and Mistry will find them in the UK. We'll get the one who got Ah Meng. But the killings are over."

"You sure or not?"

"I'm positive. The killers were just naughty boys." Low gestured towards the main attraction behind the glass. "We've caught the Messiah."

Chapter 56

Father Hodgson loved his church. The spring sunshine brought out the best of his stained-glass windows. The priest closed his eyes and savoured the warmth. Winter had been cruel to his arthritic bones. The changing seasons offered a temporary reprieve. He felt better this morning.

But then, Essex always looked better in the spring. The season was kind to every English country garden and Father Hodgson's churchyard was no exception. The daffodils danced in the breeze. The grass grew faster. Life started over. Even Nature understood the importance of resurrection.

Father Hodgson gripped his cassock as the elderly man hurried through the nave. Churches looked terrific on the glossy pages of *Country Life*, but not on an electric bill. The stone floor was freezing. Medieval architects were not without their faults. There were too many parts of the church that the sunbeams could not reach. At least the vestry was small and easier to heat.

Father Hodgson closed the door, just in case. His Essex flock continued to shrink, year on year, but his remaining parishioners were nothing if not committed. His door would always be open to them.

They would turn up soon enough, the neglected

housewives and the cynical pensioners, either looking to kill time or earn points for the impending afterlife with a homemade Victoria sponge.

Father Hodgson didn't have long. The priest checked the clock on his wall, a gift from the North Essex choir, and picked up the phone. The call was answered immediately.

"Hello."

"Oh, hello, Father Hodgson here," the priest said, shaking his head. The call was prearranged. "Well of course it's Father Hodgson. How are you?"

"Hungry."

Father Hodgson's laughter filled his tiny vestry. "Same. Going to have some jam on toast. Need the sustenance. Busy day today. I have a fundraising meeting after breakfast, then a clothes donation drive and then an evening of confessions."

"What did you think?"

Father Hodgson quietly admonished himself.

He didn't do small talk.

He didn't do banality.

He didn't do anything, beyond the mission.

Father Hodgson took a deep breath and started again.

"Yes, well, I'm terribly disappointed. In fact, I was devastated when I heard the news. I'm just so, so, sorry, for you and the foundation, everything really."

"It was never about me."

"No, I know. I understand that."

And Father Hodgson really did. The priest had never seen such an unswerving commitment to a higher cause. They had only met once, at an Essex casino of all places, but their brief encounter had left Father Hodgson in no doubt.

He was a true believer.

And he didn't fill the gaps in trivial conversations. Father Hodgson had forgotten again. "Sorry, I'm just a bit stunned.

I didn't expect you to speak to me so soon, if at all, with your, you know, position."

"It's not about me."

"Yes, of course. So why did you want to speak to me?"

"To make sure the work continues."

"Right. Yes. Of course." Father Hodgson felt his cheeks tingle. Suddenly, the vestry was too warm. "But the supply chain has been disrupted, after, well, you know."

Father Hodgson did not want to broach the subject. The priest had read the stories, about Steve Robertson, being nailed to his own pallet, crucified for his sins.

He really was a true believer.

"I will find more."

"Can you do that from there? Because you cannot return to England; I mean, hopefully you can, in the future. I'm praying for you."

Father Hodgson gripped the phone to check himself. He was babbling.

"Don't pray for me. Pray for them."

"I will. I do."

"We must save those who cannot save themselves."

"Of course."

"I'll arrange a new supplier."

"Should we not wait until things, perhaps, settle?"

"Things will never settle for these poor women. You're not here. I am. Singapore. Malaysia. Indonesia. Myanmar. Cambodia. Laos. It never ends. They all need us."

"Yes I know. It's just ... difficult." Father Hodgson's voice drifted. "How did we end up here?"

"I don't question His will."

"No, I know. But those three people ..."

"Will be judged. I don't know of their motives in England, but they were stopping the work. Now, we can continue."

"Are you sure?"

"Absolutely. Aren't you?"

"Oh, most definitely," Father Hodgson said. The priest was picturing Steve Robertson being nailed to a pallet. "Most definitely. What will you do now?"

"Eat. I'm starving. I've got to go."

Father Hodgson hung up and hoped, against all reasonable expectations, that he would never call again.

He was satisfied with the phone call. He needed confirmation from Father Hodgson that only a brief delay was required. He would establish new suppliers, fresh connections, even from here.

He would find a way.

He stepped outside. He enjoyed the fresh air, before they inevitably called him back in again. Rules. Regulations. Routines.

But the exercise, walking round in circles, made him hungrier. He could practically smell the food.

He was going to enquire about the dish when a hand grabbed his elbow.

"Hey, it's you, right?"

He turned around, slightly suspicious. "I don't know. Who am I?"

"Yah, yah, my friends told me about you. You're famous."

"Not really."

"You're famous to us. Can you help me?"

He noticed the slashes on the upper arm. "I'll try. Let's go inside."

Clearly delighted, the young domestic helper followed Father Fernandes into his church as the smell of Hainanese chicken rice drifted across the car park.

Chapter 57

The Pohs hesitated before venturing inside. The Punggol location was local and discreet, buried beneath a housing block, and the name certainly appealed.

The Perfect Helper Agency.

If only.

The perfect domestic helper had eluded the long-suffering couple for years, testing both their faith and their generosity. They always seemed to get the lazy ones.

But they needed another. The date for the court case was still pending and their clothes wouldn't iron themselves.

The heartland shopping centre was quiet, but Angela Poh had worn her favourite Dolce & Gabbana sunglasses just in case. Plus, they were both wearing face masks. Singaporeans still erred on the side of caution.

Poh Cheng Hong had his hand on the stainless steel handle. He looked for his wife for guidance. "Can or not?"

"No choice, right?"

"But cannot get a permanent one. Just get a temp one, like a daily one."

"Cannot. Too expensive. Come on."

Angela Poh nudged her dithering husband aside and

pushed the door open. Her first impressions of the Perfect Helper Agency were underwhelming.

There were no domestic helpers sitting on benches or performing domestic chores in the window. How was she expected to make an informed choice?

Angela Poh grabbed a seat at a desk, beckoning her husband to join her. Poh Cheng Hong preferred to hover at the door. His wife handled domestic matters.

"Hello, we need a new helper," Angela Poh said, refusing to remove her sunglasses.

The Perfect Helper Agency manager found the woman's appearance distracting. The storm clouds had already gathered outside. An equatorial downpour beckoned. The sunglasses were unnecessary. But he had been trained not to judge, particularly in his line of work. He fished out the relevant forms and introduced himself.

"Sure, thanks for coming in. I'm Peter Yap. Have you had maids before?"

"Yah. Many."

Angela Poh glared at her husband. His sarcastic comment was uncalled for.

"Our boy found it difficult," Angela Poh added quickly. "He's comfortable now."

"OK. Any preference for where they come from?"

"The cheapest."

"Understand." The Perfect Helper Agency manager really did. Cost was a real concern these days. "So probably Indonesia, maybe Myanmar. That OK?"

"Can. When *ah*?"

"Wow, you really are in a hurry."

"Must get back to work."

"Understand. You stay around here?"

"Northshore Crescent."

"Ah the new BTO flats? Very nice. Got sea view." Yap took a form from a nearby pile. "And you said you had helpers before. Any issues last time?"

Poh Cheng Hong faced the window. The drizzle had started. He watched residents scurry for the covered walkways. He envied their shelter, their protection. He had none. He closed his eyes and waited for his wife's inevitable lie.

"No. They just never settled."

"Understand. So you're familiar with all the guidelines?"

"Of course."

"And you will give them a fixed day off every month?"

"Yeah, *lah*, of course, as long as not Sundays."

"Why is that?"

"Must go to church," Angela Poh said, proudly.

The phone rang again. James Richmond took a sip before answering. His voice was already hoarse from a day of meetings and workshops on migrant workers' rights. TWC2 was short of volunteers so he had offered to cover the night shift again.

Nights were always the busiest. The women were offered respite at night. Whispered, tired voices called from inside locked toilets or beneath thin sheets. They spoke as one voice, scared and desperate. Only the locations changed. And the injuries.

But Richmond always answered the phone. Every call. Every query. Because he was Singaporean.

Richmond looked at the small Singapore flag on his desk as he reached for the phone. His colleagues mocked his patriotism. The more strident social workers ridiculed his naivety. What exactly was he celebrating? He interviewed the victims. He met with the recalcitrant offenders. He dealt with indifferent civil servants. He knew the economy of a first world nation was maintained on the backs of domestic helpers and migrant workers. He saw kids kicking helpers in the shopping mall, calling them stupid, humiliating them, without being censured or scolded. He recognised Singapore's unofficial caste system endured, from one complicit generation to another, passed like a grubby baton from father to son, mother to daughter. Domestic abuse begets domestic abuse. Richmond knew all of that and more.

And he still picked up the phone. Every call. Every query. Because he was Singaporean, like most of his TWC2 staff and volunteers. The Singapore flag on his desk was not an act of naivety, but an expression of hope.

In his office, day and night, Singaporeans were literally answering the call.

The voice was calm and kind. "Hello, is that TWC2 *ah*?"

"Yes, sir. This is James Richmond speaking. How can I help?"

"I think the maid next door, *ah*, being abused one. Heard neighbours shouting and then heard her screaming. Can come take a look."

Out of habit, Richmond tried to focus on the positives. Singaporeans were now making the call, too. "I really appreciate you calling. We will try to send someone over." He reached over for a pen. "Have you got an address?"

"Punggol." The voice sounded weary. "Northshore Crescent."

Xavier Ng still couldn't look her in the eye. The rookie detective found the lock and pulled hard on the heavy handle.

The hand on his shoulder almost crushed him. He didn't deserve such support.

"Don't worry about it, Xavier. I don't blame you," Mistry said.

"I do. Shouldn't have spied on you at the airport."

"You were doing your job."

"No, I wasn't. You've got five minutes."

Mistry waited for Ng's footsteps to fade before venturing through the doorway.

Christine Yeoh's holding cell was typically austere. A thin mattress on a hard floor, a table with rusted legs bolted to the concrete and no personal possessions.

"Even your maids wouldn't be able to clean this shithole," Mistry said.

The former manager of the Happy Maids Agency didn't rise to the provocation. She remained still, lying on her mattress and focusing on the ceiling's mould stains.

Besides, her hands and feet were manacled.

"Anyway, I'm going back to England, so I just wanted to thank you for your help."

"Didn't help you. Help my son."

Mistry realised she was nodding. A mother's love trumps all. "And they'll help him. Your son Noah. He's not involved in this. No reason to punish him, right?"

"No."

Mistry stepped inside the cell. The oppressive, concrete walls were stifling. Condensation trickled through the cracked paintwork. "I've made them promise me. They'll look after your son."

"Thank you." Yeoh dried her face with an elbow sleeve. "Why you being so nice?"

"Mothers and sons, right? I nearly died trying to save mine."

"Really?"

"Yeah. Seems so long ago now." Mistry found herself staring at a trail of ants, making their way across a concrete wall. "But we'll do anything for them. *Anything.*"

Mistry reached for her pocket. "Just like her."

Yeoh sat up slowly.

Death had visited her prison cell.

The face on the screen was waving at her, showing her something.

"Cannot be."

"Oh, it is," Mistry said, turning to her phone. "Do you want to say anything?"

"Hello, Miss Yeoh," Dewi said, grinning on screen.

"Wow. She still calls you 'Miss Yeoh'. Even now. You stick her on the back of a lorry, leave her for dead and she still calls you 'Miss Yeoh'."

"But she's dead."

Mistry crouched beside the manacled prisoner and held her phone screen in Yeoh's face. "No, she played dead. For us. To catch you. You see, you thought if you stalled us long enough, your billionaire nutcase could send someone to silence them all. You thought you could play both of us. Tell us where the girls are, pleasing us, but allowing Patrick Lin to have them all killed first, pleasing him. But you pleased neither."

Yeoh started shaking her head. "No. It's not true."

"Oh, it is." Mistry tapped the screen. "Do you see what Dewi is holding there? Her teddy bear. The only connection she had to her boy. And you tried to take her away from her boy. Can't do that. You know that. Mothers and sons. Nothing like it. And she loves that teddy bear. *Loves* it. But luckily for us, she hates you more. So she agreed to smear it with red paint, to catch you. It was washable paint. So it's gone now. See?"

Mistry held up the phone again. "But some stains can't be washed away, can they?"

"No, no, you're a liar," Yeoh said, pulling against her

330

manacles. "I don't listen to you. I only listen to Him. I only listen to Him."

"That sounds exhausting."

"Fucking bitch," Yeoh screamed, taking exception to the Indian's sarcasm. "You're going to hell."

"No, I'm not." Mistry faced her phone screen. "Hey Dewi, tell us where we're all going."

"You go see your son. I go see my son," Dewi said, in broken English. "And Miss Yeoh go to jail."

Chapter 58

Standing outside a crowded departure hall, Mistry watched the farewells. They all had reasons to stay and leave, loved ones on both sides of a long-haul flight. Mistry knew she had her son, husband and widowed father waiting for her at Heathrow, all giddy faces and homemade banners, ready to resume their lives. Together.

Low only had the job. Relationships were beyond him.

Mistry watched as Low left the baggage trolley beside a long line of connected trolleys, defying the orderly precision of Changi Airport with a petty act of rebellion.

"You did that deliberately, didn't ya?"

"It annoys 'em," Low said, swaggering over while adjusting the belt on his jeans. They were clean, along with his white T-shirt. He had shaved, too.

"Why can't you just put the trolley back in the right place?"

"And be like everyone else?"

"You sound like a stroppy teenager."

"You sound like a Singaporean. You should stay."

Mistry might have offered a polite, fake laugh in the past. But she cared too much to insult his intelligence. "Anyway, thanks for your help."

"Thanks for yours." Low delicately moved Mistry's fringe away from her forehead. "The bruising has mostly gone. How's the shoulder?"

"Sore. I'll see a doctor when I get back."

"On the NHS? You'll be retired by the time you get an appointment."

"You're not working for the Singapore Government now."

At the entrance to the departure hall, a pair of ICA officers checked the passports of travellers, dutifully, carefully. Low studied their robotic movements. "I'll always be working for the Singapore Government," he muttered.

"Why?"

"They're the only bastards who'll have me."

Changi Airport hurried around them. Frail uncles pushed lines of baggage trolleys from one end of the cavernous terminal to the other. Aunties mopped gleaming tiles that did not require mopping. Holidaymakers wandered beneath ostentatious art installations as business class ticket holders privately seethed over the need to queue, at all, in one of the world's busiest airports.

Mistry took in the dizzying scene one last time. "It is funny when you think about it. Everyone's always rushing to be somewhere else in Singapore. Except you. You'll always be here. You're like the one constant in this place."

"Bloody hell. I'll have to tell the therapist that one."

"Oh, come on, you're such a bloody martyr. The grass is always greener with you. But you're exactly where you need to be."

"In Singapore? Why?"

"Low crime doesn't mean no crime, right? So they're stuck with ya."

Low laughed this time. "Yeah. Everybody gets what nobody wants."

"That's democracy."

"I'm Singaporean. Don't know what that is."

A portly Chinese man shuffled past, pushing a trolley loaded with suitcases. He looked too much like a recent crime scene. "I will catch Ah Meng's killer," Low said, reading Mistry's mind.

"I know."

"Will you go after the bastards who got the driver and Robertson?"

"Of course."

"Crack the first one. That's the key. Lin was right. It's blackmail. The driver was silenced. Speak to the other Chinese drivers that Robertson was using."

"We have solved cases without you, Stanley."

Low held up his hands. "*Wah*, so *hao lian ah*. OK, fine. Go back to the *ang mohs*."

"Yeah, I'm going." Mistry checked her watch. "Where did you get that 8.52 from?"

Low looked up at the flight departure screen. "I knew it was eight something. Couldn't remember the exact time."

"The fifty-two seemed very specific."

"It was five and two. You gave me that the other day."

Mistry's eyes narrowed, seeking clarification.

"Fifth of February," Low said. "That's when we went to the Big Splash. Fifth of February. I know because that was our last proper day together, before you left."

Mistry nodded. "Yeah, well, it's closed now. The Big Splash. It's gone. Move on and stop wallowing."

"Oh, I'm not really."

"Yeah, all right." Mistry kissed the Singaporean on the cheek. "At least you've smartened up. First time you've had a shave in a month."

Low looked down at the gleaming tiles. "Yeah."

"Are you blushing?"

"No."

"Yes, you are." Mistry surveyed his appearance again. "Hang on. Clean shaven. Hair brushed. New T-shirt. Washed jeans. Even those trainers look new. You didn't do this for me, did ya?"

"*Wah lau*, I gotta dress like an *ah beng* all the time is it?"

"Who are you meeting?"

Low cleared his throat. "Well, Grace is arriving soon on a later flight."

"What Grace? Grace from the back of the lorry Grace?"

Low appeared defensive. "Yah, so? I promised I'd look after her. What's wrong with that?"

"No, nothing. Nothing at all." Mistry grinned at her old friend. "I think that's great."

She grabbed her hand luggage and joined the queue for the departure gates. She did not look back. This time, she didn't need to.

The confessional was in need of urgent repair. The climate was harsh on old timber. A fundraiser had been considered for some time now, but unlikely for the foreseeable future, considering recent events. Besides, the campaign for the stained-glass windows had cost the parish's generous benefactors enough money.

It was too soon to ask for more.

The doors were closed and the curtains drawn, but there was a reluctance to speak through the latticed opening. Anonymity didn't alleviate penitent men's wariness. They had already crossed a line once. Crossing it twice, by reliving the experience, was a daunting proposition.

"It's OK. Take your time."

The priest's words were comforting in the confessional.

"I just want to clarify, really, that what we say in here . . ."

"Cannot be disclosed in anyway," the priest interrupted. "There are no names in here. Any information cannot be shared outside the confessional."

"Any information?"

"I would be excommunicated if it were disclosed."

"Even murder?"

The priest took a moment to compose himself. It wasn't the question that concerned him, but its familiarity. His parish benefitted from low crime rates. But he'd still heard too many penitent men seek clarity on this subject too many times.

"There is only one judge."

"Precisely. That's why I'm here."

"Go on."

The priest heard the discomfort on the other side of the confessional. The latticed opening picked up the hesitation, the fidgeting, the guilt. "It's OK. Go on."

"I'm responsible for the death of two men and, in a bizarre turn of events, indirectly responsible for one more."

The tone of voice caught the priest off-guard. The delivery was measured and calm. He opted for a professional, mechanical response. "Go on."

"I got caught up in a crime syndicate. Extortion. Corrupt individuals duped me into doing something entirely out of character."

"Which was?"

"I slept with sex workers."

"That was out of character?"

"No, I've slept with many sex workers."

"And what happened?"

"Their driver always provided the women, until he decided that his financial package was not to his satisfaction anymore. He threatened to inform his boss and I wasn't entirely sure if he was serious or not. So I killed them both."

Father Hodgson clasped his hands together in a pitiful attempt to stop the shaking. His arthritis did not help, nor did the draughty conditions of a medieval church in Essex.

"Why did you do that?"

"We can't afford any more scandals," Nigel Fielding said. "The public will only swallow so much."

"And so, you, you personally . . ."

"Oh good heavens, no. There are enough disgruntled, tattooed types in Essex, friends of friends, that sort of thing. Unfortunately, the blackmailer was carrying a lorry-load of women at the time, which made the incident snowball somewhat. Bad timing on my part."

"And the second one?"

"Oh, the second one was an unexpected consequence of the first one. A cauterising procedure really, to stem the flow as it were."

"And did it? Stem the flow?"

"Oh, yes, which was rather fortunate as the guy got a little florid with the second one. But it's almost certainly over now. Almost certainly. I heard there was a third one elsewhere, but that was nothing to do with me."

Father Hodgson managed only a rueful nod. "And so we return to the root cause again. Adultery. Why?"

"Sex workers fulfil my needs in a way that my wife should not. She's a very religious woman, as you know."

Father Hodgson leaned back. The timber did his back no favours. "So why are you here today?"

"Local elections. Wanted to make sure He's still in my corner."

"He's always in your corner, as long as you atone." Father

Hodgson pulled a splinter from his seat. "That's something we might discuss after the church fundraiser."

"I'll take care of it."

"Good. And do consider the wishes of your wife."

"I do. That's why I always insist on sex workers. Never any real women."

"Your restraint is a virtue."

Feeling much better, Fielding thanked Father Hodgson for his time. The MP for South-East Essex then left the confessional and strolled through the nave, pausing only to feel the reassuring warmth streaming through the stained-glass window.

Glossary of popular Singapore terms and Singlish phrases

(in order of appearance)

Lah: Common Singlish expression. Often used for emphasis at the end of words and sentences.

Wah lau: A mostly benign expression that can mean "damn" or "dear me" in Hokkien. (See: *wah lan eh* for a more vulgar variation.)

Ah Meng: The name of the female Sumatran orangutan and a tourism icon of Singapore.

Chee ko pek: Hokkien slang for "pervert" or "dirty old man".

Kena: Malay term that loosely means "to get" or "got".

Talk cock: To speak nonsense.

Lor: Common Singlish expression. Similar to "lah", but often used in a resigned or cynical tone.

Hong bao: Red envelopes presented at social and family gatherings, especially Chinese New Year.

Heck care: A Singlish expression to show indifference or a nonchalant attitude.

Tekan: A Malay term meaning to hit or whack someone, but not always in the literal sense. *Tekan* means to abuse or bully.

Ang moh: A Caucasian (the literal Chinese translation is "red hair").

Ah Lian: A pet name for an unsophisticated Chinese woman.

Kranji: A northern town in Singapore with a large industrial estate.

Pasar malam: Malay term for night market or night bazaar.

Ah long: Hokkien for loan shark.

Chee bye: The rudest term for vagina in Hokkien.

Ikan bilis: The Malay term for anchovies, but often used to describe something small or a skinny person.

Kai lan (or gai lan): A green leaf vegetable.

Cai xin (or choy sum): A long, leafy green vegetable.

Kang kong: A tropical plant vegetable known for its tender shoots, similar to spinach or watercress.

HDB: The Housing Development Board, which oversees Singapore's public housing projects.

Kelong: A colloquialism for cheating, corruption or fixed, often used in a sporting context. (In Malay, *kelong* is a wooden sea structure used for fishing.)

Towkay: The big boss or leader (in Hokkien, *towkay* means "head of the family").

Makan: Malay for "meal" or "to eat".

Ah beng: A popular stereotype, an *ah beng* is often depicted as a scruffy, skinny Chinese guy who favours Singlish and Hokkien vulgarities.

Atas: Malay for "upstairs", used to describe a snobbish person or institution.

Cheem: Hokkien term for deep or profound.

Ah pek: Hokkien for uncle, used generally to describe an old man.

Kaki: Buddies or mates.

Bak kut teh: A popular pork rib dish in Singapore and Malaysia.

Kallang Roar: A term used to describe the intense atmosphere of football matches played at the National Stadium in Kallang.

Aiyoh: To express frustration, impatience or disgust.

Beef kway teow: A SouthEast Asian dish of stirfried, flat rice noodles with slices of beef.

Lorong: A lane or street in Malay.

Longkang: The Malay word for "drain". But *longkang* is commonly used to describe manmade water passages.

Win liao: A local expression used to concede an argument, often jokingly or ironically.

Chope: To reserve or hold something, such as a seat at a coffee shop table.

Tehc: Tea with evaporated milk and sugar.

Kan cheong: A Cantonese and Hokkien term meaning anxious or nervous.

Gahmen: A colloquial term for the Singapore Government.

Enbloc sale: In Singapore, the term is often used to refer to property sales where residents of an older development agree to sell their homes simultaneously to a particular buyer.

Tai tai: A Chinese colloquial term for a woman of privileged means.

Hao lian: Arrogant.

Wayang: Malay for "theatrical performance", also applied to someone being overly dramatic.

Tahan: Malay expression to take or endure. (e.g. "cannot *tahan*" roughly means "cannot take it".)

Wah lan eh: A naughty relative of *wah lau*. In Hokkien, it means "oh penis" or even "my penis".

Teh tarik: A popular tea in Singapore, particularly at roti prata stalls. Literally translated as "pulled tea", the hot, milky drink is poured into a cup from a considerable height, giving it a frothy, bubbly appearance.